HAAZINU
(LISTEN UP)

A Book of Prophecy

A NOVEL

YERACHMIEL BEN-YISHYE

Scripture taken from the New King James Version. Copyright © 1982 by Thomas Nelson, Inc. Used by permission. All rights reserved.

Copyright © Yerachmiel ben-Yishye
Jerusalem 2011/5771

All rights reserved. No part of this publication may be translated, reproduced, stored in a retrieval system or transmitted, in any form or by any means, electronic, mechanical, photocopying, recording or otherwise, without express written permission from the publishers.

Cover Design: S. Kim Glassman
Typesetting: David Yehoshua

ISBN: 978-965-229-534-7
3 5 7 9 8 6 4 2

Gefen Publishing House Ltd.
6 Hatzvi Street
Jerusalem 94386, Israel
972-2-538-0247
orders@gefenpublishing.com

Gefen Books
600 Broadway
Lynbrook, NY 11563, USA
1-800-477-5257
orders@gefenpublishing.com

www.gefenpublishing.com

Printed in Israel　　　　　　　　　　　　　　　*Send for our free catalogue*

Contents

Chapter I	Caleb	1
Chapter II	Joseph	11
Chapter III	Stitches	27
Chapter IV	John	38
Chapter V	Tom	45
Chapter VI	Caleb	60
Chapter VII	The Group at Breakfast	75
Chapter VIII	Caleb	82
Chapter IX	Mitch	87
Chapter X	The Group at Dinner	99
Chapter XI	An Abominable Ending	116
Chapter XII	Jerry	124
Chapter XIII	Joseph and John	146
Chapter XIV	Jerry, Caleb, and Leah	150
Chapter XV	Isaac	152
Chapter XVI	Joseph and John	156
Chapter XVII	Tom	160
Chapter XVIII	Caleb	162
Chapter XIX	Father Conlin	163
Chapter XX	Captain Bakchos	170
Chapter XXI	Leah	175
Chapter XXII	Caleb and Jerry	186
Chapter XXIII	The Argo at Sea	199
Chapter XXIV	Arriving in St. Thomas	203

Chapter XXV	In St. Thomas	208
Chapter XXVI	Taino	211
Chapter XXVII	Diving Deep for the Staff	223
Chapter XXVIII	Tom	235
Chapter XXIX	Prelude to Sailing	238
Chapter XXX	Cain	249
Author's Note		264

Chapter I

And I will make your descendants multiply as the stars of heaven; I will give to your descendants all these lands; and in your seed all the nations of the earth shall be blessed.

Genesis 26:4

So you shall serve the LORD your God, and He will bless your bread and your water. And I will take sickness away from the midst of you. No one shall suffer miscarriage or be barren in your land; I will fulfill the number of your days.

Exodus 23:25, 26

And the LORD said to Moses: "Behold, you will rest with your fathers; and this people will rise and play the harlot with the gods of the foreigners of the land, where they go to be among them, and they will forsake Me and break My covenant which I have made with them. Then My anger shall be aroused against them in that day, and I will forsake them, and I will hide My face from them, and they shall be devoured. And many evils and troubles shall befall them, so that they will say in that day, 'Have not these evils come upon us because our God is not among us?'"

Deuteronomy 31:16, 17

Caleb

January 27, 1986

H<small>E HAD BEEN A RENOWNED</small> pediatric oncologist until the dying of innocents got to him. The god that parents took him for burned out quickly once he'd lost his sure touch for miracles. So he took an extended sabbatical and embarked on months of intensive theological study pursuing the reasons why horrors such as he'd witnessed happen to children. He came away fully convinced of a highly controversial thesis: the Hebrews, or Israelites – a people the world now calls the "Jews" – were to blame. But while many thought the Holocaust would have been the most fitting conclusion to the Jewish people, Dr. Caleb Call had begun formulating the ultimate final solution.

"Dr. Caleb Call," John Hauser said, introducing him to the group. John was a psychiatric social worker at the medical center where they were now meeting. He initiated group therapy sessions for families and friends of terminally ill patients. "As a new group member, Dr. Call, tell us something about yourself, whom you're visiting, and your relationship to that patient."

"Call me Caleb," he said, disowning any pretense to a continuing medical practice. "I'm here visiting Michelle Levy, whom you may know as 'Mitch.' She was a college girlfriend, a woman I haven't seen since my abominable ending of our relationship sixteen years ago while I was in medical school. I'm forty, and if you come to know Mitch and me, you'll realize I've become in the last few years very much like her: I always tell the truth as I know it. I've become a religious person, too, but without a formal religion, who senses he has a special relationship with God. You may think that's absurd, especially in light of what's happening to Mitch, a person I pray for and would die for. But that only confirms the premise on which I've been operating in recent months: Mitch, and those innocent children who died in my care, would be as healthy as you and I if it weren't for the Jews!"

"Hold it, Dr. Call!" John ordered. "I didn't invite you into this group to start a war! Just tell us about Mitch and you, please!"

"John, I meant it as a backhanded compliment!" Caleb rejoined. "But it's true: the Jews do control our fate."

"What do you mean?" Joseph Kallman asked. His twin sister, Goldie, was a cancer patient at the center.

"When I took leave of my medical practice," Caleb answered, "it was to find meaning in my life – to remodel the arrogant SOB I'd become. I knew it meant eventually locating Mitch and asking her for her forgiveness. She's Jewish, I'm not; although like most of us, there's some Jewish blood lurking somewhere. So I thought I should understand her religion's views on atonement and forgiveness before asking her for a second chance. Gradually, I saw it – the outsider looking in – saw what those rabbis couldn't or wouldn't see: your Goldie and my Mitch are here because of them!"

"What are you saying, Dr. Call?" Joseph pleaded.

John rushed to Joseph and put his arm around him. "Why don't we take a coffee break," he said, "and be back in fifteen minutes."

Alone now, Caleb sat down and replayed the day's events. He remembered heading outside for an early morning run when a telephone call caught him: Mitch had been located at the medical center. He'd been searching for her unsuccessfully for over a month, and he immediately made a call to a colleague on the center staff to get a feel for what to expect. The shock of learning about her terminal condition drove him out the door despite his need to pack and make airline reservations. But this was to be no ordinary run. For by the time he'd run a mile, his mind had become convinced that stopping would have fatal consequences.

That in itself was not unusual. At the track, for instance, he'd often pretend that misfortune would befall him if another runner overtook him. And at night on the road, he'd frequently prod his tired limbs with a fear of the devil in pursuit. These extremes seemed real enough at the time, although he later recalled them as only the mildest of playful distractions.

His fixation this morning, however, was unusual, for it lacked even the slightest pretense of promoting a greater distance or better time. On this snow-clad winter's morning, only one truth was known to him: his heart would fail at the end of the run.

Compulsively he ran on: three, six, nine miles. His body ached and sweated, and only his constant fear of stopping pushed him on. His legs were fully exposed to winter's chill; yet at ten miles he felt so suffocated by the heat of his body that he pulled off his sweatshirt and tied it around his waist.

At eleven miles, every step he took required a concerted effort. He could no longer distract himself from the pain by focusing on his spiritual being – the partnership he thought he'd forged with God to make him into a better person – one who would never have done to Mitch what he did. Waving his hands high in the air, then dropping them loosely to his sides, he instinctively turned homeward, grimacing upon realizing how ill prepared he was for death: no will, no loved ones to mourn for him, no forgiveness from Mitch.

At thirteen miles, the rising sun brought the distant lie of a silver coin to his attention. At another time its precarious position in the midst of an intersection would have challenged him to snatch it on the run. This time, however, he crushed the temptation for the sake of maintaining his pace.

But as he traversed the intersection, the coin's brilliance made him think again about retrieving it: he'd begun giving all the money he found during his runs to charity. So he started toward it, only to be jolted by the blare of an approaching vehicle. He raced toward the sidewalk, but the car, in passing, played its horn again, jarring him as he mounted the curb. The ball of his right foot hit the point of the curb, and he stumbled forward amid vain attempts at righting himself. Some ten feet beyond, he grabbed a protruding dead tree limb, clutched it tightly in his hands like a staff to break his fall, and with a rolling motion, came to rest on his side in a sun-melted puddle of water.

Frozen like an unoiled machine, he jerked his face upward and questioningly allowed the sweat at the wells of his eyes to sear his vision. Still, he saw.

He breathed deeply and felt his ears pulse to the easing rhythm of his heart. Still, he heard.

Turning his face downward, he smiled at the purity of the snow surrounding his soul's anticipated flight. Nonetheless, the snow's chill merely numbed the bare flesh of his already-tightening legs.

At last he stood, prepared to see Mitch, and, after glancing about in embarrassment at his spill, started slowly limping home. A quarter mile into that walk, however, his resolve began crumbling, and as if a knife were piercing his chest, he winced at the unfairness of it all. Despairing once more at Mitch's condition, hurting and lame in limb, his mind demanded deeper soul searching, and he chose to run again.

"Caleb," John said on returning, shaking Caleb's shoulder, "now that you've calmed down, why don't you tell us how it went today during your first visit with Mitch. After sixteen years, there must have been some roughness around the edges."

"You know the disaster that happened, John," Caleb replied, "That's why you invited me here!"

"But the others don't," John said, "and that's why we're here; it's a session that has no boundaries and no secrets."

"It probably had to do with that abominable endin' of your relationship with her," Zachariah Alfred Potter, nicknamed "Stitches," offered, quite certain that it had. His wife, Jo Jo, was awaiting a heart transplant at the center.

"I'd rather not discuss it," Caleb answered. "Besides, I want to see how personal we get before I disclose the intimate details of my past with Mitch."

"If Dr. Call wants 'personal,'" Joseph said, "I'll give him 'personal.' But before I start, John, I'd like to ask Dr. Call a question, okay?"

John nodded reluctantly.

"What did you mean by blaming the Jews for my Goldie's condition?" he asked. "I'd do anything to save her."

"This isn't the time or the place," Caleb responded, noting John's irritation. "What I will say is that…you're Jewish, Joseph?"

"I don't see –" he muttered.

"You don't have to answer," Caleb continued. "I grew up in a WASP environment that made it a point of knowing whom to exclude. It's just that at your age I would have thought you'd stop hiding it. What I will say –"

"Yes, I am," Joseph interrupted.

"Thank you. What I will say," Caleb went on, "is that the first five books of the Bible, revered by Jews, Christians, and Muslims alike as the Torah, the Pentateuch, the Five Books of Moses, or whatever you'd like to call them, present a written contract between the human race and God in which God promises to bless humankind with peace, prosperity, and freedom from all diseases – like cancer – if our representative at the table, the Jews, reciprocally perform all of their obligations under the contract. The Jews were chosen as our agent not because they were more gifted or God's favorites, but because they were the first people to step up to the plate, to be burdened with the tremendous responsibility of representing all of humanity in our attempt to live in God's image, to be holy, and become godlike. And if the Jews were to achieve it, if they showed God that to obtain the contractual blessings they were willing to relinquish their moral free will – their right to do evil as well as good – in favor of submitting fully to God's will, then the rest of humanity would be blessed through them. It's that simple: the Jews are a human sample being put to the test, just like Abraham was tested with the binding of his son Isaac.

"So, Joseph," Caleb continued, "before you grab Exodus 23:25 as your Goldie's salvation, you'd better ask yourself whether you're truly ready to be put to that test."

"Of course I am!" Joseph exclaimed.

"John, two more minutes and I'll be done," Caleb said, noting John starting to rise.

"When God distinguished humankind from the rest of the animal world by giving us moral free will," Caleb went on, "He anticipated that the choice between exercising our free will to do evil, or submitting to His will to do good, would be our toughest battle. Adam and Eve told Him so with their first bite of the apple, and Noah's heirs soon rejected their covenant through their actions at the Tower of Babel. Abraham was the first to succeed in fully submitting to God's will, culminating in his binding of Isaac. But the Israelites chose free will over God's will in worshipping the Golden Calf only days after God's revelation at Sinai. Not since the days of Joshua, after the death of Moses, has the conflict between the Jews' submission to God's will and their passion for free will gone consistently in God's favor.

"And since God's contract with the Jews promises all of us blessings of health, peace, and prosperity, we should focus on the Jews' performance of the contract to regain those blessings and deliver a second Eden, a heaven on earth, and freedom from Goldie's and Mitch's cancer. So, Joseph, let's go to the Jewish roadmap to those blessings in your Torah. Do you eat pork? And remember, I sat next to you in the cafeteria at lunch earlier."

"Some bacon every now and then," he answered hesitantly.

"Caleb," John broke in, "there are more important things on our agenda!"

"John, let the man finish!" Stitches said. "It's a fascinatin' subject, and it's exactly what we're here for: to find meanin' in what we're experiencin' – why bad things happen to supposedly good people, who, it seems, may not be so good after all. So let the man speak, John."

John nodded reluctantly.

"Joseph, do you know that Leviticus 11:7 bars you from eating pork products?" Caleb went on.

"I don't know where it comes from," Joseph replied, "but I do know that I'm not supposed to eat it, that it's not kosher. Why?"

"Don't take offense at what I'm going to say," Caleb said, "but if you intentionally eat bacon, you really don't believe in your God, *Adonai*, as you Jews call Him. What you've done is create your own personal god, the Joseph Kallman god, who permits eating pork. In which case you've violated the commandment directing you to have no other god but Him. And that puts your Goldie in this medical center as surely as you put that BLT in your stomach!"

"You've got some nerve!" Joseph shouted.

"Perhaps," Caleb rejoined, "but it's my understanding that your Torah contains 248 contractual dos, which represent all the good Jews can do, and 365 don'ts, which represent all the evil Jews are prohibited from doing. It's like Eden revisited, but instead of calling the Torah the Tree of Life, as the Jews now do, it should be called the Tree of the Knowledge of Good and Evil. Fortunately, many of the don'ts are universally proscribed and embedded in our civil and criminal laws, so you have to follow them no matter what. Others apply to outdated practices like the treatment of slaves, or to priestly practices in a temple that no longer exists, so you don't have to follow them now. Even so, there are enough other ones – ones that conflict with today's lifestyles, like eating bacon – that I doubt, Joseph, you'd be willing to make the necessary sacrifices to restrict your free will and bend it to God's will.

"And because of the Jews' failing – *your* failing, Joseph," Caleb concluded, "God has turned His countenance from all of us – that's Deuteronomy 31:16–18 – and my Mitch and your Goldie are doomed. Stitches, that's why bad things happen to good people: because God's turned His face from this world, leaving everything to chance, the free will the Jews have opted for instead of God's will. Only when the Jews return to Him and abide by their contract terms will we get the proverbial heaven on earth, our second shot at Eden, those blessings. There are no lightening bolts that punish us for straying, just His turning away and leaving us with a redemptive, prophetic

Torah poem that begins with the Hebrew word *haazinu*, that all Jews are commanded to memorize but obviously never do."

"And what do you suggest we do about it?" asked Dr. Tom Petersson. His brother was in a coma at the center, brain dead and awaiting the harvesting of his organs, which Tom had authorized.

"We get the world community as the contract third-party beneficiary to demand that the Jews perform their contract terms," Caleb replied. "I propose a twenty-year trial period for the strict observance of the Torah by the Jews, nurtured by the rest of us to make it happen. That's the true intent of the command to 'love thy neighbor': so that each Jew by his concern for the good of his neighbor helps bring the blessings to all of us. And those Jews unwilling to play ball are excluded from the group – just what God prescribes throughout the Torah for intentional violators of His teaching. Then we'll see if those blessings of health, peace, and prosperity actually rain down on us."

"You're assuming the world will accept your thesis," Tom stated, as the anthropologist he was, "but the world would never honor the Jews that way."

"Of course not," Caleb replied, "but that's the beauty of it. They'll certainly use it as a legitimate means of punishing the Jews for resisting. For some, it'll be a chance to prove that the God of Israel doesn't exist, or that no god exists at all. Then there'll be those looking to prove that the God of the Old Testament has swapped Christians for Jews as the new chosen people. Even Muslims should be drawn to it, and that's enough of the world to make it happen. Everyone wins, even the Jews, who can now shed the stigma that being Jewish was to them."

"And what if the test is done to the letter," Tom asked, "and nothing happens? No blessings, no nothing?"

"Then there'll be no need for Jews anymore!" Caleb responded. "And their historical, God-given right to the Land of Israel will disappear – just what the Muslims have wanted since 1948. That's why the most vocal opponents will not be the anti-Semites, but the rabbis, who live off the Jews and have never followed God's teaching anyway."

"And what do you do with all the rabbis," Tom inquired with a smile, "assuming there are already too many diamond merchants?"

"Frankly, there shouldn't be non-Levite rabbis in Judaism to begin with; that's the primary cause for God's turning away, and why all those supposedly righteous Jews faced the Inquisition, pogroms, and the Holocaust," Caleb replied. "Rabbinic Judaism violates Deuteronomy 33:10, and the rest of the Torah as well. All teachers of Torah must be Levites; it's their sole, eternal inheritance, unlike all the other Israelite tribes who got land in Canaan and Transjordan.

"Funny thing, there's a Ramban that bases the utter destruction of the Levitical Hasmonean monarchy on its usurping Jacob's blessing of kingship, given solely to the tribe of Judah. But then the Judean rabbis introduced their Rabbinic Judaism and usurped Moses' blessing to the tribe of Levi to be the sole teachers of Torah to the Jews."

"What's a Ramban?" Joseph asked.

"A commentary on the Torah by the sage Nachmanides," Caleb started to reply.

"That'll have to wait for another day, Caleb," John interjected. "We've strayed far enough as it is. Joseph, it's time for you to tell us about you and Goldie."

Chapter II

You shall not add to the word which I command you, nor take from it, that you may keep the commandments of the LORD your God which I command you.

Deuteronomy 4:2

At that time the LORD separated the tribe of Levi to bear the ark of the covenant of the LORD, to stand before the LORD to minister to Him and to bless in His name, to this day. Therefore Levi has no portion nor inheritance with his brethren; the LORD is his inheritance, just as the LORD your God promised him.

Deuteronomy 10:8, 9

For the LORD your God has chosen [Levi] out of all your tribes to stand to minister in the name of the LORD, him and his sons forever.

Deuteronomy 18:5

They shall teach Jacob Your judgments, and Israel Your law. They shall put incense before You, and a whole burnt sacrifice on Your altar.

Deuteronomy 33:10

Thus no inheritance shall change hands from one tribe to another, but every tribe of the children of Israel shall keep its own inheritance.

Numbers 36:9

Joseph

"As you already know, my name is Joseph Kallman. I'm a semi-retired New Yorker, visiting my twin sister, Goldie, who's been my best friend and business partner my whole life. To know us, you have to understand the time and place we grew up in, a world miles apart from today. Every chance I get, I read, to anyone who'll listen, a memoir, as Goldie calls it, that she wrote last year before her cancer came out of remission. Today you're my captive audience, so here goes."

* * *

The stone buildings were razed quickly after New York City condemned them, but the foundations of other worlds soon stalled their excavation. Three hundred fifty years before, this lower part of Manhattan was untaxed swampland, spreading out from New Amsterdam and down to the East River. Now, construction of the Beekman Downtown Hospital, having unearthed tenants of the Swamp's recent years, was ineluctably dredging up remains from its murkier past.

We were logged into the Swamp's history at an early age, though we were born above a candy store in nearby Brooklyn. Raised in that store by our wonderful mother, Molly, we were weaned on the insatiable demands of our father Sam.

Our father could neither read nor write, not even to know that they'd changed his surname at Ellis Island to Kallman, to sound more American. Arithmetic was his scourge – too often he'd erode his old-world nest egg making wrong change at the candy store cash register.

In the early 1920s, my father heard of a business that guaranteed profits: everyone wore shoes, so he sold the candy store and became a finder of heels and soles for the shoe repair trade. At the time, Joseph and I were eight years old, the eldest of five children, and to my disappointment, our father chose to name the business S. Kallman & Sons.

That name, of course, instantly belied the venture's true identity, for Joseph and I quickly became the truant "Sons," who would, during school hours, pick up and deliver merchandise and keep Sam's books. Fortunately, I was the darling of third grade math, and Joseph was a sturdy youth. But unlike the freedom my father found on coming to America, we were fettered forever by his heartless demands at our tender age to the stench of hide leather, like doomed steers in a slaughterhouse corral.

There was a day in the beginning of the venture when I remember Joseph returning from deliveries with tears in his eyes. He'd just turned nine, his long face was puffed out, and his shoulders were sagging more than usual. I ran to him immediately, and I remember how the redness surrounding his green eyes frightened me.

"You late!" my father bellowed in his flawed English. "The delivery was not so far that the day be wasted. Hurry, Joseph, orders must go!"

Joseph stared at me and hesitated. His eyes widened and his breath shortened. "Pa," he whispered haltingly, "the horse broke loose on the bridge!" It seemed he couldn't breath. I blinked and tightened. I felt his arms twitch.

"What!" Sam shouted, racing outside. The wagon was not there, and only the resounding creaking of the wooden floor on his return made the world seem real. "Where is the wagon?" he demanded.

Towering over us, he raised his hand as if to strike, but I pulled Joseph away. My father's hand hovered for a long time, trembling from his own frustration, before descending aimlessly to his side. "At the bottom of the bridge, Pa," Joseph said at last. "The wagon's at the bottom of the bridge. I tried to hold her, but the harness broke when she reared. It was on the bridge, Pa. It was so high, and the water scared me."

He began whimpering, and my father palmed the scruff of Joseph's neck to pull him from my grasp. "I ran after her, Pa," my brother added as my father yanked him away, "until I couldn't no more!" He twisted back toward me and shouted, "It wasn't my fault the harness broke, Goldie, honest!"

"It'll be all right!" I yelled back. "Pa will talk to the liveryman about the broken harness. You'll see, it'll all be fine. Just don't worry about it!"

Delivered to a table loaded with women's heels, Joseph began the boring task of sorting, counting, and boxing. He hated it. Soon I came over and wiped away his tears. "Goldie, will I have to work harder for it?" he asked. "Will Pa make me work even later than now?"

"The horse'll find its way home," I answered, smiling, "You'll see."

"Are you sure, Goldie? The other boys don't even have to work. They go to school and play!"

"I know, Joseph. I watch you stare at them."

"Joseph!" my father shouted from the storefront. "We fetch the wagon!"

Joseph bounded to our father's side, as much to escape the monotony of what he was doing as to assuage our father's anger. Sam embraced him and said, "I, too, drove a wagon at your age."

"You did, Pa?" my brother exclaimed. "When you was a boy?"

"Yes, Joseph, my son, it was hard then too."

"Did you ever lose a horse?"

"No, my son, but there was other things. You got to be strong. It is not easy in this world. Today you got horse sense. Tomorrow – well, tomorrow will be better because you learned today. You will see."

"Will I always have to work hard like this, Pa? Forever?"

"Maybe you will be luckier than me. For me I must work, even though I have such helpers as you and Goldie."

"But Pa, if I make us rich, could we stop working then?"

"It is in me to always work. I am not happy without owning things to sell. I know nothing else."

"Is it in me to always work too?"

"I do not know, my son," he chuckled as he tightened his grip on my brother's shoulders, "but maybe if you make us rich, the working bug will go away."

The late 1920s brought my family marginal prosperity: Sam paid his bills, but not on time. Only my math skills were kept current.

Across the East River, the Swamp was aswarm with tanners and wholesalers, who attracted the breadth of leather goods manufacturers and finders. One wholesaler of particular repute was Louis Goldberg, exclusive holder of the premier tannery line. He was the despised autocrat of the Swamp's leather district.

It wasn't often that Joseph went to the Swamp, even after my father conferred on him at the age of thirteen the full responsibilities of a buyer. The merchandise there was too expensive, and transactions were exacted on too stringent terms.

In late 1928, however, with our existing suppliers tightening credit, Joseph and I plotted with our father to improve the quality of our customer list by offering better quality merchandise. Cash management was survival, and in deciding to reduce the heavy cost of our slow payers by replacing them with more creditworthy customers, my brother went to the Swamp to buy.

Walking briskly across the Brooklyn Bridge, then meandering apprehensively along Gold Street, Joseph finally confronted the stone building on Spruce Street housing the Louis Goldberg establishment. He took a deep breath, fidgeted with his coat and hair, and stepped through double doors onto Goldberg's main inventory floor. It was like another world to him. The floor was crowded with merchandise of all types: full bellies and bends, soles and taps of all grades – A's, B's, C's, D's, and tannery runs that were mixtures of all those grades – and of the most desirable thicknesses, 12 iron and up.

Louis Goldberg was walking the floor with a customer when Joseph arrived. At first, their impeccable dress, diamond rings, and Havana cigars made my brother feel like running. But after minutes of being ignored, he calmed down enough to eavesdrop on their discussion of hide futures, particularly the excellent prospects for the prime leather bends against which Goldberg was leaning. I had guessed right about what we should hold in inventory!

As the customer departed, Goldberg noticed my brother and assumed he was picking up merchandise. He pointed next door at the loading platform, and Joseph meekly said, "Mr. Goldberg?"

He pivoted and said disdainfully, "Loading is over there!"

"No, Mr. Goldberg," Joseph quickly countered, "I came to buy! S. Kallman & Sons, Howard Avenue, Brooklyn. I'm Joseph Kallman," he introduced himself, extending his right hand, as he'd practiced with me.

"Oh, I see," Goldberg said, visibly amused. "S. Kallman & Sons, you say?"

"Yes sir, Howard Avenue, Brooklyn!"

Disregarding Joseph's outstretched hand, Goldberg plucked a black notebook from the left breast pocket of his suit coat and studied it. "Ah, yes," he said at last. "Six years in business, slow pay, minimal capital. You're Joseph, the oldest?"

"Yes, sir!" he answered. "I'm Joseph Kallman." There came a flood of confidence from his name being in that book, and again my brother extended his hand.

This time Goldberg grasped it like a vise, but Joseph was prepared. He returned the pressure, to the extent he could, with a smile and a direct gaze into Goldberg's beady, brown eyes.

"How old are you, Joseph?" the man asked as their hands fell away.

"Fifteen," he replied. "And a half!" he hastily added on seeing Goldberg wince.

"Well, Mr. Kallman, what can I do for you?"

Walking to the prime bends which had been the earlier topic of conversation, Joseph examined them for thickness, firmness, and grade. Each bend ran over four feet from the steer's shoulder to its butt. Each was closely trimmed and near perfect.

"What's your price?" my brother inquired.

Immediately grinning, Goldberg soon was choking with manufactured laughter. "I'm interested in a few bales," Joseph went on, a bit unnerved. "Do you have a quantity discount?"

"That's the best!" Goldberg said abruptly. "Aren't you a bit confused, my boy?"

"No, Mr. Goldberg," my brother responded, "I'd like three bales. I'd like them cut if it's not a problem."

Instantly the man's facetious manner ceased, and pointing toward a tannery run of bends, he shouted, "Those are for you!"

Blanching, Joseph turned and walked to the designated bends. Quickly recognizing their poorer quality, too much like what he already had in inventory, he said softly, "No, sir, you don't understand. I want first quality, only the best! Just three bales, please."

"No, young man, *you* don't understand!" Goldberg shouted. "You want bends, you'll get what I decide! And for you, it's these or nothing!"

"Please, Mr. Goldberg, we're trying to improve our inventory. I know what I need; I'll pay cash!" The last words found little air to push them out. The embarrassment, the degradation made my brother want to escape.

"Cash? Not for gold!" Goldberg ranted on. "Not for the likes of you! You're buyers of crap, and you'll stay that way so I can move it after I sell the cream! If you don't want it, get out! Out! There's nothing in here of first quality for the likes of you!"

Joseph raced for the door, and from the intersection of Gold and Spruce streets, where he stopped to catch his breath, he glared at the Louis Goldberg building. Then he ran for the Brooklyn Bridge.

But a block from the bridge, he hesitated. The prospect of disappointing me after all my planning and encouragement stopped him from returning, and soon he was recalling stories we had heard of the successful Pearlman brothers who, like my father, could neither read nor write.

Suddenly Joseph began smiling. With him now was the confidence he'd gained in exploiting our father's idiosyncrasies, for it had occurred to him that the Pearlmans were just like Sam. Except that of them all, only Max Pearlman was still signing his name with an 'X.' My brother raced through the Swamp again.

Peeking around the corner, he glanced ruefully at the Louis Goldberg building, before entering the Pearlman establishment. Greeted warmly by Max's brother, Julius, and without the appearance of a black notebook like Goldberg's to thwart him, Joseph roamed the Pearlman floors in search of prime merchandise.

At last he arrived at prime bends he could comfortably substitute for those at Goldberg's, and he offered to buy three bales. "No!" Julius Pearlman declared, and my brother froze. "Of *this* you can have three bales," he added quickly, as he led Joseph to some adjacent inventory.

Sighing in resignation, my brother moved toward the hides. Once there, his eyes grudgingly focused, at length recognizing the prime quality of the bends. And when he finally realized that he might indeed return to me with what I'd hoped for, he began choking with confusion. "But why not those?" he asked cautiously. "It's the same quality, isn't it?"

"Yes," Julius Pearlman said, smiling, "but the others are for no one. They were bought at a higher price, and they will sit until the market returns. These were bought recently, and they are for sale."

That was in 1928. By 1933 so many in the Swamp had perished. An economic famine had ravaged the land and destroyed almost all predators and prey. Some said Louis Goldberg, the worst of the predators, had committed suicide; others distilled the rumor that he had absconded with his creditors' money. Incongruously, S. Kallman & Sons thrived. Guided by Joseph and me, five hungry siblings were in the business to garner whatever business there was. People still wore shoes; heels and soles still had to be replaced. And with viable customers to service, my father's shift from the candy store seemed vindicated.

At twenty, Joseph was an extremely competent businessman, devoted to the daily trading games that occupied him. I was instrumental in making him feel good about himself, for I'd often tell him that his stallion black hair and tiger green eyes dazzled everyone into submission. But he knew, as well as I, that his talents really came from the math skills I'd instilled in him. Far superior to the rudimentary calculators of the day, those skills proved time and again to be the crucial ingredient in most of his bargaining successes.

In addition to my back office responsibilities, I was also a peacemaker. For every time our father would appear on the floor, there would be a confrontation between Joseph and him. Most often it was caused by Sam's desire to retain control, while at times it resulted from my brother's desire to be acknowledged as boss.

I'll never forget one particular encounter between them. In 1934, as Joseph was going over some unnecessary goods that Sam had ordered, Sam praised the frivolous purchase and Joseph exploded in anger. I rushed to them from the back office and shouted down their heated words. "What's such a problem that everyone should hear! It's not like we have so much success that we should have time for this!"

"He's gone and done it again, Goldie!" Joseph said. "Whenever we get our heads above water, he goes and spends our last nickel on more inventory, and too often it's what's not selling!"

Cupping my father's face, I was caught momentarily by his accelerating aging. How much older he looked than he really was! I wondered for some seconds whether I would age that way, and then I asked, "Pa, why do you do it?" I dropped my hands into his large, coarse ones, caressing them and saying, "Pa, explain it to Joseph and me so we can learn from it."

A softness in my father's eyes turned watery, and a tear fell. I looked at Joseph, and we watched an unexpected mellowing of this complex man. "Pa," I said again, "why do you keep buying when we can hardly pay for what you bought last week, and the price we have to pay for what you just bought is more than what we sold it for yesterday?"

Our father remained silent, as if he knew that no answer he could give would satisfy us. Tears began streaming down his cheeks, as strains of an old world infected his attempt at aloofness. Finally he turned to me and whispered, "I know from a distant time, the past was much worse, much worse." He sighed, cringing from painful memories.

"If I have debts and no inventory," he went on, "I have nothing." His palms opened upward as he shook his hands free of mine. His shoulders shrugged. "But if I have even more debt and a little inventory, I still have a business to dream of for tomorrow."

Immediately I embraced him. But as I tightened my clutch on his body, he shook himself free, sprang away, and was out the door. I remained motionless.

My father's confession did little to stem his foolhardy purchases or mitigate Joseph's impatience with him. Serving mainly to educate my younger brothers and sister in the art of turning inventory into sales, those purchases also seeded Joseph's first thoughts of breaking away into a business of his own. Encouraged by Julius Pearlman, who had my brother in mind as a suitor for his only daughter, Joseph honed a passion for a business of his own until his desire was sharp enough to cut him loose.

"Goldie," he said one morning when we were alone in the back office, "I'm going out on my own." I closed my eyes, breathed deeply, and a sense of emptiness invaded me. He must have realized how cold he'd sounded, and added, "Things will only get worse between Pa and me, and besides, with the rest of the kids in the business now, there's not enough room for me here."

I stared vacantly at him as I absorbed the full meaning of his intentions. "I've taken a room and rented a building in the Swamp, the old Goldberg place," he went on, in response to my pained expression, "stole it in fact, with an option to buy. This is the only way, Goldie, but I don't know how to tell Pa. Would you do that for me?"

"It's not just Pa, is it?" I asked. "It's been a long time since we really talked."

"You won't change my mind, Goldie!" he said sharply. "It's just Pa and the boys. I can't breathe, that's all!"

"There's got to be more than that!" I shouted. "You wouldn't break us up just for that! You'd suffer along with me like always – for the sake of the others!" He turned away. "You owe me an explanation, Joseph!"

"Okay, if you must know," he said, turning back, "I can't stand the thought of becoming like him! If I stay here, I'm sure that'll happen!"

"I don't understand!"

"Everything with him is work; there's never any time for us. And the way he treats Ma – I can't stand it no more!"

"And what about Ma? She needs you!"

"She knows already, I told her yesterday." I stiffened at the finality of it, and he hurried on, "I won't be far away. You'll see, it'll be better without the fighting, and Ma and you having to side with Pa or me."

"And in your new business," I said, forcing a smile, "will you do the books?"

"Of course! I had the best teacher in the whole world!" He hugged me tightly and added, "It'll be the wholesale side of the business – no competition with you – and who knows, I might even sell to you on credit!"

"Then you must have been a lousy student!"

"Why?"

"Would a good student give credit to a business that just lost its best man?"

We laughed uncomfortably; there was nothing more to say. I took his hand and walked him to the storefront. "What will you call the new business?" I asked at the door.

"J. Kallman Company," he said, "plain and simple."

"No '& Sons'?"

"Never that!"

I smiled and shooed him out the door.

Nineteen thirty-seven was the worst of years to start an undercapitalized business in the Swamp. Were it only ambition and toil that assured survival, J. Kallman Company would surely have thrived. But Joseph was a novice in the deadly games of the Swamp, and he failed to anticipate the killer instinct of his competition. For unbeknownst to him, there was a concerted effort among his neighbors to "welcome" him by directing all their insolvent accounts his way. Short on cash to begin with, Joseph learned quickly the misery of being prey, and for the next few years rarely labored in a creditable world.

Months later his wholesale business stabilized, but something was still missing. Partly by intuition, and partly because of things that were said, I joined Joseph, and by 1942, with Joseph working the outside buying and selling, and me the inside, shipping, receiving, and doing the books and other paperwork, J. & G. Kallman Company became the preeminent wholesaler in the Swamp. Few in search of sole leather passed through Manhattan without calling. One visitor, however, stood apart from the rest.

It was a cool fall evening in 1943 when a haggard, lame man arrived on our main inventory floor as we were closing up. The man's defeated air slowly evaporated as he limped toward me in the back office.

"Hello, Joseph," he turned and said as my brother overtook him. The sound of his voice made Joseph speechless. "How are you?" he added, continuing to look around.

"Is that you, Mr. Goldberg?" my brother asked.

"Yes, Joseph, it's been a few years. I thought I'd become active again. Retirement hasn't been good to me." He tapped his lame leg with his cane and added, "I see you've done well for yourself. I always valued this building; you were wise to acquire it. It's got a perfect floor plan for our kind of merchandise." He limped away and Joseph followed.

"I see you've got the exclusive on that premier line now," he went on, pointing to the prime hides. "They're gentlemen in their dealings, and the credit they give is unbeatable." He stopped at a skid of prime bends and added, "I could use some of these to fill out my inventory."

"Would you like thirty or sixty days to pay?"

"That depends on the price."

"Mr. Goldberg, do you remember fifteen years ago when I was a young boy and came to buy from you?" The memory was chasing his breath. "I wanted so much to succeed. You took all the pride I had away from me in how you treated me. It was as if you'd slapped me on both of my cheeks."

"I didn't mean –"

"Of course you did, Mr. Goldberg! It was your way with 'people like me,' you said it yourself. No, I'm sorry, there's no merchandise in here for you, not even the tannery run you offered me back then. Why don't you go see your brother-in-law down the street."

"I just did. He threw me out."

Struggling to contain his desire for revenge, Joseph stalked the lame man. Finally he screamed, "No!" before whispering, "Please get out. There's nothing in here for you."

Limping away, Goldberg disappeared quickly into the darkness outside. Moments later, however, as Joseph was bolting the double doors, there came the cry of a wounded animal. For several seconds my brother halted the bolt throw, as if the turn of his wrist would end the lame man's life. I had run out from the back office when Joseph screamed at the visitor, and now watched in amazement as he remained frozen at the door. After everything Goldberg had done to him, despite what the man had become, Joseph still held him in awe.

I walked to his side and grasped his hand, still resting on the lock. "We're all creatures of the Swamp," I said, throwing the bolt. "We're its inventory, Kallman prime, and we've got to live by its laws of selection." I pulled Joseph from the hideous sounds he knew were still out there, and hand in hand, we walked back to the office.

* * *

"It's now over forty years later," Joseph said, putting Goldie's memoir down, "and Goldie and I are still one soul. But unlike the Swamp, which has been revitalized, we've merely aged into a woman with terminal cancer, and a man horrified by a future without her.

"It's funny," he went on, "the more you reach into your past for comfort, the colder the present becomes. I'm constantly amazed at how much like my father I've become. Everything I've ever enjoyed has involved work: I've kept my real estate business alive after retiring from the leather business because I can't cope with the prospect of doing nothing – it's where my life is. My father worked until the day he died, but Goldie, who was into a lot of charitable work and continually read the best-seller lists, was confident we could liquidate our businesses and retire with ease. She could do it, she was into so many things. But for me it was a disaster – and it's a disaster now not being able to tell her I love her, when she's all I have and ever will. Sure it's understood between us, but she's going to die and I can't tell her what she means to me. All I keep doing is eating for the two of us, ever since her weight loss became the first sign of her cancer. I never had a weight problem until now.

"And as for you, Dr. Call, I went to a synagogue near the hospital the other day to sort my feelings out. It felt strange. Except for occasions like family marriages, deaths, and bar mitzvahs, I haven't been in a shul for my own needs since 1937 when my new business in the Swamp almost went under. At the time I became crazed with Jewish tradition – even stopped eating bacon for a time – because I needed God; He was all I had to share my fears and suffering. When I got my big break in 1941 by landing a Russian lend-lease deal, I forgot my roots and haven't really explored them since.

"Maybe that's why Dr. Call's comments got to me. If it could be shown that there was some truth to those blessings, I gotta believe you'd see a lot more Jews practicing being Jewish, me included."

"As an anthropologist who has an interest in the belief systems of primitive cultures," Tom said, "I can assure you, Joseph, that the only truth in those blessings lies, no pun intended, in the same quicksand as every other attempt to prove that God exists. Even your sages rejected the God of those blessings when they began rebelling against the Torah's Levitical hierarchy in the last centuries before the Common Era. Then they overthrew it completely at the time your Second Temple was destroyed. That date marks the clear beginning of modern, or Rabbinical, Judaism, a new religion based on an oral tradition that anointed the rabbis, mostly from the tribe of Judah, as Caleb pointed out, with exclusive teaching status despite the continuing line of priests and Levites, who were ordained directly by God to do it. That oral tradition became the Talmud when it was finally reduced to writing, and it did exactly what your Torah prohibited: it added and deleted so much to the Written Law, the Torah, that Moses himself wouldn't recognize it, even as those rabbis linked everything they did to Moses at Sinai to give it legitimacy. So Joseph, don't count on any blessings from your God, when the rabbis crucified Him just as surely as the priests did Jesus."

"You could say," Caleb added, "that if God had wanted the Jews to live by Rabbinic law as well as Torah law, and for rabbis from all the tribes to minister to Him and teach the Jewish people instead of just the Levites, He would have had Moses write it that way in the first place!"

"Sounds like it's gonna be real hard to get those blessin's even if they real, Joseph," Stitches commented. "Sounds like the Protestants and Catholics goin' after each other in Ireland."

"That's why the world has to force the Jews to be like the Israelites in the time of Joshua," Caleb said, "but rather than a holocaust annihilating the Jews, the world has to nourish and motivate them to do what's best for society. Maybe after twenty years – the first five to convene a Sanhedrin of seventy elders, Levites who would establish what the written Torah expects of the Jews, and then fifteen years for their strict performance – we'll see if God's face returns and becomes active once more in blessing our lives."

"What you and Tom seem to be saying," Joseph said, "is that the rabbis and their Talmud are the real culprits in giving my Goldie cancer. I find that hard to believe!"

"What I'm saying, Joseph," Caleb rejoined, "is what Tom described. The religion that God, through Moses, set before the Israelites was Levitical Judaism, a demanding yet simple prescription for relinquishing your moral free will to God's will, and by doing so, gaining heaven on earth, no Messiah needed. Just as Moses would be shocked by what Judaism has become, you should be, too!"

"As the only Jew among us, Joseph can be our own guinea pig," Stitches laughed. "Let's force him to be a true Levitical Jew and see what happens. Maybe like his old business was saved from what he did with his religion in 1937, Goldie could be saved now if he did the same thing!"

"Stitches, this is no time for your sense of humor," John broke in. "Instead, why don't you tell us about you and Jo Jo."

Chapter III

Stitches

"During the first eight years of my life," Stitches began, "bein' the youngest of ten, I had this feelin' that I was an unwanted child. And that made me treasure my nickname, Stitches, mostly because, in my world of hand-me-downs, it was an original possession. It also became a trademark of my handsome ability to make people laugh – you know, keep 'em in stitches.

"But on my eighth birthday, my father, in one of his drunken stupors, revealed the true origin of my nickname to be the stitches he asked for to close my mother's womb after I was born. And so I fled that disappointment by becomin' the practical joker that I am. I also became your typical black high school dropout, and while I continued to use my once-cherished moniker, sometimes in jest I'd use the initials of my given name, ZAP.

"So I give you fair warnin' about my jokin'. It got me my Jo Jo and a fair measure of success, beginnin' thirty-five years ago when I was a mere shadow of what I've become. Then, I was a lonely thirty-year-old man, peddlin' an overloaded bicycle along the dirt roads of Mississippi, offerin' a prudent selection of pins, needles, and thread to the bountiful tenant farmers of that gawd-awful place. I used to see those tenant farmers as my true stock in trade, 'cause it was through my pranks on them, and not my pins, that I cushioned my despair."

* * *

So it was on that spring mornin' thirty-five years ago, that after spendin' a restless night in a nearby field, I was churnin' toward Isaac Brown's farm. My body ached from the disagreeable earth, but that didn't diminish my black humor. In fact, it was tickled immediately when Isaac, who would later become my father-in-law, prevailed upon me to replace his broken mechanical alarm clock with the one I used for travelin'. The isolated farmer had no sons, only a wife and daughter, and without livestock to crow the farm awake, he had come to rely on a timepiece instead.

My clock read precisely 7:00 a.m. as it changed hands, for fifty cents as I recall. But in the midst of the exchange, I mischievously exclaimed, "It's daylight savin's time!"

Isaac's eyes lit up, like he had heard the phrase before, and I added, "Spring back, fall forward!"

"What?" Isaac said.

So I says to him, "You moves the clock hands an hour back in the spring – that's spring back – and that's how you saves time. Here, let me do it!"

I retrieved the clock and set it at 6:02. "Now you have an extra hour to do your work today and every day until the fall."

Isaac took the clock, studied its face, and gazed at the sun. "Don't understan'," he said at last.

"It's easy," I said. "You moves the clock an hour back so's you gets more time for farmin'. Spring back, fall forward! That's a radio jingle. You got a radio?"

The jingle captured Isaac's attention. "Electricity, you got 'lectricity?" I added playfully.

"Nope!" came a voice from behind. The farmer's daughter, Jo Jo, appeared, shakin' her head. At the time she was in her early twenties and a little plump, but cute as a button. I must say I was instantly smitten.

"Then jus' remember," I said, "you moves the hands forward in the fall, that's fall forward, and back in the spring, that's spring back." I fell forward and jumped back in rhythm with the jingle, and Jo Jo giggled. My antics also regained Isaac's attention.

"How'd you hear about spring savin's time?" I asked, surprised by his earlier recognition.

"A fella come 'round here sellin' wrist clocks tells me that," Isaac answered, "but I seen no need for it. This here's plenty."

* * *

"Well, actually," Stitches interrupted himself, "you wouldn't understand what he really said – he an' his daughter spoke the local way, which is so incomprehensible that I could hardly make it out myself, even after years of peddlin' there. But I'll jus' speak it out in my own words, regular, so you can understand."

And with that he resumed his narrative.

* * *

Isaac studied the clock again before lowerin' it to his side. He was clearly uneasy with the extra hour. "Day's comin'," he muttered, and without even a nod at me, moved off with his daughter.

"What time's it?" I called after him.

Isaac turned and held up the clock for me.

"Can't see!" I shouted.

Hastily Isaac returned. Grinnin' in embarrassment, he traced the clock hands with his index finger, and I realized that he couldn't read time by the numbers, only by the position of the hands.

During the followin' fall, I eagerly awaited my next visit to Isaac's farm, and on finally greetin' Isaac, I gleefully spouted the radio jingle, "Spring forward, fall back! Spring forward, fall back!"

At first Isaac squinted his eyes questionin'ly, as if recallin' a different verse. But then he strutted to the farmhouse while whistlin' the jingle and returned with the clock. It read 7:15 a.m.

Acceptin' it with a broad grin, I set it back to 6:15. For some seconds after retakin' it, Isaac shaded his eyes and gazed at the risin' sun. Perplexed by the divergent positions of the clock hands and sun even more so than in the prior spring, he bowed his head, and bypassin' a hoe he'd rested against the storage shed on my arrival, lumbered to a chair on the farmhouse porch and reclined there.

Those past spring and fall mornin's foreshadowed my approach to Isaac's farm the next spring. Yet that spring mornin', unlike the others, seemed totally unreal. Maybe it was the brilliant sun, which, in its effortless climb, appeared to spread an eerie calm over the farm as I arrived. The unearthly silence seemed to seal the success of my prank, but it bothered me considerably. I had been expectin' some activity so late in the mornin', but after noisily mountin' the porch steps, I decided against knockin' and just sat on a chair and moped.

Suddenly a door clattered open and I jumped up. Jo Jo appeared, totin' a water bucket, and her plump figure attracted my thoughtful gaze. Unnoticed, I stepped toward her, and a creak of the floorboards under my feet startled her. She pivoted instantly, and raisin' the bucket to shield her chest, retreated toward the open door.

"Your pa 'round?" I asked, speakin' their way, or as close to it as I could. She stopped, stared at me, and smiled.

"Sleepin'," she answered, blushin'.

I hesitated. "You mean we all by ourselves?" I finally said. My heart was poundin', and my breath was all but gone. I didn't even catch her nod that we were alone.

"You makes some mighty fine magic with that clock o' yours," she said when I began to fidget with my suitcases. "Things changin' mighty good 'round here since we got it." She paused, grinned oddly, and added, "What's your name, Mistah Magicman?"

"Stitches," I said.

"Where you from, Mistah Stitches?"

"No," I said quickly, "Stitches is my nickname, my first name. You can call me Stitches, not Mistah Stitches." She nodded coyly and rolled her eyes.

"I'm from the North," I went on, "from Ohio, but I spends most of my time down here sellin' this stuff." I kicked the two suitcases with my foot.

"You likes it here?" Jo Jo inquired.

"Not much afore today," I answered, "but now I likes it jus' dandy!" I smiled sincerely. "What's your name?"

"Jo Jo."

"Where's that from? I never heard of no Jo Jo afore." She quickly stepped away, but I pursued her. "Where's that from?" I asked again.

"From the Bible," she whispered.

"From where?"

"From the boy Joseph in the Bible. Pa needs a boy 'round here real bad, and I'z it!" She tried to say it proudly, but I could tell it saddened her.

"That's nothin'!" I exclaimed. "My name's from my pa's not wantin' me to get born!"

"Born?" Jo Jo chuckled. "How's that, Stitches?"

I pondered an answer for the longest time and said, "You gots to live with not bein' wanted the way you are, that's all." I bent toward my suitcases, as if to lift them, but really only to toy with their handles. Impulsively, Jo Jo grabbed my hand, probably to change my mind about leavin', and she pulled me toward the storage shed.

"Where you takin' me?" I asked.

"To the 'ventions!" she said. "Pa calls 'em that 'cause the lan' owner does!"

The shed door opened to an overhead clang that scared me. But before I could investigate what the noise was, Jo Jo had pushed me inside – just as Isaac's anxious figure appeared in the farmhouse doorway. He saw us disappearin' into the shed, noted my suitcases, and withdrew into the house.

The shed held many surprises: some mounds of dirt molded into strange plowin' contours, and innovative farm implements that maximized mechanical advantage. Jo Jo continuously gauged my reaction, as if my impression could give her the self-respect she'd never known, and I didn't fail her. I was awed by the display, as good as the best around.

"Jo Jo!" a voice called from outside the shed. "Where's you at? Is Mistah Stitches with you?" Then Isaac thundered, "Jo Jo, now! It's spring savin's time!"

We emerged from the shed carefully distant, beamin' an indiscretion that hadn't occurred. Isaac was fondlin' the clock in his left hand, and he took my right hand in his, and like some mysterious ceremony, he delivered the clock into my left hand. Put off only momentarily by Isaac's gaze, I turned the clock an hour back and returned it to him.

There was now a four-hour difference between reality and the counterfeit world I'd created on that tenant farm; yet Isaac seemed perfectly content with it. "You knows the ways of the lan' owner, Mistah Stitches," was all he said, fully ignorin' the sharp incongruity between the sun and his imaginary time. But then he spun around, stared at me, and as Jo Jo came to his side, said, "Teach me the magic o' the clock, Mistah Stitches, please. I works so much less with your magic; promise you'll keeps it here always!" He reached for his daughter and hugged her.

"I gives you my Jo Jo and the lan' over there if you do," he added, lookin' straight at Jo Jo.

I studied Isaac intently. When I glanced at Jo Jo, she smiled approvin'ly. "Why you needs the magic so bad?" I asked.

Isaac motioned me into the shed. "See this here?" he began, once inside. "That's my 'vention for the seedin'. The wheel turns and the seed falls jus' right. But I needs time for finishin' it. I gets it with your clock, but I never had no time afore like your clock gives me now."

"I don't understan'," I said, aghast at the gift my prank had become. "You seems to work less with my clock, not more! I comes here after the sun's up and the farm's still sleepin'. Why you likes the clock time instead of sun time? 'Cause you don't likes to work?"

"No, Mistah Stitches!" Isaac cried out. "I likes to work jus' fine! But I don't needs to work at farmin' so much no more. I takes the extra time I gets workin' the farm less to work on my 'ventions more. Then the 'ventions lets me work the farm even less! And maybe I even rents some more lan' from the owner with the money I gets from the winter crop no one gets 'round here."

It was incomprehensible to me at the time. The world seemed to be spinnin' on its head. Less work suddenly meant more output. It didn't figure, unless Isaac was after his own pound of flesh for my practical jokin'.

The shed door began swingin' in ever-increasin' arcs while I planned my escape, and soon Jo Jo meekly appeared. Isaac immediately eyed her, but before he could expel her, she'd breathed deeply and said, "Pa, I knows you don't likes me bein' in here now, but I'z smart too! Stitches here knows this family real smart."

"That's *Mistah* Stitches, girl!" he chided her, but she merely swept her eyes toward mine to confirm her special status with my name. "Girl, jus' go helps your ma!"

"But Pa, I'z already been in here with Mistah Stitches! I already showed him your 'ventions!" She sidled next to me. "Can I stay if I'z quiet?"

Isaac shrugged his shoulders and looked at me. I nodded. "She'll make a mighty fine woman for you," he said. "I seen that you likes her, and if I gets the other piece o' lan' from the owner, we can makes two families livin' good here. You thinks 'bout that, Mistah Stitches, while you tells me the magic o' the clock. Then I don't says nothin' to Jo Jo's ma 'bout you bein' in here alone this mornin' with her little girl."

I nodded uncomfortably, sure now that revenge was his motive. "You gots the clock and the jingle," I said, inchin' toward the shed door, "why you sayin' you needs the magic?"

Isaac stepped among his inventions and deliberated an answer. Twice he began to speak but stopped. I was at the door and would have broke for the outside, except Jo Jo had been takin' every step I had, like we was doin' some dance, and she ended up blockin' my way. That turned out to be right lucky 'cause Isaac finally started talkin'. "Afore, I never had no time for 'ventionin'," he said.

He turned toward his contraptions, and staring at them, went on, "These 'ventions jus' likes the owner has. They makes for good farmin' and less workin'. Afore I works from sunup to sundown, and always the time it cheats me. The workin', my eatin', my sleepin', they use up all my time. But the magic o' the clock, it says to sleep even after the sunup, and I listens to it and still I gets the work done, like the same amount o' work fills up the day no matter how long or short it is.

"In the beginnin' I works mighty hard 'cause the clock keeps shortenin' the farmin' time. But then I gets more time in the night for thinkin' 'cause I sleeps more in the mornin' and I ain't sleepy at night like I used ta been. Then from the thinkin' I makes this 'vention for the tillin' and I gets even more time for thinkin' and 'ventionin' at night.

"This here winter I gets my first crop ever, and the owner he likes that 'cause no one 'round here gets the winter crop, and the owner he offers me the extra lan' over there for rentin', and I'z gonna do it too, after I gets me a man for my Jo Jo and a horse from the winter crop. Then I be like the owner!"

Isaac began walkin' among his inventions, and the compellin' honesty in his manner chased my fears of reprisal. I debated confessin' the prank and zappin' his good fortune, but I immediately recalled my father's thoughtlessness on my eighth birthday and squelched the temptation.

"Come see the extra lan'!" Jo Jo said, pullin' my mind back from the past with a tug of her hand.

"I'd be pleased to see the land," I said, drawin' on my long-forgotten Cleveland public school education.

"You talks funny," she remarked cautiously and giggled tensely. "You still the same ol' Stitches, ain't you?"

I smiled at her, but my mind was on Isaac's proposition. Jo Jo nudged me. "You still the same ol' Stitches, ain't you?"

I squeezed her hand. "If we's gonna be like the owner," I said, "we gots ta talk like the owner." And with those words, I broke from her grasp and pranced ahead.

Reassured, Jo Jo began imitatin' my antics. Then I saw her stop and look back at her pa, who was returnin' to the farmhouse with the clock. And with Isaac's implicit approval, she resumed skippin' after her future mate.

* * *

"That was a carefree past, but over the last year, ever since our daughter died from cancer, Jo Jo's been bearin' a heart condition like a trouper, and I've been ferryin' between her in hospitals and Isaac on the farm. Then there's been the farm machinery business, which seems to get along fine without me these days. It just seems like everythin's wavin' goodbye, and like Isaac might say, I had my time in the sun, and darkness is ahead. They give my Jo Jo a week at the most if they don't locate a match by then."

"Stitches, you know we take one day at a time!" John broke in. "Remember, nothing is fixed in concrete – like the Mississippi peddler who became a tremendous success in farm machinery. From childhoods of rejection, you and Jo Jo have blossomed with your love for each other. When I was a child in Germany, I had issues at home just as you did, and I became a priest to find comfort in God and my fellow man. I remember reaching out for my mother's affection, but she never returned it like she did with my sisters, never touched me. You overcame childhood adversity as I did, so let's use that strength to overcome this trauma too."

"I'm not cavin' into anythin', John," Stitches replied. "It's just funny how you come to take so much for granted when it's come so easy, even after my earlier hardships. You sort of forget the bad times until they come at you again. Last week Jo Jo out of the blue tells me that if a match doesn't happen by the end of this week, she wants to go home to die. Then I go home at Jo Jo's urgin' to check on Isaac, even though I'd just done it the week before, and I get clobbered by him."

* * *

We're sittin' together on the farmhouse porch and out of the blue he says, "Stitches, when's spring savin's time?"

"In a few months," I answered.

"That's a special time for me," he goes on. "Remember the magic o' the clock?"

"Yes."

"It ain't no more."

"Of course not, Pa," I said. "I explained about that prank a long time ago!"

"I knows 'bout that magic. I'z talkin' 'bout the clock itself – it's runnin' so long without fixin'."

"Yeah, that's amazin'."

"Well, it don't work no more. It jus' up an' died this mornin'."

"We'll get it fixed, Pa, don't worry. I'll take it into town tomorrow. Okay?"

"No, son," he said, "there ain't no fixin' what ails it, jus' like my Jo Jo. The hands can't do what the body's directin', and the face is tellin' its own time. No, Stitches, the wakin' force is gone, from the clock and from my Jo Jo."

"I keep tellin' you, Pa, this new heart transplant surgery works miracles. It's like God's given it to us to resurrect the body, new life from old, to allow the body to repent its sins like the soul. Jo Jo'll have a new wakin' force soon enough, you'll see!"

"But the Lord ain't intended us to be like farm machines gettin' replacement parts to go on forever," Isaac said. "There's only evil that comes from playin' with God's creation. And the more we try fixin' them sins of the body, the more our souls see only the possibility of sinnin' anew." He fell silent, and his head sunk to his chest as his rockin' chair swung backward. It was Isaac's way of shuttin' down a conversation when there was no more to let out.

✳ ✳ ✳

"You should be thankful that there's still hope," Joseph said. "I go to sleep every night thinking I might wake up without Goldie. I look back over the years – it's been just the two of us – and I think how selfish I've been. If I truly loved her, I would have made it easier for her to leave me and marry. Instead, I clung to her, didn't let her go over the years, and can't now." He buried his head in his hands.

"That's not fair to yourself, Joseph," John interjected. "You're damning your past as if it's the cause of what's happening to Goldie. Too often we look back and redefine history so it's understandable, but what we're really doing is trying to control what's ahead. We figure that by understanding how we acted when we got a bad result in the past, we can avoid doing the same thing in the future. We become more religious, more charitable, whatever it takes to give us the hope that misfortune won't repeat itself. The trouble is, we never really understand the past the way we need to in order to truly help define the future."

"Maybe I am doing that," Joseph responded. "I used to see people on the streets and subways of New York talking to themselves, and I used to think how crazy they were. Now I do it all the time myself, and all I'm doing is attempting to change what was said or done years before, as if I now know what was right then. I'm trying to replay my life as it could have been if I could return to the past and, like the poem Goldie always quotes, choose one of those roads not taken."

"You know, Joseph," Caleb said, "your desire to return to the past has its roots in your own roots: in the Torah. In Leviticus 26:38, God states the last of a litany of calamities to befall the Jews if they depart from His teaching. That verse describes the Holocaust.

"And in Deuteronomy 30:1–10, He sets out your road not taken, the one the Jews should have taken. There are two 'returns' described in the latter verses, and the first, the UN sanctioned return of the Jews to the land of Israel as a Jewish state, was fulfilled by reason of the Holocaust. The second, however, is yet to be fulfilled. Can you guess what it is?"

"Your return to Levitical Judaism," Tom blurted out.

"Sorry, gentlemen, but I'm going to cut you off and break with tradition here," John interjected, now with a noticeable German accent. "I've never told a personal story in front of one of my therapy groups, but this group has some unique characteristics that compel me to do it. So, as long as we're talking about redefining our histories, let me tell you a story about my own escape from the past."

Chapter IV

And Cain said to the LORD, "My punishment is greater than I can bear! Surely You have driven me out this day from the face of the ground; I shall be hidden from Your face; I shall be a fugitive and a vagabond on the earth, and it will happen that anyone who finds me will kill me." And the LORD said to him, "Therefore, whoever kills Cain, vengeance shall be taken on him sevenfold." And the LORD set a mark on Cain, lest anyone finding him should kill him. Then Cain went out from the presence of the LORD and dwelt in the land of Nod on the east of Eden.

Genesis 4:13–16

John

"After more than thirty-five years in America, I'm still running from the young German priest I once was. Maybe it's all in the work I do with the families of terminally ill patients here at the center, or maybe it's just that I constantly remember – like Joseph when he talks to himself – the day in 1946 when I fled Berlin, the Catholic Church, and the memory of Jews I'd refused to protect.

"On that day in 1946, I entered a burned-out synagogue in an attempt to reconcile past events with the guilt I felt."

* * *

My palms glided effortlessly over the smooth, cool edge of the one remaining uncharred wooden bench. I began talking aloud to God as I fought off images from my ugly past that had brought me to that place.

Unaware of an old man hobbling in the back, I sat down on the bench and continued to berate myself for my failings as a priest. A noise startled me, however, and I turned to see the old man placing prayer books in the back racks of the bench I was sitting on. The man noted my presence and said in German, "Are you a foreigner?" I gave no response.

The old man touched my shoulder, and I pivoted to face him. "You are a foreigner?" he asked, in English this time.

"No," I replied in English, assuming my new lay clothes might be suggesting it. "Who are you?"

"I am the *shammes*, the sexton of this shul," he said.

"Why do you ask if I am a foreigner?" I inquired.

"There are some who return to see what is left, mostly those who fled years ago," he replied. "I know every Jew in the area – there are so few now – so it is not difficult to tell. I would like to help if I could: a name, a street, a house perhaps. There is a slight possibility something remains."

"Is the rabbi here?" I asked.

"No, and may his soul rest in peace," he answered, "but I used to pride myself on being his ears. Maybe this one time I might speak for him too."

I stood and faced the sexton, who effused an unusual warmth through his aged eyes. "I have an interest in the biblical Cain," I said. "Did God ever forgive him?"

"That is a very interesting question, and a very difficult one to answer," the sexton said, "but it is not one with which I am unfamiliar." He thought for a while and went on, "The text says that Cain was punished for murdering his brother Abel. He was given a sign to protect him from his enemies and was banished from the Lord's presence to the land of Nod, a place for wanderers. It was the second time, but not the last, that God's countenance was turned from man, allowing evil to befall him."

The sexton looked at me with a refreshing smile. But all I returned was a sense of disappointment. "You are not satisfied with that answer?" he asked. "We can verify it if you would like."

"It is not that I doubt what you have said," I answered reassuringly. "I was just hoping for more. There is no biblical chronology of Cain's life like there is for the other ancients who died. Was it perhaps because God never forgave him?"

I could see that the sexton felt compromised. "I think I have your answer," the old man whispered after much deliberation, "but I must caution you that it is an obscure idea, a legend, not authentic. Are you interested in that?"

"Yes, certainly," I replied. "What is it?"

"Well, this legend maintains that Cain never died," he said, "that after the pronouncement of his punishment, Cain was unrepentant. God had created man with the moral ability to become godlike in His image, along with the free will not to. And He had placed man in paradise so that man would have no desire to exercise his free will toward evil. Yet man still opted for the forbidden fruit, inviting God's wrath and provoking Him to turn away from man for the first time, thereby planting the seeds of the first murder.

"So the Lord allowed Cain into the Garden of Eden to eat of the Tree of Life, which had never been forbidden," the sexton concluded, "and Cain became the eternal embodiment of evil, wandering outside of God's presence."

The sexton searched my eyes once more and found tears running down my cheeks. "I do not know what more I can offer you," he said, patting my arm. "If I have not been fully informative, you must forgive me. If I have confused you, please let me try again. But I have not misled you, of that you can be sure."

We stood together, my pained expression challenging the old man's credibility. "Maybe I am grasping for something that does not exist," I said at last. "Maybe you cannot understand the real question

I am asking because you did not turn away from saving others like I did."

The sexton touched my arm again. "There is no shame in having survived," he said softly.

"Many died that I could have saved," I said. "There was a Jewish boy the Gestapo took from the church when I could have protected him. For that, I too should be an eternal wanderer."

"Cain killed!" the old man exclaimed.

"I let others die!" I cried out. "I killed!"

"We do not know that Cain became immortal," he said to ease my pain.

"But you said –"

"That was a legend, not authentic!" he reminded me. "I never would have revealed it had I known the pain it would cause!"

"Then what happened to Cain?" I asked again. "I must know!"

The old man looked upward, then closed his eyes. After a few minutes he sat down. Considerable time elapsed, and thinking myself forgotten, I stepped uneasily toward the door.

"I am sorry to have taken so long," the sexton called after me. "I was caught in a memory on the very question you have posed. It was brought to my attention years ago, even before the first war, by an English Jew, a historian, who was visiting the rabbi, may his soul rest in peace. The rabbi's ancestor was one of the rabbis involved in a great debate the historian was researching.

"It seems that once there was a Torah study session in Lublin, which focused on the life of Cain," he went on. "The session raged until it finally provoked invitations to Talmudic scholars from all the major learning centers of Eastern Europe for a full debate, which occurred six months later. The resolution of the issues seemed to be centered on an ancient scroll, part of which amounted to a riddle. This fascinated me and so I memorized it. I suppose the riddle was also the source of inspiration for that legend about Cain – that he became an eternal wanderer – because one interpretation of the riddle is just that. Let me recite the riddle to you as the English historian recited it to me:

> *If God made Cain to e'er walk the earth,*
> *He surely watched Satan's birth.*
> *If God made Cain to be a while,*
> *'tis no man's need for human trial.*
> *But shouldst Cain the earth walk still,*
> *He surely shall make reign His will.*

I sat down, and the old man helped me memorize the riddle. The sense of it wouldn't come, however, and staring at the sexton in bewilderment, I said, "The meaning eludes me. What did the debaters conclude?"

"The debate resulted in a confusion similar to yours on the life of Cain," the sexton replied, "but it did not stop there. The rabbis assumed, for argument's sake, that Cain was still alive, and they discussed the benefit of finding him to prove the existence of God. That discussion was settled on purely theological grounds.

"Their pronouncement was based on man's need to believe in the possibility that God exists without any absolutes, because if all doubt in God's existence were removed by finding Cain, man would end up forfeiting God's gift of free will. And that would be disastrous for humanity. Instead of voluntarily offering our love to God, which comes from a mixture of doubt in His existence and hope in our salvation through Him, leading to divine blessings, we would become rebellious slaves to a divinity seen as a taskmaster, vindictive and not just and merciful, thereby inviting divine curses. Can you understand?"

"Yes, but that begs the same question I've been asking!" I said sharply. "Cain may be alive, an eternal sinner like me!"

"If he lives, he lives in all of us, not just in you," the old man replied. "Remember the riddle! If he lives, he serves the Lord's purpose: perhaps to test man's free will to choose between good and evil, life and death, just as you – along with those who died – serve a purpose we may never comprehend. Do not feel shame or guilt for having survived; there is a reason."

The old man extended his hand in a parting gesture and returned to his chores. Down the street from the synagogue, I transcribed the riddle from the sexton's recitation, and became puzzled by certain possible spelling alternatives: "reign" could be "rein," "a while" could be "a wile," "birth" could be "berth," and every capitalized "He" and "His" could be lower-case "he" and "his."

I returned to the synagogue to obtain the sexton's written version of the riddle, preferably in the original Hebrew, but found the building closed, shuttered – as I had heard might be the case when I first sought directions to it. I became perplexed, even frightened.

Suddenly I knew I had to leave that place, that country, and I began running without conscious intent. "There is a reason," I kept repeating to myself as I raced past gutted structures toward the train station.

* * *

"And through all my years of wandering, I've sought, without success, that reason the sexton said was there. So, Joseph, maybe through my own experience you can learn to accept your past as having its own reason for being."

"That's easier said than done," Joseph replied, "especially when you're over seventy and have nothing to live for. But I'll think about it, just like I've absorbed what everyone's been saying here. And you know, Stitches, Isaac was right about God not wanting the human body to be like a machine with replacement parts. Goldie and I discussed donating our organs or giving our bodies for medical research, and we were told that it's not generally permissible under traditional Jewish law, except if it would save a specific life."

"I thought you weren't an observant Jew," Caleb commented.

"When you're near death, your belief in a 'world-to-come' somehow renews itself," Joseph answered, smiling. "Well, anyway, even autopsies are generally forbidden; it's all about prohibiting the desecration of the human body, whether dead or alive, which is supposed to be treated as holy, as a loan from God. The truth is, though, that Goldie and I have no children to leave as a legacy of our having been on this earth, and we wanted so desperately to leave something of us behind. The donations seemed a good idea until we got rejected by rabbinic opinion."

"Of course, the whole issue of transplants, bodies for medical research, and autopsies would become moot," Caleb inserted, "if the Jews scrupulously followed the Torah as written, enabling us all to receive the blessing of good health until death do us part – at one hundred twenty years."

"We've heard that already, Caleb," John interjected, "and now it's time for Tom to tell us why he's here."

Chapter V

Tom

"I'M DR. TOM PETERSSON, brother of Jake. He's an organ donor on life support, awaiting a match for his heart before they harvest all of his transplantable organs. I'm a professor of anthropology, and if you'd like to read on my field of interest, I've given John a copy of an article I recently authored.

"What I'm about to tell you is very personal and will shock you more than anything Caleb can throw at us about his relationship with Mitch. That, I'll guarantee.

"Jake, my younger brother, was a mentally challenged man in his thirties. Misfortune accompanied him throughout his shortened life, but life was what he respected most, even in death."

* * *

The night Jake ejaculated in Lulu, a prize sheep, he seeded a nightmare no man should suffer. And when the vet later pronounced Lulu pregnant, my brother concluded in his own simple way that he wasn't a man at all, not even the slow learner we had told him he was, but rather a sheep in man's clothing. And so it was that on the day he learned of Lulu's condition, Jake wandered aimlessly about the ranch that had sheltered him for the last thirty years.

"What's up, Jake?" Charlie, a ranch hand, asked in passing.

"Nothin', Charlie," Jake replied. "Say Charlie, what does 'abort the fetus' mean?"

"Come on, Jake, even you know that!" Charlie said. "It means an abortion. You know, pull out the baby and step on it. Why, you gonna have one?"

"Nah, just askin'," Jake said. "They gonna do it to Lulu I think."

"That ain't no abortion then, Jake," Charlie said. "Abortions only happen to people, not sheep. Probably it's called a 'fleecing.' Get it, Jake?" He slapped Jake's back and laughed loudly.

"Say, Charlie," Jake asked, "where can I find out more about abortions if I feel like it?"

"In town at the library," Charlie replied, "or you can go over to the clinic. They got this awful lookin' counselor there who talks to the girls about the pros and cons of it if they ain't sure. She'd put out for you if you played it right!"

"Ya think she'd really see me? Ya know I ain't no pregnant girl..." Jake said.

"What's really up, Jake?" Charlie asked, punching Jake's arm. "You got a girl in trouble, is that it?" He had a weird grin suddenly. "Good ol' Jake. That bit o' fool in you ain't stopped the urge. Heh, heh, so you finally done it! Well, sure she'll see you. Only don't go gettin' taken by any knocked-up girl – it's her fault, her problem! She made the mistake! You start dishin' out them big bucks, and we'll all be in trouble. Them girls'll take a fool like you and trick ya inta thinkin' they're knocked up so's you give 'em money for the abortion, and they never go to no clinic! Or maybe they're knocked up all right, but they're chargin' every guy like it's theirs, a real racket. They –"

Jake began walking away from Charlie as I'd instructed him to do with all insensitive bastards, but Charlie went after him anyway. "I ain't finished, you gimp!" he shouted. "Don't go pullin' your 'walkin' away' routine on me, you retard!" Jake moved faster. "Hey, you freak, come back here when I tell ya!"

"I ain't that, you bastard!" Jake shouted back. "My brother's a college professor!" He limped to a bus stop, and while waiting there, set his deformed left arm in a makeshift sling he carried in his pocket.

The clinic wasn't nearly as scary as Jake had imagined it to be. He filled in a card and was attempting to read a brochure on first- and second-trimester abortions when a short, homely woman in her early thirties approached. She was smiling pleasantly while reviewing the card Jake had scratched out. He smiled back.

"Hi, I'm Jenny," she said and offered him her hand, which Jake shook. "We don't get many men coming in here alone, and I'd like to set your case up right. Is there someone waiting for you outside, in your car perhaps?"

"Nuh-uh," Jake stammered.

"I see," she replied, somewhat puzzled. "Well, then follow me into my office and tell me your problem."

Jake remained standing after they'd arrived, and Jenny motioned him to sit. He sat and stared at her.

"Your problem, Jake," she said, "please." Jake's eyes promptly shifted to the desk in front of him.

"About aborting the fetus," he said slowly and carefully, "what does it mean?"

"Well, that depends," she replied, looking at his card again, at his sling, and at him. She decided he wasn't a prankster like they'd gotten on occasion, just another uneducated ranch hand. "Jake, I can't tell from the card what your problem is; you didn't write it out well."

Jake was thinking of leaving. "Did you break your arm?" she asked to put him at ease.

He nodded and settled back in his chair. "So the problem, Jake," she went on, "what is it?"

"I asked you already," he answered. "Abort the fetus, what does it mean?"

"That's it?" she inquired.

Jake nodded.

"Okay," she said. "It means terminating a pregnancy before birth, normally before the fetus becomes viable. That's in the third trimester, the last three months of a nine-month pregnancy. We don't do third-trimester abortions here."

"Is it the same with sheep?" he asked.

"With sheep?" she chuckled. "You've got to be kidding!" Jake nodded excitedly. "That was a pun," she added when Jake didn't smile.

And when he didn't even grin after that, she threw her hands up and exclaimed, "I don't know!" Then she started to laugh but quickly calmed herself. "I guess so," she went on, softly, after a few seconds. "They're viviparous – they give birth to live young – so I guess so. Only the nine months, I don't know about that. But why sheep, Jake? We don't do abortions on sheep here."

She was laughing again, and Jake got up to leave. She apologized quickly and said, "Go on, Jake, tell me about the sheep. Please, I promise I won't laugh anymore."

"Lulu has an abortion tomorrow," he said, sitting down again. "What do they do with the lamb? That is what I really would like to know. I would take care of it if I could get it!"

"The lamb will die," Jenny said. "That's what I meant by not being viable, so you won't have to take care of it."

"That is not right," Jake said.

"What's not right?" she inquired.

"Its dying," he answered. "Everything should live if it can!"

"Jake, off the record, the right thing is what the mother needs – in humans anyway," she said. "You don't want to destroy a mother's life because of some accident that's occurred to get her pregnant. If she hated the child for being born, what kind of a life would the child have anyway? It would be brutalized. And if there's a birth defect involved, it's even more reason the fetus should die."

"At the ranch they told me birth defects make you special," Jake remarked. "My brother always told me that, and he's a college professor!" He closed the open end of his sling to conceal the stubbed fingers of his left hand, which were protruding slightly. "The lamb would be special too!"

Jenny looked at her watch, stood, and said, "I'm sorry, Jake, but I have a lunch date I can't miss. Why don't we finish up this afternoon, anytime after two."

"I can't," he replied. "I promised someone I'd be at the ranch before then."

"This afternoon is all I can offer, unless you'd like to return tomorrow," she said. "I'm sorry."

"Can I go with you until wherever you are going?" he asked.

"I guess so," she said reluctantly, "but it's only down the street." She walked briskly out of the clinic, and Jake hobbled after her. There was no chance to talk.

"Why didn't you ask the vet about these things?" she asked, as Jake approached her in front of the Italian restaurant where she'd stopped.

"Mr. Carter kicked me out of the barn when he found out about Lulu," he replied. "She is a prize sheep, goin' to the fair next month, and he blamed me for its happening. I was supposed to watch her all the time. An' I did too!"

"Look, Jake," Jenny said, "I'm meeting someone in two minutes, and I don't want him to get the wrong impression with your being here. So if you can't see me after two today or anytime tomorrow, why don't you find the vet and ask him all the questions you want. You'll get much better answers from him anyway. Okay?"

Jake limped away dejectedly, but he didn't go far. He stood and watched Jenny from a distance. Fifteen minutes later, he was back.

"You again!" she shouted. "All you men are alike! All you want is your own gratification! I met this guy last night at a singles bar, bought him three drinks, and spent what I thought was a beautiful evening with him. All I got was a promise for lunch today, but he didn't show!" She began walking toward the clinic.

"I would buy you lunch," Jake offered, scrambling after her.

"Why?" She turned and demanded, "Because you feel sorry for me? Or is it because you have some more weird questions on sheep? What the hell are you, anyway, a pro-lifer for sheep?"

"A what?" he asked.

"Oh, all right, Jake!" she said, clearly exasperated. "If you want to take me to lunch, you got me! Just let's go inside. I'd like to see if the stinker even reserved a table." He hadn't, and the two were seated.

"So you're a right-to-lifer for sheep?" she queried.

"A what?" he asked.

"A lifer!" she shouted. "Jesus, what's the matter with you, anyway? It's someone who opposes abortion because the fetus, any fetus, has a right to live. It's solid Christian morality: let 'em be born and then turn your back on them when they're abused. Right?"

"I don't know," Jake said. "I want to talk about Lulu, please."

"Jesus, I need a drink!" she declared. "You buying me a drink?" Jake nodded. "On second thought I'll just have some pizza and beer. You in the mood for that?" Again Jake nodded, and the waiter took the order.

While Jenny searched the restaurant for familiar faces, Jake studied her. He decided Charlie was cruel in the way he'd described her. But then, he knew Charlie to be cruel in everything he did. Gradually Jenny's eyes returned Jake's gaze, and he blushed, turning away. She took that as a compliment, and addressed the appearance of the man sitting across from her. She saw a ruggedly handsome face; even the twisted character of his nose, which had been broken numerous times, pleased her. Only his makeshift sling, pronounced limp, and lack of class put her off. Still, she was happy to be seen with him at the table.

"How long have you been at the ranch?" she asked, having forgotten Jake's request to talk about Lulu.

"Thirty years," he answered.

"How'd you get into it?" she asked.

"Mr. Carter took me in when I ran away from home," he replied. "I was real scared and he took me in."

"How old were you then?" she asked.

"Nine," he replied.

"Why'd you run?" she inquired. "We get a few runaways at the clinic each year."

"My pa, he got drunk an' beat me all the time," Jake confessed. "My brother too, when he protected me. When Pa killed Ma an' hisself, we picked up an' run, Tommy an' me. But we got separated right near the ranch – I don't know how, Tommy never told me – an' Tommy went somewhere else. Now he's a big college professor. He writes an' visits sometimes, an' someday he's gonna come an' get me. He will too, some day!" His voice sank to a whisper as he repeated, "He will."

"I'm sorry about your parents and brother," Jenny said, touching his right hand and marveling at the breadth of it. She instantly recalled how huge and soft it was when he shook her hand, how there was no roughness to it; yet there was power.

The pizza came, and Jenny reluctantly removed her hand from his. She ordered more beer, and for some minutes playfully pulled oozing pieces of pizza apart with Jake. The cheese had gotten all over, and Jenny laughingly plucked a string of it from Jake's cheek.

"Why can't you go back to the clinic after lunch?" she asked after the giddiness had subsided.

"I promised Mr. Carter I would do something," Jake replied. "He taught me to always keep my promises."

"Then if we can't talk later," she said, "tell me why that sheep's abortion is so important to you?"

"You promise you won't make fun of me?" he said.

"I promise," she responded.

"Nuh-uh," he replied.

"But I promised!" she exclaimed.

"Nobody keeps promises to me," Jake said. "Even Tommy when we was little. He'd promise, and then he'd run to my ma and tell her the bad thing I did."

"Look, Jake," Jenny said. "I've heard everything under the sun in my job. Nothing shocks me anymore, and I don't laugh at anybody but myself. Look at me! I got stood up today, for the thousandth time, and you were even there to witness it! So don't tell me about broken promises! Oh, I'll admit I'm desperate to get married and have a kid. In fact, forget the getting married part. I thought last night was a shot, but no such luck. There's just no man in sight! Maybe I've just become too aggressive, what more can I say?"

Jake was totally confused by her outburst. "Please," she said, sensing that her comments had been lost on him, "just tell me about Lulu's abortion, why it's so important to you."

Her plea melted Jake's resistance, and he said, "I will tell you: Someone made Lulu pregnant."

"A person?" she asked.

Jake nodded.

"Impossible!" she exclaimed.

"Yup!" he said.

"No, Jake," Jenny said, laughing, "there's no way a man could get a sheep pregnant. Nature doesn't work that way. A ram must've gotten to her."

"I protected her the whole time," Jake replied. "Only this one person was able."

"So let them do the abortion then!" Jenny responded. "What better reason could you have? Do you want some freak being born anyway?"

"Don't say that!" Jake demanded. "I would take care of it!"

"My, how righteous we've become!" she shot back, sarcastically. "Maybe, just maybe, I could empathize with certain pro-life arguments on human abortions. But on sheep? I mean, it's all hogwash!" She smiled for a second, then continued, "Ah, I get it! You're afraid we'll be killing the next Charles Lamb, right? It'll be called a lamb-child, or should it still be a love-child?" She saw no reaction from my brother and took a deep breath before saying, "This whole conversation is plain stupid! I mean, we eat lamb chops, don't we?"

Jake got up and began walking toward the door. Jenny rushed after him. "Look, I'm sorry," she said, tugging at his good arm. He stopped. "Please, we still have some pizza left."

His face flashed a confused and pained expression. She took his hand and led him back to the table. "I won't say those things anymore," she said as he sat down. "We'll concentrate on your problem only, okay?" My brother nodded.

"Let's go back to the conception issue," she began. "It's genetically impossible for a human sperm and a sheep egg to fuse."

"It must've," he argued.

"Let me finish!" she rejoined. "What likely happened was that someone let a ram into Lulu's pen when you weren't around, and when he heard that Lulu was pregnant, he played a joke on you by saying he did it. Just to get your goat." She smiled, but Jake merely reached for the last piece of pizza.

"He did it for real," Jake said after devouring the piece. "I know."

"Why are you so sure the guy didn't let a ram in?" she asked. "I mean, who the hell can watch a sheep, even a prize sheep, twenty-four hours a day? And what about exercising her? She's got to get out with the flock every now and then for a little socializing, doesn't she?"

"I just know," he replied.

Jenny studied his face once more. My brother felt her eyes on him for what seemed like hours. "You're the guy, aren't you, Jake?" she said at last, plucking a wad of cheese from the pizza tray and eating it. "Aren't you?" she demanded when no answer came.

Jake was startled by her triumphant tone. He nodded in fright and bolted for the street. Jenny grimaced. She dropped twenty-five dollars on the tray and ran after him.

Two streets down she had almost caught up to him, but as she was crossing an intersection, about to tap my brother on the shoulder, a car screeched to a halt, tapping her on her rear as it came to a stop. She halted her pursuit immediately and sat on the curb. Jake looked back at the noise and ensuing commotion, ran a bit more, then turned around. He stared at the crowd surrounding Jenny and limped toward her. As he approached, she stood, leaned against a mailbox, and began waving the driver back into his car. My brother inquired about her condition.

"I think, okay," she panted, "but I'm a little too shook up to go back to work. Get me a taxi, please."

When the cab arrived, Jake helped her inside and sat next to her. "You don't have to feel obliged to take me home," she said apologetically. "It was my fault for not looking, and fortunately nothing serious happened. I can make it back on my own. Thanks anyway."

"I'm sorry I ran like that," he said. "I will take you home."

The taxi arrived at Jenny's apartment building within minutes, and after paying the fare and bringing her to the main entrance, Jake turned to go. Jenny pulled him back.

"I can't let the one chivalrous act in my life go unrewarded," she chuckled. "Besides, I do need some help getting up the stairs." My brother acquiesced.

Once in her apartment, Jenny called the clinic. Jake scanned the living room and marveled at the furnishings. They were much more, he thought, than a single woman should have. He decided to wave goodbye and leave, but Jenny was off the phone before his hand reached the doorknob. She motioned him to the couch, and while he sat down, she kicked off her shoes and scurried into her kitchen for two beers.

Popping the top of one, she handed it to Jake and sat beside him. He inched away. "I keep cold beer in the fridge for special occasions like this," she said, popping her own can. "Do you have a girlfriend?"

"Nuh-uh," he replied, standing and walking to the window overlooking the street. "The guys always told me about girls, but I never been alone like this before. Sometimes I went into town with the other guys, but I would not let them make fun of me with girls. Except Charlie one time, he made a girl do things to me with him lookin' and laughin' at me."

"I won't ask what she did, but it sounds interesting," Jenny remarked. "How'd you get that limp? I almost caught up to you before getting stopped by that car." She patted the adjacent cushion for Jake to sit on.

"I was born with it," he said, cautiously seating himself on the cushion she patted.

"Is it congenital?" she asked.

"Huh?" Jake said.

"Or is it genetic – does your brother have it?" she said.

"Tommy's perfect, like I would've been," he replied proudly. "They said it was from my ma's doin' the drinkin' an' such that it happened, but I don't like sayin' it about it. You get kidded enough when you're not like everyone else without tellin' even more things to laugh at."

"That's why you're so defensive about abortion," Jenny noted, mostly to herself, before adding, "You know, we're a lot alike. You can say that the way I look is a birth defect of sorts."

"No, you are pretty!" Jake declared. "Like my ma!"

"Thanks, Jake, but it's not necessary," she said. "I've been told too often how ugly I am. In fact, just like you, I really haven't had a date in years and then only with some hard-up guy who wanted to take advantage. In a way, not dating is good – no pressures, no regrets like last night – but then there's no marriage or kids either. Men have been cruel to me, just like the guys have been to you. Sometimes it makes you want to scream! But let's talk about your problem with Lulu, now that I know your own involvement. What exactly did you do to her?"

"Nuh-uh!" he responded.

"Please, Jake, it's important if I'm to help; I've got to know the whole story," Jenny said. "We're too much alike not to share our secrets."

My brother pondered her sincerity and finally said, "The guys talked about how good it was that way, better than any girl. They laughed at me always for never havin' done it, so I took Lulu one night, one time…"

"Jake, listen to me," she said. "There are certain times when abortion is acceptable even to some hardline pro-lifers. That's when a pregnancy occurs from rape or incest or when there's a significant probability of a major birth defect. I won't argue with you about what or who made Lulu pregnant. If it was you, though, Lulu's fetus fits all those categories I just mentioned. You didn't ask her permission, so there's rape; you took care of her like a father, so there's incest; and if the fetus is really yours, then there'll be major birth defects for sure."

"I do not know about those things," he said. "I just want to save the lamb. I will take care of it!"

"Jake, I understand your intent, believe me," she said. "I want a part of me to live on too. Children give us a reason to hope in the future; certainly they help us make sense of all the cruelty we've suffered. But the irony of it all is that my life right now is limited to helping terminate life before it begins. Crazy, isn't it?"

"Will you help me save it?" he asked.

"Gee, would I love to have a little boy of my own," she mused, ignoring his question, "a blank slate to mold into my ideal, compassionate man. If only women could do that, there'd be no need for most abortions. Either the woman would want to keep the child to make a better world, or the men that came from that kind of nurturing would be sensitive enough to avoid getting a woman in trouble in the first place. But that's not the way it happens."

"So will you help me?" Jake asked again.

"With what?" she said.

"To save it," he replied.

"Jake, there's nothing to save if there's an abortion," she said. "Do you mean you'd like to kidnap Lulu to prevent the abortion?"

"Okay, we can do that," Jake responded. Jenny sat quietly, thinking. Jake didn't move at all.

"Jake, do you like me?" she said at last. Jake nodded. "Would you kiss me if I asked, to seal our helping each other?" Jake froze. "Just one kiss and then we'll make our plans for the kidnapping," she added when my brother didn't move toward her. She gulped her beer and put the can on the floor. "Then we'll make the plans for Lulu, I promise."

Jake started to rise, but Jenny reached for him and pulled him back. "Just a little peck," she cooed as she slipped one hand behind his neck and the other to his thigh. "Just make me feel how pretty you said I was, and I'll help you. I promise." Her lips moved to his, and he didn't resist.

Increasingly uneasy as her aggression accelerated, Jake soon found her tongue in his mouth and her hand exploring the bulge at his crotch. She smiled at her achievement and slid his right hand to her breast, gently massaging herself with it. But his hand fell away as soon as she returned her hand to his crotch. It didn't matter anyway: his pants were wet, and the bulge was receding. Jenny groaned and cursed. Before she could vent her frustration, however, my brother was out the door.

On the street he instinctively hid behind some cars until he was sure Jenny wasn't pursuing him. He might have remained there all afternoon if a bus hadn't stopped within ten feet of him to let off passengers. Only after he'd boarded and sat for awhile was he calm enough to seek directions to the ranch from the bus driver. Jenny's abuse continued to upset him, though, even while he fulfilled the task he had promised to do on the ranch. Shortly after dinner, the distress turned to rage.

As night arrived, he felt completely abandoned, perhaps realizing for the first time that I would never be coming to get him. Only Lulu was his friend, a companion to fill his emptiness, a body with which to snuggle on cold winter nights. She seemed always infinitely pleased by his smallest attentions.

With those conflicted feelings, Jake limped toward the barn where Lulu awaited her fate. His face reflected the light of the fire he'd set in the bunkhouse to distract the ranch hands from his purpose with Lulu, and hastily he cradled her under his powerful right arm. Out of the barn he hobbled toward a nook in the bluff overlooking the ranch. But Charlie spotted them as they snuck away.

In the mouth of the nook, Jake and Lulu snuggled against each other at the approach of the ranch hands below. The bunkhouse fire was now out, and in the darkness, startled by calls from the ranch hands below, Lulu attempted to shake loose from my brother's hold. The pings of thrown stones against the walls of their hiding place further aggravated her, and Jake withdrew as far as he could into the nook.

"Watch the stars with me for a little," he pleaded, "at least until they get us." Nothing he said soothed her.

In frustration at Lulu's efforts to free herself, Jake squeezed her ever tighter. "Please, Lulu," he whispered, "love me." Unwittingly he was choking her, and finally she kicked free. Jake lunged for her and caught a hind leg on her way out of the nook. But his chest hit a protruding rock as he landed, and he let go. Lulu leaped into the night, falling into the depths below.

Realizing what had happened to Lulu, and hearing Charlie at his heels, Jake began crying for me to protect him. Suddenly, Charlie was at him from the side. With a smart shove he yelled, "Fly, birdbrain, fly!"

For a second Jake seemed to be soaring, and a smile found his lips. Then he began falling toward Lulu, and he cried out for me again.

* * *

"I never gave my brother enough of myself while he was alive. The distance, my research, but mostly an anthropologist's embarrassment at recognizing in his brother all the defects in his own family tree – what I wouldn't admit to myself, much less to my wife, kids, and colleagues – that's what kept me away, and drove me to keep him away. It's funny, I'm spending more time with him now than I ever did, even when we were kids. It's like his parts are worth more than the whole."

"I wish he'd been a match for my Jo Jo," Stitches said, "especially with all the heart he seems to have. And then he wouldn't have ended up bein' a neomort."

"A what?" Joseph said.

"I read somewhere in all the materials I've studied on transplants," Stitches responded, "that they're thinkin' of creatin' special hospital wards called neomoratoriums to keep the blood flowin' in brain-dead people while the search is on for transplant matches. That way no precious organs would go to waste. They say that while the bodies are on life support, they could also be used for drug testin' and –"

"That's enough, Stitches," John broke in. "Why don't we close out this evening with some of Mitch's story. Caleb, if you will, please relate the story you thought earlier might be too personal. After what you've heard from the others, it's got to seem less of a problem now."

"I think I can handle it," Caleb said, "but I've never acknowledged in public the repulsive scoundrel I was. Now's as good a time as any, I guess. What follows, in all its crude detail, is what happened the night I met Mitch."

Chapter VI

Caleb

WITH A LEG CURLED BENEATH HER, she nestled into an armchair and leaned back from the banter. The other girls in the parlor of the college dormitory were conjecturing on whether the ball-peen hammer was named after *it*, and what the Mohs scale reading would be in its erect state. Hardness was in issue; once before, its size and weight had been reduced to the absurd.

The doorbell rang but no one stirred. It was a Friday night in late April, and as usual, it was assumed the boys on the Hill would be stag that night.

The girls giggled, and the chimes persisted. Finally, the girl in the armchair responded, striding lazily to the door. Involuntarily, her fingers found the center part of her curly brown hair and brushed stray strands into neatness. She reached for the doorknob.

As the door swung open, he was there. That was pretty much the way she'd pictured her dreamboat, she later told me – about six inches taller than her own five-foot-six frame, the straight, light brown hair, and the light blue eyes, even the dimpled cheeks. But still, her mind hadn't fully developed him either – certainly not the patch of whiskers in a deep cleft in his chin, just like on her older brother, whose cleft hairs too often also had escaped the razor.

Instantly, there was an awkward, orthodontic smile between us. I traced her figure, and she caught my pleasant surprise. "How about a swim?" I blurted out.

"A what?" she said.

"A swim...at the falls," I answered. "It's hot out!"

"You're crazy! Where you from?" she inquired.

"Guess!" I said, ticked off at the interrogation.

"What year you in?" she asked.

"Third," I replied. "Look, my roommate's got his car and girl outside, just grab a suit."

"Who's your roommate?" she asked.

"Ed Haley," I said, irked that my standing with her might be based on his name.

"Oh, and Sue –," she began to say.

"Yeh, that's right," I broke in, "and Sue Lassiter is the girl."

She studied my face. "I'm afraid not," she said, remembering certain vows she'd made following her older brother's recent death. "The water's freezing this time of year. Maybe some other time." She turned slowly, and I caught her arm.

"Sue suggested I ask her roommate," I said, "but..." I saw her wince, "I'd rather be with you."

"What's your name?" she asked, smiling.

"Caleb," I replied.

"Caleb what?" she asked.

"Call, Caleb Call," I shot back.

"I'll be right back, don't move," she said, disappearing into the parlor. The giggling within instantly ceased, replaced by a hushed chatter. Seconds later she returned. But she didn't move toward the door. Instead, she turned toward the stairs opposite me and said, "I'll be right back," adding after a few steps, "Don't go away."

I wasn't alone for long. A gaggle of girls soon emerged from the parlor, most of whom hastily ogled me before retreating down the hallway. Others stared and scurried up the stairs.

Five minutes later, she returned. She had a tote bag with her. "Michelle Levy is ready to go!" she announced with a broad grin.

"Michelle Levy," I repeated, somewhat surprised, only to realize how asinine I must have sounded. "The name rings like a movie star's," I added quickly, to minimize the damage.

She didn't take advantage. "Just call me Mitch," she said as we reached the car.

The water at the falls was cold, dark, and scary. Stripping to our bathing suits, I fantasized about swimming nude. She cursed herself for having committed to swim at all.

We jumped into the water together, on mutual dares, and surfaced screaming. We bounced and bellyached about the cold, but neither of us left the water. Then I touched her, to warm her, and we froze. Waist deep, without words, teeth chattering uncontrollably and eyes roaming deceptively, she searched my lean, muscular body, and I the fullness of her breasts. Defying gravity, droplets of water clung to her high cheekbones, capturing in miniature the full moon. That image of me touching her arm, the life of one melding with that of the other, would remain with me, haunting me, forever.

Her face drew me closer, and I stroked her cheeks to tame for her the cold, dark, and scary water. And she allowed me that; a kiss too, lingering in the warmth of tongues caressing chattering teeth to rest.

Then, laughing, she ran from me toward the car. Debating her expectation, I hesitated only momentarily before pursuing her into the company of Ed and Sue.

From the falls, Ed's car managed the dirt road reluctantly, until it finally balked. With only nickels and dimes to feed it, the car once more had run out of gas. Except this time it had Mitch and me as companions while Ed and Sue went off in search of fuel.

There was an exaggerated silence that settled over our isolation. Making a point of her extreme misgivings, Mitch gazed at the gas gauge even though it was unreadable in the moonlight. She was peeved at having allowed a kiss at the falls, and only her trust in Sue kept her from abandoning me to this false pretense she was certain Ed and I had concocted.

I stared at Mitch and struggled for the right words and moves. I cautiously stretched my arm over the back of the rear seat and mentally tested several lines. All of them came off lame. Finally, with nothing better to offer, I grabbed at a rejected one. "Can you imagine running out of gas like this," I said flippantly.

"No," she replied with an edge to her voice. She flinched her shoulder as my fingers alit there. I remained steadfast.

"Do you suppose it's Ed and Sue's way of getting alone?" I said, smiling at the innuendo.

"For what?" she asked.

I swallowed hard. "Oh, come off it, Mitch!" I said. "Maybe just because it's nice to be alone with someone you like!"

"Then what does it mean if you don't like being alone with somebody?" she said. I ignored the question.

"Say, are you cold?" I asked, then realizing an unintended meaning, added quickly, "I mean with a wet bathing suit on."

I could see she was enjoying my discomfort, which became her way, I'm sure, of compensating for the bitter aftertaste of our kiss. "It depends on whether I like being alone with you," she whispered.

"What does that mean?" I inquired.

"It means I don't on the first date!" she declared.

"Don't what?" I asked. "What are you talking about now?"

"Don't kiss on the first date!" she stated.

"But you already –" I said, befuddled.

"All right," she interrupted, "then I don't *undress* on the first date!"

"Jeez, Mitch, all I meant was that I'd take a walk while you changed," I explained, realizing at last where her weird comments were coming from. "It seems the least I can do for getting you into this mess."

She must have decided she was being too cute, because she said, "No, I'm not cold. Besides, how could I be cold when I'm alone with you?" I withdrew my outstretched arm, and for some minutes only crickets appeared to exist. While Mitch agonized over the wordplay, I decided to act the injured party.

"I enjoyed the falls tonight," she said at last, assuming correctly that I wasn't about to volunteer another word. "I've never been there like that. Have you?"

"No," I said.

"No, never, or no, once or twice?" she inquired.

"Okay, once," I replied honestly.

"With a girl?" she asked.

"Does it matter?" I replied.

"Yes," she said.

"Why, because you like being alone with me so much?" I said.

"No, because I like the games you play," she said, smiling. "Like how hurt you want me to think you are. Tell me, am I the only one who's pushed you to be so creative?"

"You don't let up, do you?" I said. "I try for pleasant conversation, and all you do is turn everything I say into some sexual plot. No, I don't have lines that I feed my dates; no, I've never run out of gas before!"

"Not even the way your mouth keeps running?" she shot back.

"Let me finish!" I raged. "You know I did like being alone with you. Yes, damn it! I mean, Jesus, I was supposed to ask Sue's roommate, remember? But there you were, and I asked *you*, didn't I!"

"You'd never know it!" she shouted back.

"Oh, come on, Mitch, that's got to mean something," I retorted. "My asking you has got to mean the lines, the physical stuff – yeah, including that kiss – ain't everything!"

"You mean I'm not going to hear your best lines or get to kiss you again?" she giggled.

"Look," I said cautiously, "all I really wanted when I asked you about changing was for you to be comfortable, believe it or not! Did you think I was going to just sit here while you stripped and ogle your naked bod? No, ma'am! I would have helped you!" I smiled to show I was joking. "No, what I really would have done was gone down the road until you called. Really. Boy, you must be one shell-shocked lady!"

Mitch didn't know what to say. I thought she'd apologize, but she wasn't sure she'd misread me. She thought to debate my points, but figured an argument would inevitably lose the cause. "I'd like to change now," she said finally. "If you don't mind, that is."

"Are you serious?" I asked.

Mitch spied the sound of victory in my words. "Yes," she whispered, "so I can finally be alone with someone I like."

"How far should I go?" I asked.

"There you go again!" she exclaimed.

"There *you* go again," I retorted. "All I meant was how many steps should I take from the car before I turn my telescope on you?"

"How far does the crow fly?" she said.

"How the hell should I know?" I shot back. "Look, Mitch, you'll just have to trust me!" I opened the car door and went about fifty paces behind the car. Then I shouted, "Yell when you're ready!"

"Ready for what?" she shouted back.

"Do you really want to know?" I said.

"Yes!" she answered.

"Ready to kiss and make up!" I said.

"Never!" she shouted.

"That's a long time!" I answered.

"Not long enough!" she said.

"Should I keep walking?" I asked. She sensed a sting to my ego.

"As far as the crow flies!" she replied.

"How far's that?" I said.

"Close enough to hear me yell, 'Ready!'"

Alone, down the road from Mitch, I became uncertain when the first ten minutes passed without a sound from the car. Then, pressed by a desire to strut before her in the absence of Ed and Sue, I discreetly approached the vehicle.

A few feet from the rear bumper, I softly called Mitch's name, as if my reserve would mellow her likely abuse for peeking. There was no answer, however, and concern for her safety prompted me to shuffle forward to the side door of the car to peer in.

But as I took the last step, something caught my left instep and toppled me. I tried to grab the doorknob, before twisting to break my fall. Anxiously attempting to rise, I failed to perceive the hurtling body coming at me from behind. The body hit my rear solidly and collapsed my immature stance. Again the dirt road came at me, but I pivoted to my back after hitting the ground, only to receive the well-timed weight of my attacker on me. It knocked the wind out of me. With arms and legs working in unison, my attacker hastened to pin me to the ground.

Belatedly recognizing my attacker, I began guffawing in silence, for the earlier impact of Mitch's weight was still cheating me of the sound of laughter. My jocular animations, however, were enough to further antagonize her and fuel her continuing efforts to pin me.

"You pervert!" she yelled. "I knew you would peek! That's all you've got on your mind!"

I twisted my right arm free and plucked Mitch's blouse from her pants. A one-piece bathing suit was still in place. "You stinker!" I shot back. "You never intended to change! You set me up, you –"

I didn't finish. In the seconds of our playful rebuttals, we experienced a spontaneous surge of emotion. I rolled Mitch beneath me and cupped her face in my hands. She didn't resist. Tenderly, my fingers traced the contours of her face, and like a pecking hen, I swiftly kissed the tip of her nose. Then, pulling my head back abruptly, I searched her eyes for the acceptance I already knew would be there. Her mind couldn't forestall where we were going, and imploring me to continue, Mitch readily palmed the nape of my neck and urged me toward her.

Our lips and tongues eagerly played together, and while she constantly thwarted my hands in touring her body, both of us became marvelously excited.

Several minutes into our newest dimension, with each body irrepressibly manipulated by the other's clever maneuvers, I reached an exclamation point. There was no denying the mass in my pants, which had creased her hand seconds before.

Normally, I would have submitted to a clandestine ejaculation, thinking it better to wet my pants than unilaterally expose myself. But Mitch was a Jewess, and at the time – I hate myself for this – I was thinking of all the Christian fantasies I'd had of being with that kind of sexually liberated woman, who was there for the asking. So with the deftness of a lock picker, I surreptitiously unzipped my fly and released myself from conscience's restraint. My joint hung out there, throbbing to its heart's content.

Rejoining Mitch's more traditional movements, I soon became overwhelmed by the psychology of my transparent condition. With vanquished control I grasped Mitch's hand at my neck and led it forcefully to my groin. Her surprised touch of hot skin, or maybe just the shock of what must have been so demeaning, seemed to magnetize the objects in play. Seconds later, spurts of semen again surprised Mitch, and, perhaps numbed by the double deal, she lay submissive to my premature assault.

As if cemented into an eternal hold, Mitch was oblivious to my shrinking penis. Even my renewed lip readings of her face in a naive afterplay were ignored. Her mind was clearly elsewhere, but to me at the time her mindless state was just another indication of the accuracy of my initial assessment of the situation.

It took jolly noises in the distance to separate us and bring a more immediate awareness to Mitch. On returning to the car, Ed and Sue noticed only the remarkable quiet in the back seat. And although the subject was indirectly broached, like fellow travelers on different journeys, neither couple begged the other for an explanation of the lapse of time.

Ed and I shared our apartment with another undergraduate, who was intentionally not at home when we finally arrived from the falls. Jerry Watkins' absence, however, was the least of things that needed explaining as we entered the building far behind Ed and Sue. After my abuse of Mitch, I'd struggled for conversation. Mitch had kept conspicuously to herself, not even voicing her preference to return directly to her dorm. And neither of us seemed to want to renew the verbal combat which had previously captivated us. Without the needling and baiting, I was at a loss to resurrect our earlier camaraderie, whatever it was.

"That your high school ring?" I asked, touching Mitch's right hand.

"Uh huh," she said, pulling her hand away.

"I didn't get one," I remarked, and added, "Didn't see the need for it."

"You don't have to make excuses," she said drily.

"I wasn't," I rejoined. "There just wasn't a need."

"There's always a need if you want something badly enough!" she said testily.

"What do you mean?" I asked somewhat conciliatorily.

"I mean –" she started to say, then exploded with, "Oh, what difference does it make after what just happened!" She caught herself and added a bit less vehemently, "I mean you could've bought it for memory's sake, but fond memories don't seem to be worth a damn to you!"

"May I see it, please?" I whispered, taking her hand again. I tried to remove the ring and stumbled on a step.

"Can't you do anything right!" she said derisively as her hand fell away.

"I'd rather do something wrong," I said, "than not do anything at all."

I took her hand firmly in mine to look at the ring without removing it. "Your hands are freezing!" she exclaimed.

"Warm hands, cold heart!" I responded.

"You mean 'cold hands, warm heart,' don't you?" she said.

"Do I now?" I replied. "You see, you've got the warm hands, but I've got the warm heart!" Lacing her fingers with mine, I sensed a slight recovery in the evening.

"You forgot to inspect the ring," she chided as our woven hands swung downward. "White gold, yellow gold; rich girl, poor girl."

"I did inspect it," I said. "I just have a quick eye for precious things." I squeezed her hand, but she broke away and bounded up the stairs into the apartment.

Roaming around her date's den, Mitch sought the nitty-gritty of my existence, things she readily made light of but never forgot. They compelled her to reassess her own intentions too.

"Whose room is that?" she asked at Jerry's door.

"That's our third roommate's, Jerry Watkins," I said. "Boy, what an animal!"

"Must be a precondition for living here," she said. "Why's he an animal?"

"It's not important," I said.

"Of course it is!" she said. "Everything on your mind is important."

I went to the kitchen and returned with a box of pretzels and two cans of beer. "Want some?" I asked.

"Only if you tell me about Jerry," she answered, taking some pretzels and the one can that was already open.

"Tell you what?" I asked.

"Why you've got an animal in the apartment," she said.

I looked at Ed and Sue. They were on the couch making out. "Okay," I said. "There are a dozen things you'll see for yourself when you meet him." I paused to let the hint of our future meet the present. "But the one thing that stands out just happened. Jerry stayed here over spring break and by the time we got back, he'd packed the kitchen to the ceiling with trash. And the first night we were here, the landlady came up for the rent, and we had all this garbage to get rid of or we would be out on the street!"

Ed overheard the comment and sauntered over. "So what happened?" Mitch asked, unaware that Ed's arrival had chilled my desire to continue.

"We ended up shutting the kitchen light before she came in," I hurried on, "so she couldn't see into the kitchen."

"And whose idea was it to kill the light?" Ed broke in, grinning broadly.

"Come off it, Ed!" I rejoined. "So you've had one good idea."

"Caleb!" Mitch scowled. "Just because you didn't think of it?"

I ignored her and said, "What an animal that Jerry is!"

"Must be contagious," Mitch muttered.

"What'd you say?" I asked, already having a pretty good notion.

"I said, 'He must be outrageous,'" she answered.

"Say, how about some slow music?" Ed stretched out the words, sensing the tension between us.

"Great!" Sue responded from the couch. "Put on you-know-who," she added, winking at Ed.

The lights evaporated, and the romance of mood music charged the air. Mitch allowed me to hold her close, my feet stationary, my arms draped around her waist. "It's been an interesting evening," I whispered, brushing her ear with my lips.

She didn't answer. Minutes and songs passed. "Are you doing anything tomorrow night?" I asked, pulling my head back from her cheek to gaze into her eyes. She stared back blankly. "Are you?" I repeated.

"Yes," she replied hesitantly, still looking into my eyes. "I have to go home for the weekend." And like I said before, Mitch always told the truth, as she knew it, although at the time I didn't know that. "Sorry," she added as my disappointment registered. But I didn't think she was sorry, either for not being available or for torturing me with her delayed response. I dropped my hands from her hips to her buttocks. She didn't react.

Ed and Sue disappeared into his bedroom, and even though I'd bombed earlier when mentioning their departure for gas, I swung Mitch around so she could see the withdrawing couple. Again she was nonresponsive, and I decided dominos wasn't her game. Instead, I settled for kisses to her neck and nose, and the teasing of her lips with mine. Still there was no resistance, and my hands pulled her groin against mine. She grinned.

The last record on the spindle played itself out, and without an automatic retraction, the needle's annoying scratching finally broke us apart. Leading Mitch to the record player, I silenced it, and reassessing what I had to lose, I wrapped my arm about her shoulders and led her to my bedroom.

At the flick of a switch, the room was imbued with a red glow. The bed was made, books were neatly stacked, and a letter from home was on the dresser. I locked the door.

There was a marked stillness which blended perfectly with the manufactured atmosphere, and was disturbed solely by my bedsprings as we eased onto the mattress. Mitch seemed amenable to a prone position, and my routine of the dirt road repeated itself.

Realizing the onset of activities that earlier had surprised her, Mitch again allowed me the liberty of her hand. But this time she only let her hand hover over my deliverance, and when unable to hold off any longer, she bolted upright.

Mitch's reaction had confused even herself. She had intended an abusive scene no man would have forgotten. It just wouldn't come, and she got off the bed.

"What's the matter?" I asked, somewhat dazed.

"Guess!" she mustered with peppery sarcasm.

"Come on, Mitch," I said. "It's not the time for twenty questions!"

"Okay, I'm not in the mood for another biology lesson!" she shouted. "One a night's enough!"

"I still don't understand," I said. "What'd I do?"

"Just look at yourself!" she ordered. I looked and became embarrassed, but not enough to bury my manhood – at least not without another try. I reached for her and brought her adjacent to the bed. She shrugged me off.

"Mitch, you excite me," I blurted out. "It's a compliment if anything. What's wrong with that?"

"Maybe you don't excite me!" she said, hesitated, and added with care, "Oh, Caleb, you keep making me say things I don't want to. This is stupid. I wanted to start a relationship tonight, not end one. I just don't want a repeat of what you did to me before; I couldn't handle it.

I don't know who was to blame – I've got to think it through. But let's not add to it now. Please."

The agony in her words didn't escape me, but I was too preoccupied with my own ego to let it go at that. "Mitch," I pleaded, "it's going to hurt if we don't. I thought you wanted to – you didn't stop me." I reached for her hand, and she stepped back. "Just this time, Mitch, please! I'll know for next time." Again I extended my hand toward hers, but she walked to the door and unlocked it.

"Caleb," she said, "you got yourself into it, you get yourself out! Whatever pain you feel can't hurt nearly as much as I do inside. Please take me home."

Stunned, realizing at last the heel I was, but really the heel I thought she thought I was, I redeposited myself in my pants, stood, and faced her. Falteringly, I inched toward her, reached out, and, cupping her face in my hands, advanced until my nose was touching hers. She seemed mesmerized by my actions and accepted a brushing kiss with the words, "I'm sorry."

Mitch didn't know how to respond. She chose to remain silent.

The only other words spoken before Mitch was dropped at her dorm came from me. "Mitch," I said plaintively, "we both have much to think about from what happened tonight. I meant what I said before about being sorry. I also meant what I said about wanting to see you tomorrow night. Maybe you have to go home," I paused to give her the chance to reverse her earlier statement, "but time is what we need anyway. I'd like to call you next week, after you've had a chance to think things through."

She stared at me and cocked her head as if to speak. I quickly put my fingers to her lips. "Don't say another word," I added, feeling an expanding emptiness. "If you don't talk to me when I call, I'll know why."

I didn't attempt to kiss her at the door. She later said that she would have preferred that I did.

* * *

"That's it for now on Mitch and me," Caleb concluded. "Someone else take up the banner."

"I never had a relationship like that with a woman," Joseph volunteered. "Goldie sometimes reads that kind of romance novel, and from the pages I've read in them, you could write one just as good, Caleb. It's strange how women create private worlds that men, no matter how intimate with them, are barred from. Even Mitch back then seemed to have hers, or was I imagining it?"

"I don't know what you mean…," Caleb said.

"Come on, Caleb," Tom said, "even the insensitive bastard that you were should have sensed something going on in her life that kept her on edge. For one thing, you did mention her older brother's death; that had to have an effect, whether you knew about it or not. And your abuse of her highlighted it, at least to me. You know, on campuses today you'd be brought up on charges mighty close to rape for what you did. Probably you didn't catch the undercurrent because you had only one thing on your mind.

"How'd he die anyway, and did you ever find out what vows she'd made because of it?"

"I don't know…," Caleb said, his voice trailing off.

Tom snickered. "You mean you went with this woman two, three years –"

"Three," Caleb inserted.

"Three years," Tom continued, "and you never asked her how her brother died? You're putting us on."

"Nope."

"Are you sure she didn't drop you for a lack of interest?" Tom added.

"Okay, so I know how he died – she accidentally ran over him with his car!" Caleb shouted. "Does that make you happy?"

"Quiet down, Caleb!" John interjected. "If you've forgotten, we're in a hospital lounge, and it's after visiting hours. Let's call it a night and get together early tomorrow morning for breakfast at my place. Let's make it around seven. The address and directions from the hospital are on this paper I'm passing out. Seven o'clock in the morning, so we can continue our conversation over some good home cooking and still get to the hospital early enough for visiting hours. Is that okay with everybody?"

Everyone nodded.

"Caleb, why don't you stay after the others leave," John went on, "and tell me how I can be of help tomorrow."

"John, as long as we're getting together so early tomorrow, let's save it till then. I'm exhausted, it's been a long day, and we've got to do it right. Okay?"

"Sure," John said. "See you first thing tomorrow morning."

Chapter VII

'But if you do not obey Me, and do not observe all these commandments, and if you despise My statutes, or if your soul abhors My judgments, so that you do not perform all My commandments, but break My covenant, I also will do this to you.... I will scatter you among the nations and draw out a sword after you.... You shall perish among the nations, and the land of your enemies shall eat you up.

Leviticus 26:14–16, 33, 38

Yet for all that, when they are in the land of their enemies, I will not cast them away, nor shall I abhor them, to utterly destroy them and break My covenant with them; for I am the LORD their God. But for their sake I will remember the covenant of their ancestors, whom I brought out of the land of Egypt in the sight of the nations, that I might be their God: I am the LORD.

Leviticus 26:44, 45

Now it shall come to pass, when all these things come upon you, the blessing and the curse which I have set before you, and you call them to mind among all the nations where the LORD your God drives you, and you return to the LORD your God...that the LORD your God will bring you back from captivity, and have compassion on you, and gather you again from all the nations where the LORD your God has scattered you.... And you will again obey the voice of the LORD and do all His commandments....

Deuteronomy 30:1–3, 8

The Group at Breakfast

When Tom entered John's apartment the next morning, he walked in on an argument between Caleb and Stitches concerning the article Tom had written and given to John. Caleb had arrived early at John's apartment to enlist John's support in seeing Mitch, and he'd happened to peruse Tom's article while waiting for John to finish preparing breakfast.

"That article," Tom interposed after catching the gist of the conversation, "through my study of Caribbean Indian civilization, documents that the rise and fall of the various cultures there was the result of the increasing intelligence of the dominating culture under generally equivalent environmental conditions. You could say that the conquerors had more supermen going for them. Any way you cut it, the conqueror's weapons, their development of natural and human resources, even their war strategies, were clearly superior to the vanquished. My conclusion is irrefutable: the Ciboneys lost to the Arawaks, who lost to the Caribs, because each was less developed than its successor.

"Now, don't get me wrong. I'm not advocating genetic inferiority. All I'm reporting is that with basically the same resources available to each, one people dominated the other, and never – and this is important – never did the subjugated people ever regain their former stature."

"Before you came in," Stitches said, "I was about to agree with your position based on my own, home-grown philosophy, more or less a reflection on the genius of my father-in-law Isaac. What I've seen is that the world population is made up of three classes without any race or gender bein' involved: Supermen, Men, and Nomen, named by yours truly. I came up with this theory way back when Jo Jo and me first discussed bringin' kids into this world, which we decided against – until our lovely Becka was born, anyway, some fifteen years ago. It came to me during one of those soul-searchin' periods we all have in assessin' how far we've come against the odds. Well, I concluded that there's a special breed of man, the Superman, who, findin' creative ways of bein' released from society's constraints, plays the game of life smarter than everyone else. And I just thought that with Caleb dumpin' on your article, I might tease him with my own thinkin' that since there've been Supermen, well, maybe, there've also been super-civilizations, like your Caribs, that simply play the game of life smarter. Just so ya know, in my thinkin' a civilization is a place where the inhabitants sleep without fear."

"Interesting definition. Yes, I'd like to hear about your three classes and the game of life," Tom said, whetting Stitches' desire to expound.

"I start my theory by definin' the Noman as a primitive. He lives unproductively off society, either on welfare or some other charity, pretty much drainin' the world's limited resources. The class of Man, on the other hand, is skilled and productive, what you'd call your typical blue- and white-collar workers. Man delivers hard work for a day's pay and gives society back as much as he takes from it. At the other extreme is the class of Superman, the advanced men of civilization, who constantly replenish society's limited resources, counterbalancin' what's taken by the Noman. So you have the prospect of a perfect balance, sleepin' without fear, right?

"Fortunately, a Superman can never be anythin' but that. It's the essence of his intellectual and moral makeup. So the objective is to stimulate each Superman to reach his maximum potential, and in that way to constantly build up society's resources bein' subjected to an ever-increasin' drain as more and more of the class of Man falls into the class of Noman: the homeless, the downtrodden, the dropouts."

"When you arrived this morning," Caleb interjected, "I was contesting your article from the perspective of the Jews: they keep coming back and dominating their conquerors and oppressors. Or did you forget about them?

"You'll recall that Leviticus 26:44–45 says that despite all the bad things that will befall the Jews because they exercise their free will to reject God's laws, they will rise, like the phoenix, from their ashes when they return to God. The odd thing is that the Jews use the Holocaust and other horrors that devastated them to question God's mercy and justice, and whether He exists at all, when those horrors by their very occurrence actually validate the divine authority of the Five Books of Moses. You see, what has actually happened to the Jews over the last three thousand years is expressly foretold in Leviticus 26 – like the Holocaust in verse 38 – and, if anything, certifies that God exists."

"So, according to you, the Jews should be thrilled that the Holocaust happened," Tom snickered. "Caleb, just look at the Jews in Egypt or even the Ciboneys: their slavery is a consequence of losing. But let's go back to the Superman, Stitches. I'm curious: how did you think the world should choose this elite class to rule over us? Better yet, how does a Southern black man, to mirror your racial concerns – even a brilliant and successful one like you – ever become a Superman in a white-dominated world?"

"That's a good question," Stitches replied, "so good, in fact, that I never could answer it, and, as I said, that's why we once thought never to have a family. To think I could bring a Superman into this world only to be thwarted by racism was, until Becka, too much for Jo Jo and me."

"So let's get back to the Jewish phoenix," Caleb said. "The Jews have been our most identifiable Supermen: Einstein, Marx, Freud, to name a few influencing this century alone. Isn't that the real reason Hitler went after the Jews? Because as Supermen, the Jews rejected God. I mean – without condoning his inhumanity – Hitler may merely have been a pawn in fulfilling biblical prophecy. Someone had to remind the Jews of the contract that made them into Supermen in the first place, especially when they'd failed to remember the Torah poem, '*Haazinu*,' that was supposed to remind them of it!"

"And maybe, Caleb," Tom countered, "it was Stitches' Jewish Supermen who created God in the first place, as one innovative way of keeping the Nomen in check. By offering the have-nots the promise of a heavenly afterlife to make up for their current misery, the Supermen kept the Nomen from overwhelming them with their numbers, if not their brains. So, as Stitches would say, they could sleep without fear."

"Gentlemen!" John exclaimed. "I've never had such an argumentative group. It may take our minds off what's happening at the hospital, but that's not what we're here for! After we leave here, we're still going to have to grieve, and we've gotten nowhere on that score!"

"I'd say we're bondin' just great, John," Stitches said, quite pleased with the reception given his theory, "and what more effective way is there to grieve than with friends?"

"Jews and blacks have been partners in suffering and the struggle for civil rights since I can remember," Joseph offered, eager to contribute after arriving late. "Goldie worked hard and long in the civil rights movement, so I wouldn't want this conversation to end with the suggestion that Jews and blacks aren't equals in all respects."

"That's not true, Joseph," Tom said. "Jews have always exploited blacks. My research on Caribbean history found a number of instances of Jewish slavers. Maybe their activities weren't the most egregious, but they were there where there was money to be made."

"Let's not stereotype," Stitches remarked. "For example, I wouldn't say that Dr. Rosenberg, who'll perform the heart transplant on my Jo Jo when a match is found, exploits blacks. Why, the minute he saw we were black, and without knowin' we could afford whatever he charged, he said he would charge us only what we could afford."

"Enough of your humor, Stitches," John said. "When do you visit Isaac again?"

"Probably the day after tomorrow if nothin' develops here," he answered. "By then I may be goin' home to plan Jo Jo's return to die, not just to see Isaac. But I got good vibrations about the next few days. And as for Isaac, I got rich sellin' his simple contraptions to the local tenant farmers, who were poorer than hell, and those sales cascaded into more sophisticated equipment, which we eventually sold to whites as well as blacks. Maybe a Jew or two, like Joseph's friend Louis Goldberg, sold my customers some machinery that was more than they could afford, with the intention of repossessin' it and sellin' it to another dirt-poor farmer down the road in some vicious cycle, but it wasn't some Jewish conspiracy of Supermen keepin' the Nomen down – it was everybody, includin' me, havin' a field day with the ignorant. Eventually I stopped exploitin' them, made my money helpin' them, and came out on top. The Jews may not have seen that end, but for a time I was no different."

"Stitches, you were stereotyping Jews with that comment on Louis Goldberg," Joseph argued. "Jews got killed for your civil rights, so comments like that, as much as you try to soften them, start things you can't stop. It's the old story about biting the hand that feeds you."

"I don't think Stitches did that, Joseph," Tom said. "Besides, the blacks owe the Jews nothing. Whatever actions the Jews took were to promote their own civil rights too!"

"Talking about biting the hand that feeds you," Caleb said, "the Jews do that constantly with the hand of God that chose them in the first place."

"So, Caleb, you propose a mandatory period of full observance, forcibly placed on the Jews by society to test their contract with God," Tom said. "Talking about biting, I'd say you're biting off much more than you can chew!"

"Perhaps," Caleb replied, "but I'll hazard the guess that if the proposal were fully aired, it would take off."

"But doesn't the need to use force contradict your position that the Jews are the Supermen of civilization, chosen by God expressly to represent the rest of us before Him?" Tom argued. "If they do all these self-destructive things, how can they be our elite, especially when, as Supermen, they themselves should see that full observance of God's laws is the easiest way to replenish the earth's resources? With blessings of health, peace, and prosperity, who'd care how many Nomen were around? In fact, we'd all be able to laze around like Nomen."

"It's the world that says the Jews are our Supermen, not me," Caleb rejoined, "and then it punishes them for being it by alleging all sorts of conspiracy protocols. According to Stitches's philosophy, the world should be nurturing the Jews, not designing the next Holocaust."

"You still haven't answered why they're so self-destructive when they're supposed to be so smart," Tom said, "and why they don't realize that gaining the blessings for all of us makes great business sense."

"They act that way," Caleb replied, "because their rabbis know that if they preach strict adherence to only the Written Law in the Torah, which means a return to Levitical Judaism in lieu of today's Rabbinical Judaism, the rabbis will be out of power. And as we all know, power corrupts. The nice thing about the test period is that even if nothing happens, they'll be out of a job anyway. Maybe that's why the rabbis foster such self-destructive ideology. They don't really want to find out about God, and in the process find themselves on the outside looking in!"

"What you keep saying," Tom said, "is that if the Jews were to conclude from a failed test that there really was no contract and no difference between their God and the God of the Christians or Muslims, then a lot of Jews would convert, because it loses them nothing if God is truly what they seek. And if that's the case, Caleb, your test might indeed become the final solution for the Jews – and a good incentive for Christians and Muslims to push for it!"

"Caleb, time is running out before visiting hours, and this group could go on forever," John said. "Why don't we send the others along so we can finish discussing your problem in visiting Mitch. Unless, of course, you want all of us involved."

"We're here for you, Caleb," Stitches said.

"With what happened yesterday," Caleb said, "I guess I need all the help I can get."

Chapter VIII

Caleb

"Before I get into my disaster with Mitch," Caleb began, "I'll provide some additional background so you can assess my mental state from the second I got to the hospital."

* * *

When I arrived yesterday, I immediately scanned the hospital entrance for familiar faces from Mitch's and my past. Fortunately, there were none, and I survived the first tier of horrors I'd envisioned on the plane in. I also looked to the weather as a predictor of my success with Mitch, and the sight of the dank and cranky sky spawned a sense of rank dismay. Still, I straightened my tie and suit coat and walked inside.

Normally, I'd be quite at home in a hospital, but on this occasion, on Mitch's floor, I was immensely relieved to learn that Mitch's room was barred to visitors for the next hour. Escaping to the basement cafeteria, where I saw Joseph ordering his BLT, I nursed the breakfast and lunch I'd foregone in my effort to get here. The whole time I was eating, I pondered the delicacy of confronting Mitch uninvited after so many years. Constantly with me was the fear that she would never forgive my abominable ending of our relationship. Needless to say, the reason why I ended it was, to me, as bad as the how. When my anxiety finally became unbearable, I returned to Mitch's floor determined to face the consequences of surprising her with my presence. Well, maybe not all that determined, as it turned out.

This time I was informed that Mitch was asleep and wouldn't be receiving visitors until much later in the day, after they'd finished some procedure they wouldn't discuss, professional courtesy notwithstanding. When I became somewhat irate, it was suggested that I wait in the visitors' lounge, where we were last evening, with the promise that I'd be advised as soon as I could see her.

About two hours later, I was startled awake by the nurse who had directed me to the lounge. A bit tense to say the least, I followed her to Mitch's room.

The door opened fully at the nurse's prodding. Mitch's eyes were closed, and the nurse, with a finger to her lips and a hand pointing to a chair, directed me toward the bed. The bed was elevated at the head, and a television was silently projecting bright colors from a support on the opposite wall near the ceiling.

Flowers, a noisy compressor, and Mitch's emaciated face instantly monopolized my attention, however, and I remained frozen at the door while confirming the stage to which Mitch's cancer had brought her. You see, and this is not to be repeated, her cancer has spread to her bones. They're so brittle that when the nurses turn her, they risk breaking parts of her skeleton. That appears to have happened already: her pelvis, one or more vertebrae, I'm not sure what else. The compressor is for a special mattress that has tiny silicone beads in it, which are kept in motion so that she pretty much floats in bed. An IV is delivering morphine right into her bloodstream from a computerized pump, and, of course, there are oxygen supplements being delivered through a tube in her nose. I saw all this, and the culpability I'd begun feeling from the minute I learned of her condition yesterday morning was about to explode on actually seeing it all. So when the nurse put her arm around me and gently pushed me toward the chair, I was at that moment totally incapable of approaching her. I've seen much worse in my years of practice, but the tubes and needles, the horror of Mitch's magnificent complexion gone to death's yellow cast, and her frail, wrinkled hand clutching the bed's automatic controls made me weak-kneed and sick.

Overwrought at witnessing the shocking antithesis to my dream of courting Mitch once more, I was physically helped from the room by the nurse and deposited in the lounge again. Flooding myself with coffee when a strong sedative was my true need, I paced the floor like a test rat injected with some confounding solution. After a half hour of that, I decided to steal into Mitch's room and be with her to the end. Steeling myself, I snuck in, pushed the chair next to her bed, and, taking her hand from the control panel, whispered my undying love for her.

Slowly Mitch began to respond to my voice. I stared into her eyes and concentrated my whole being on receiving a favorable response when her eyes opened. Then they did. For no more than a handful of seconds, Mitch gazed at me while the ravenous silence ate at my composure. In those seconds, I'm sure, Mitch was playing back my face to see if it matched the twenty-four-year-old's she'd last known, just as she'd probably done with my voice. I stood and leaned forward to embrace her, but she struggled upward with evident pain and screeched out the words, 'Get out! Get out!' before falling back in a coughing spasm. Nurses rushed in and chased me from the room.

"How could you, Dr. Call!" the nurse who had earlier escorted me from the room said. "The cancer's at her voice box – she hasn't spoken in days because of the pain!"

"I'm sorry," I said. "I didn't expect that. I'm sorry."

The nurse noted my pallor and relented. "I'm sorry, Dr. Call, but you may not see Ms. Levy again unless she requests it. She mustn't be upset like that anymore. Please understand."

Having half expected Mitch's reaction, I didn't contest the nurse's decree and returned dejectedly to the lounge. Gradually, however, the hospital air became stifling, and I had to escape the building. Breathing deeply outside, I began strolling the streets with one thought, one hope, in mind: Mitch had reacted that way not as a rejection of me for what I'd done to her years ago, but, rather, to keep me from seeing her as she was now. Her need was for me to remember her as she once was.

I sat in the park across from the hospital and penned a message to her that I later asked a nurse to deliver. It read:

My dearest Mitch,

The years have passed without the benefit of each other. They have been cruel in that regard. You may have heard of the emptiness of those years for me. If you have, you surely understand why I must be here.

I have heard little of what these years have held for you. I can only wish them to have been better for you than for me. Knowing where you are today, my heart grieves for not having shared your burdens these last few years.

The nurses have banished me from your weary eyes. They have disallowed that I might comfort you. We both know that I can. There will be brighter days ahead, and if you would permit me a little of your precious time, I'm sure I can bring those days to you much sooner.

Perhaps you might let me read to you, or even recount our past together. I promise not to be overindulgent nor be my witty self, but to take your directions faithfully.

I have never prided myself on being a salesman (although you always maintained otherwise, especially in certain subjects), but I wish to heaven you would permit your door to open to me now.

Please know that I would rather look upon your face with the anger in it I perceived today than never look upon you again. I have searched for you relentlessly and now have the chance to breathe serenity into both of us. I can't erase the past, but I can give you a new meaning for what you may have wished to forget. Certainly, I can bring those brighter days to you sooner.

Mitch, I love you very much. Please let me be with you, and please forgive me.

✶ ✶ ✶

"Mitch has the note now," Caleb went on, "and John, I would appreciate whatever can be done to get me in to see her. It would mean everything to me to be with her during the time she has left. I honestly believe her reaction was a result of my seeing her the way she is, and I've got to make her understand that our hearts are what matter now. If any of you can think of a way, I'll be in the lounge as long as it takes till she'll let me see her."

"Speaking for all of us," John said, "I'll see what I can do. I'll trust your medical training for the reason she threw you out, and proceed on that basis. But if there's any resistance from her, Caleb, I'm going to have to understand exactly how 'abominable' the ending of your relationship was before I take it any further."

"Thanks, John."

Chapter IX

Mitch

As John drove the group to the hospital that morning, he invited them to his apartment that evening for dinner at six. And, subject to events of the day, each accepted. John personally walked with Caleb to the lounge on Mitch's floor, and after completing a few tasks, began negotiations with the nurses in Caleb's favor.

At ten o'clock John returned to the lounge to find Caleb with his head in his hands, looking desolate. "I was with her just a few minutes ago," John said, "and she seems a lot more alert. I noticed your note near her hand so I think she must have read it. I also think it's probably responsible for her orders to her doctors to reduce her medication, which, I guess, is why she's so alert. Because it seemed to mean that she's preparing herself to see you, I shied away from attempting to convince her to do it. My guess is that if you confront her without her having built an argument against it with me, she'll more likely accept you after some initial resistance."

"I thought her medication would be my worst enemy," Caleb said, somewhat cheered, "but you say she's alert?" John nodded. "What a day it will be!"

"You know the pain she's in, Caleb," John said, bringing Caleb back to earth, "so you'd better couple your medical know-how with your lover's compassion to bring her a death with dignity. No more flare-ups, or there'll be hell to pay, especially from Mr. Watkins, who's cold as ice when it comes to getting whatever's right for her."

"I promise," Caleb said, his mind suddenly elsewhere. "John, is that *Jerry* Watkins, the roommate I mentioned yesterday when I talked about the night I met Mitch?"

"I think so, Caleb," John replied, "but I can't say for sure. You'll just have to meet him to see. He's a strange character. He's got all the time in the world for Mitch, but none for himself or our therapy sessions. My guess is he's a prime candidate for therapy, and his grief is going to explode in him."

"Let's do it, John," Caleb said. "I'm ready to see her. I know what needs to be said. She'll improve after being with me; you'll see!"

"At this stage, Caleb, that may not be best for her," John answered. "Just follow me and ask no questions."

They walked past the nurses' station with only a nod from John and were soon at Mitch's door, which was slightly ajar. As the door swung open, they stepped inside and immediately faced Mitch, who attempted to hide Caleb's note, which she had been valiantly rereading. But before a scream could issue, before the note could be buried beneath her sheets, before her frail fingers could find her distress buzzer, Caleb had her hands in his.

"Go ahead, scream!" he whispered defiantly. "Go ahead, press the buzzer!" he added right after. "I've bought the whole staff off, every nurse and doctor on the floor! I've got you all to myself for the afternoon. So you're going to listen to me for as long as it takes, and when I'm done with my say you can throw me out – if you still want to."

Gently rubbing her hands with his, as if by that contact his strength would find its way into her, Caleb gazed into her eyes, still the large brown brooding ones he'd loved so dearly, and said, "You read my note, didn't you?"

She couldn't deny it and faintly nodded.

"I love you!" he exclaimed and kissed her lips. "Do you hear? I love you, love you, *love* you! We're going to break out of here together, the two of us. But first we're going to get you well – so you can scream and yell at me whenever you like, and forgive me too." John quietly left the room.

Mitch squinted her eyes, and it further wrinkled her face. She was questioning his knowledge of her condition, as if his words had finally made her realize the futility of escaping her fate, no matter how much she invested in hope.

Caleb began talking slowly, whispering really, but soon so many utterances were rushing from his heart about things left unsaid and undone, that had to be said, even if now never to be done. There was pain, too, more his than hers, and his tears joined hers in their rush to silence the agony of time. They appeared to be successful in collapsing the dams of hate and heartbreak and in washing away the unspeakable years. His hands left hers and cupped her face to clear the streams that seemed to pardon him. So tenderly did he cleanse her cheeks of their anguish, and afterward he again kissed her lips to allow her the feel of his sincerity.

They froze in that position for many minutes, man seemingly infusing life into woman, a second creation, until her eyes closed to the sleep her body demanded despite the pain. Unwilling to leave, yet without the poetry book he intended to read to her, Caleb sat again next to her bed, grasped her right hand in his, and whispered, "Mitch, do you remember the last day of the semester we met? You feared it for many reasons, but for me it was a truer beginning of our relationship than the night we went to the falls. You opened yourself to me in many ways that day, and we shared some of the bitter and the sweet of your past.

"Every minute of that day is etched in my mind. Let me bring you back with me to that day in our lives, when time began for me."

* * *

It was a June day two months after we'd met. Exams were over, and we had my apartment to ourselves. The warm fragrance of impending summer wafted through rooms cluttered with the packings of a successful school year and the mementos of soon-to-be suspended relationships, ours included.

Our goodbye I relished little; you savored it even less. I liked you a lot, thought you were so lovable, but there was this student exchange program into which I'd been accepted before we'd met, and, truthfully, you'd become a major complication to what I'd hoped originally was to be a fun summer abroad.

You were in love, no question, though it was tainted, as I soon learned, by your brother's death just before we'd met. An emptiness was within you, impinging on your whole being, and instinctively you clung to your remaining hours with me.

At the time, there was a strong physical relationship between us, but I was more reluctant than you to go to extremes. I was content to have you explore my body and me yours without the intrusion of more consuming measures. And although you were somewhat befuddled by my restraint, especially when compared to my performance the night we'd met, you appeared quite satisfied with our current bedroom activities, having only twice playfully teased me for more.

But this early June day was subverting your complacency even more than I thought it would. You'd begun to feel some stress on my announcing a departure date, and now the tension was palpable as our time together was concluding. Unable to divorce my summer vacation from a sense of permanent separation, you seemed terribly overanxious in everything you did.

It was almost noon, and you were clearing a surprise breakfast while I was inspecting my room for overlooked articles. And when you finally caught up with me, I was rear-end up, searching beneath my stripped bed for the mate of a black sock.

The opportunity proved too attractive to you, and you mounted the play horse in front of you, slapped my rear, and roared with laughter, expecting my head to collide with the bed frame. Instead, I collapsed and avoided the reaction which would have satisfied you. Still, my movement sent a shudder of excitement through you, and you jumped to the mattress, rolled into a ball, and tightened in anticipation of my next move.

I didn't attack, and you waited. You bounced on the bed to force a grunt, but none came. Gradually, you unraveled yourself and peered over the edge of the bed. I was motionless.

"Cal, is your stuffed tummy caught under there?" you snickered. You were the only person I ever let call me Cal. Again you bounced on the bed when no response came. And once more there was no grunt.

"Come on, Cal, dear," you added, "you know what pleasure awaits you up here. Shall I presume that my sensational breakfast was all that your large appetite desires?"

Still there was no response from below, and you began poking me to get it. My non-ticklish body lay dormant nonetheless, and you became disturbed by my possum's charade.

"Caleb, that's enough fooling!" you shouted, as if your command would resolve everything. "If you don't get up here this minute, you can forget that flagpole of yours getting any attention!"

The tension of that day was now explosively mixing with your already-seeded dread of summer, and the concoction pushed you to fidget with my torso by tugging at my belt, and then shove me at my shoulder blades. Horrified, you were unwilling to join me on the floor.

"Cal," you screamed, "I can't stand this game you're playing!" I sensed an honest fear and began to relent. But before I decided to quit my gambit, I heard reflexive gasps, like monstrous sobs, coming from above, and all you could do was wail, "Caleb!"

The tone of your call instantly severed me from my game plan. I got up and was about to pounce on you to retrieve your good humor when I realized you hadn't even noticed me rise. You were twisting weirdly, perspiring, and wailing for sure. Your eyes were closed, but your lips were mouthing something I soon comprehended as your late brother's name, Larry.

Although seeming all too real, the extreme reaction suggested a possible put-on, and I was unwilling to allow you even the slightest prospect of finessing me on our last day. You'd done it all too often before under more transparent circumstances, and with what turned out to be perfect control of your emotions. The sole purpose of those other times was to turn my shenanigans into routs, and, consequently,

I was reluctant, to say the least, even in your apparently hyper state, to present you with your most skillful victory yet. My hesitation was only momentary, however – just long enough to convince me that you weren't the consummate actress – and I committed myself, at least, to sitting on the bed and stroking your face.

Immediately your twisting ceased and your rale eased. Your eyes opened wide, but they failed to recognize me or your surroundings. Minutes later you'd physically recovered with only a slight sense of disorientation.

"What happened?" was the first thing you said on sitting up. "Did I pass out? I remember tickling you and getting upset that you were playing dead. This is so embarrassing, I'm sorry." You breathed deeply, touched your blouse, and screamed, "Geez, I'm drenched!"

"Dammit, Mitch, I don't know whether to believe you or not!" I remarked. "And that's going to depend on what you meant by what I think was the name Larry before. And I don't need your hyena cackling if you're sucking me in again!"

Your reflexive gasping began again, and I couldn't ignore it this time. I forced you to lie down, returning whatever blood had drained from your head on prematurely sitting up, and the pallor of your skin panicked me into barking, "Cut the shit, Mitch!" But all that did was bring your hands into a kneading motion, which exasperated me further.

"Either you let me in on your little secret or you go home!" I stridently announced. "I've got too much to do to be suckered by you now. So about Larry?"

Slowly your hands became still and your breathing relaxed. I pressed you again for full disclosure, and although you weren't fully healed yet, you decided you could no longer contain your pain either.

"I never wanted to tell you, certainly not before this summer," you murmured, closing your eyes tightly. "No one knows, no one! Larry was my brother; I killed him over spring vacation." You said it that way, I'm sure, to get the worst behind you, and you put your face in your hands to ward off the disbelief you knew would come. It came anyway.

"You what!" I cried out. "Come on, Mitch, you mean like you kill me every day with your asinine sense of humor, right?" You returned a vacant gaze. "Aha!" I exclaimed. "There really has been another casualty of your quick wit. Now who the hell is he, really?"

You seemed to feel faint. Your stomach was upset and was thinking of returning your recent breakfast. You tried to rise from the bed, only to fall back. Your skin, already cold and pale, was becoming increasingly clammy.

Your relapse rankled me. Hastily I placed your head between your knees and squeezed downwardly on your neck, as if forcing blood to your brain by the mere pressure of my hand. I regret doing that, because I think I did it more with the intent to punish you than to assist you, and I shouted impatiently, "Mitch, are you all right? Mitch, answer me! Are you all right?"

Without an answer or a sense that you had regained control, I let go of your neck. You rocked slightly but stayed up, though bent over. Running to the bathroom, I grabbed a wad of toilet paper and soaked it. Racing back, I found you as I'd left you, and with harsh compressions of the paper to your neck and forehead, cold water ran in heavy streams down your face, chest and back. It seemed to revive you, and I ran to the bathroom again.

Soaked from the overdose of cold water, you squirmed at the chill. You smiled feebly and lay back at my urging. "It's my brother, Larry," you whispered and sat up. "I killed him in a car accident driving home spring vacation." It was no put-on; I finally had to accept it.

"Don't say another word!" I ordered. "We'll talk about it later. Right now you need some rest!"

"No, now!" you shouted, and your demeanor stunned me. Uneasy from your unpredictable behavior, I stepped over to my laundry bag and removed a towel.

"You'd better wipe yourself off," I suggested to change the subject, "I made a mess of my best intentions." I dangled the towel in front of you.

"Sit down, Caleb!" you directed. "I've got to talk about it sometime. I would have preferred to do it in the fall, but if I don't do it now, I'll have shot my summer worrying about what you're thinking now that you know."

Responding to your plea, I tossed you the towel and sat down on the edge of the bed. But to you, I still seemed unwilling to concentrate on what you had to say, and that irked you. You swiped at the beads of water on your face and wrapped the towel about your neck.

"Larry had picked me up late in the day," you began when you thought you had my attention, "and because he'd been driving for about five hours already, I was going to drive the rest of the way home. Damn! No, I won't cry! No, I won't get upset! Cal, don't you see, I've just got to talk about it. It's like everybody's known all along no matter how much I pretended nothing happened when I came back to school from vacation. I told no one, and only the newspapers might have said something. Do they talk behind my back? Maybe nobody knows or cares. Did you know, Caleb?"

I hadn't been earnestly listening like I should have. Rather, I'd been debating how best to end the discussion. To me at the time, my feelings for you were not solid enough to tolerate sharing that heavy a burden, and although I recognized your need to share it, I ignored your question.

"Did you know about my brother before?" you asked again.

"No," I answered with the realization that escape was impossible. "You never mentioned it, nothing about a brother or a Larry in particular, even when we talked about family. And I'd never stand for anyone talking behind your back – unless it was about your beauty, poise, and smartaleckiness. Certainly nothing about your brother or an accident, I swear!" I raised my right hand in front of your eyes as if to take an oath but really to break your gaze at me. You noticed only the smile that grew on my face from my teasing you, and, of course, that angered you.

"But I'll tell ya," I foolishly added without perceiving your true state of mind, "you'll never win a beauty contest looking the way you do right now."

Instantly you surveyed your disheveled self. You stood, trembling, and driven by some subliminal impulse, unbuttoned your blouse and skirt and dropped them to the floor. I was flabbergasted. Pausing for a second, as if to measure my reaction and presence of mind, you unhooked your bra and shed your panties. Completely nude now and exposing to my eyes what my hands had known only in the dimmest of light, you hastily wrapped yourself in the towel and plopped down on the bed.

From your new position, which you topped off with a sweep of your hair, you said, "Are you ready to listen now?"

Still shocked by what you'd just done, I nodded. You had judiciously set the bait, and all I could do was bide my time listening to what you had to say.

Forever steadfast, you pondered your confession until your thoughts were firm. "It was a Friday night," you began. "The sky was clear, the roads were dry, and the visibility perfect. Larry was on the passenger side dozing while I plowed ahead.

"I was going too fast, I know that now – I knew it even then – but Larry hated how slow I drove, and that was the deal. Don't you see? He wouldn't let me drive, even after he'd put in five hours, unless I promised to drive like one of the guys. He always pushed me that way, to be one of the guys. And I could take him in wrestling too, up till a few years ago."

You realized the digression and blinked a few times. I quickly became mesmerized by two teardrops, one floating at your right eyelid and the other meandering slowly down your right cheek. The incongruity in those tears readily seduced my attention from what you were saying, for only your right eye had shed them, and your left eye appeared oblivious to its partner's plight.

"I saw him sleeping, and I could've slowed down," you went on, "but I'd made the deal and I couldn't let him down. I'd never let him down before, so how could I start even if he was sleeping. Can you understand that?"

I nodded and that seemed enough for you. But you hesitated.

Suddenly you lifted your hand and squinted your eyes. Your breathing became slightly labored, and perspiration appeared on your forehead. Even so, you were otherwise serene. It was eerie.

"The truck had its bright lights on; I couldn't see." Your words seemed to creep out without sound. "It was a country road so close to home, and I thought he was coming right at me. I swerved, I shouldn't have…it was only…I was off the road spinning, and Larry was thrown out."

You spoke so calmly and evenly, it scared me. Only your hands, through a kneading rhythm, betrayed your outward composure. You stared beyond me, too, toward the wall, and I had this weird feeling that a look at me might destroy your control.

"It was a country road. I was dazed; I sat in the car, just sat there for so long. Then I remembered Larry, and I ran all over looking for him until the groans broke the silence and led me there.

"He was so cut up when I found him. I just stared and cried and didn't do anything except whisper his name, and he said, 'Help me, Mitch, it hurts,' but all I did was whisper his name and cry. Then he started coughing up blood and there was a gurgling in his throat and I think he was saying, 'Help me, Mitch, it hurts real bad!' and then I ran and ran and started waving at passing cars on the road and ran back screaming that help was coming; I remember it so well." You paused, made a fist, and pounded it into the palm of your hand three times, like a baseball mitt.

"But when I got to him," you added matter-of-factly, "he wasn't moaning, and I put my face to his to feel his breath, and I knew he was dead, knew it even before they came and pulled me away."

With the end of your story, you began trembling markedly, and I was drawn by your vulnerability into a tender embrace. It broke the towel's hold at your shoulder, and the towel fell to your lap. "Mitch, I'm so sorry," I whispered. "I'm so terribly sorry."

"I can't sleep at night, Caleb," you said. "I can't stand the thought of being alone. I keep dreaming about it, but it's not his dying that haunts every minute as much as constantly hearing him ask for help, his saying it hurt real bad. Cal, I took care of him while my parents worked. Don't you see, I could almost live with his dying, but I can't forget the pain, that I couldn't make it not hurt. He asked me to stop it from hurting, and I ran to get help. I wasn't even with him when he died, to hold him; I ran away. I let him down, Caleb, and the last thing he knew, the last thing, was that Mitch let him down."

I stared at you and felt emotionally drained; you were awakening to an emotional need. Neither of us remembered the fallen towel until you raised my cold hands to your lips and in passing they grazed your breasts. You gasped and stared at me. I hesitated and then pulled you toward me. You kissed my chin and began awkwardly working my pants loose. Your breath quickened with my excitement.

Outstripped by your ardor, I pulled at my shoes and socks and sent my pants flying. Instantly you were at my shorts and freed me with an urgency deflected only momentarily by my movement over you.

My mouth found your lips, my teeth your tongue, my hands the warmth of your body. We stayed that way for what seemed an eternity, rubbing and rocking body to body. I knew your state, from times before, and I awaited the help of your hands to bring me there too. It never came. Instead, you bolted upright and turned from me. I tried to bring you next to me, but you resisted. Another attempt at gaining satisfaction fizzled. That time, however, you sweetly announced, "I won't: maiden's privilege."

"Why not?" I gulped.

"I won't do it your way anymore," you said firmly. "I want you in me and no other way; it's a maiden's privilege!"

I wasn't really surprised. Your earlier overtures in that direction, playful as they were, had forewarned me. I suppose you had assumed the inevitability of it, and I had to agree: time was on your side.

"Please, Cal," you whispered as you finally stroked me, "leave me at least this while you're gone."

But I hadn't accepted anything at that moment, least of all intercourse. "In the fall, Mitch, maybe in the fall," I replied with my own determination.

That surprised you. Clearly you hadn't expected me to weigh time so heavily, as if the summer, your treacherous summer, could make a difference to me too.

You put your hand on my scrotum and began sucking my nipples. I lay back victorious. You kissed my navel and twirled some pubic hairs with your tongue. My eyebrows knotted as I fought the pleasure. Then you ventured where you'd never gone before, licking the shaft of my penis, and I instantly knew I had lost.

* * *

During the telling, Mitch had been uneasily asleep, suddenly awakening without orientation when her pain overcame her morphine drip, but falling off again when the pain subsided. After the vignette, Caleb maintained a vigil at her bedside for no more than a quarter of an hour, and was about to begin another vignette of their time together, when John arrived to shoo him out. He reminded Caleb of the dinner at six, which Caleb said he could make after a shower and change of clothes at his hotel.

Chapter X

If God made Cain to e'er walk the earth,
He surely watched Satan's birth.
If God made Cain to be a while,
'tis no man's need for human trial.
But shouldst Cain the earth walk still,
He surely shall make reign His will.

Translated from Hebrew
Author Unknown

The Group at Dinner

BY THE TIME CALEB ARRIVED at John's apartment that evening, the others were already feasting and conversing around the kitchen table, where everything for a hearty spaghetti dinner had been laid out buffet style. Oddly, just as Caleb grabbed a plate, John stepped back from the table and began slowly circling it until his activity drained their small talk.

"This is the last time we'll be together here," he said at last. "With Tom going back to Boston tomorrow morning and Stitches visiting Isaac on the farm, I thought we might focus this evening on our spiritual needs – not that Caleb hasn't overdosed us on that already. But, in truth, Caleb's been merely warming you up for me. You see, tonight we're going to talk about what's brought the five of us, with such varied backgrounds and interests, together. And it's not just an illness in the family.

"Yes, you may initially laugh at this, gentlemen, but by the time we leave here, this group, hardly knowing each other, will have committed itself to a journey to prove the existence of God."

"Rather than laugh, John," Tom said, arresting everyone's tittering, "I'd suggest that what you propose contradicts your own story yesterday about that debate on Cain. If God exists at all – and I give no inch on that score – He's spirit, and there's no way we're going to spot Him on some street corner selling Bibles. Theology isn't anthropology – there's no such thing as a journey to prove the existence of God. If there were, we'd see theologians in khaki shorts and pith helmets doing fieldwork in heaven."

"Are you finished?" John asked.

The group nodded in unison.

"I told you yesterday about the most significant event in my life: when I visited that burned-out synagogue in Berlin and had a conversation with a man who professed to be the caretaker of that non-functional house of worship. I was given a riddle that defies solution, and left that synagogue only to find it boarded up when I returned minutes later.

"I walked away the second time – no, I ran away – with a sense of total loss, despite having been told by that apparition of a sexton that there was a reason for what had happened to me during the war. Back then, I felt I was just like Cain – and I still sense it! I have been an outcast, a pariah, all these years. No matter how much social work I perform attempting to elevate myself from the basest things, I'm still wandering outside the grace of God, an ex-priest in exile.

"All I've had was the riddle, which has been like an albatross around my neck, until the four of you converged on the medical center to give me hope in finding that reason. We're here for only a few more hours in support of each other, so I'm asserting my seniority to request that we spend that time babysitting this old fool's fancy.

"There are a host of things that have convinced me that the five of us are here tonight to begin a journey to prove the existence of God. As we proceed, you'll realize how each of us uniquely contributes to that goal. Let's start, however, by getting away from us, and into the Book of Genesis.

"One of the principal reasons our society has lost its moral way is because the world's modern scientific revolution – from the theory of evolution and genetic engineering, to the Big Bang theory and satellite communications – has made us reject the literal, factual accuracy of the Bible and, with it, a firm belief in God. We're going to change all that.

"If you begin reading the Bible at Creation, it's hardly surprising that the first chapter turns you off and leaves you less than enthusiastic about the validity of what follows. Last night I told you about the Talmudic scholars of eighteenth-century Poland who addressed the riddle I recited as well as the issue of finding Cain to prove the existence of God. Tom just argued that those rabbis' conclusion should be our own. I disagree, partly because I believe the world has come to a juncture in its moral disintegration that demands help from above, either through the Messiah, some prophet, or a miracle beyond question. And because the pieces that each of us brings to this group couldn't have happened by chance, I've concluded that there's a guiding hand here that may be part of the miracle to come. So let's go back to those rabbis and discuss some of the things I may have omitted last night.

"Although those scholars decided that it was best for humanity to maintain its free will by leaving the existence of God in doubt, they did recognize the possibility that Cain might be alive. First in their thinking was that eating from the Tree of Life was not forbidden to those in the Garden of Eden. Consequently, immortality was initially permissible for the Garden's inhabitants – a clear dividing line between those within the Garden and those outside, who had evolved. But I'm getting ahead of myself.

"So eternal wandering for Cain, through God's sanctioning one bite from the Tree of Life before Cain's banishment to Nod, doesn't seem far-fetched, especially if God's purpose was to make Cain an ever-present reminder of the temptation of evil. Of course, one interpretation of the riddle is just that: that Cain became the earthly embodiment of the devil – Satan incarnate.

"Second in their thinking was that no chronology of the life of Cain appears in Genesis, unlike for the other biblical ancients, who did die.

"Third in their thinking was the sign God gave Cain to ward off his enemies – that's Genesis 4:15 – a sign we have come to call the Mark of Cain. It was those scholars' conclusion that the Lord intended the mark to be an eternal identification alerting His faithful to the temptations and presence of evil.

"Of course, you're saying: who believes in that nonsense? You've joined the crowd that accepts the Bible as merely compelling fiction, and no more. It's seen as an outdated tool of useless theologians who should have been made extinct by evolution, just like the dinosaurs. Tom's probably a proponent of that philosophy.

"But if you'll humor me a bit longer, I'll give you another view, one that will demonstrate that this three-thousand-year-old biblical contract, as Caleb calls it, is alive with modern scientific thought and totally consistent with it – and like an immortal Cain, shouldn't be discounted so easily. Then I'd like to talk about the things in each of us that make our convergence here so miraculous, things like Tom's article, Caleb's contract, and my riddle. I won't even hint right now at what Joseph and Stitches uniquely bring us, but they're as potent as the rest."

John paused, obviously intent on slowing his momentum and regearing his thoughts. Tom had become captivated by John's mention of his article, as had the others by their respective roles. The apartment was suddenly energized by the prospects exposed, and John sensed the tension.

"The two most controversial areas between scientific and religious thought today deal with the creation of the universe and the evolution of mankind. Because the conflict between what we think we know, and what we would like to believe, is so unresolvable, we have relegated the biblical story of Creation to that of parable: a story filled with moral lessons and little fact. While probably not yet in the category of Aesop's fables, the Bible seems to plead its case from an unsure foundation that taints the rest of it.

"Before hearing Caleb yesterday – and I thank him for sparking this thought – none of us would have given much credence to, much less accepted, the statements throughout the Pentateuch claiming that Moses wrote it over forty years of desert wandering. Some of us have heard theories about possible non-Mosaic authors who not only put the Pentateuch together, but did it much later than the books themselves would like us to believe. Caleb's argument yesterday, however, has convinced me that the Pentateuch is indeed a contract between the human race and God, written by Moses as a result of negotiations that occurred over time in the desert. If you can accept the possibility of that, we're more than halfway there!

"Now," he said as he handed out photocopies, "let's take a look at these copies of the first chapter of Genesis to find an equivalent to the Big Bang that created our galaxy and solar system. Keep in mind that we're reading the first chapter of a huge document. The chapter was written to express information Moses received on Sinai concerning events not personally witnessed by him. This caused three problems as I see it – but correct me if I'm wrong, Caleb, since you're the one who seeded my newest view. First, since it was the earliest of his writing, recorded at the time stated in Exodus 24:4, the chapter was inevitably the most poorly drafted. We can accept that God didn't write it – nowhere does it say He did, like it does with the Decalogue – and we can assume that it wasn't transcribed by Moses on an 'as told to' basis. That's because it's only when he came down from the mountain that it says he wrote the Book of the Covenant, which recorded the Bible's Creation story. So, but for the writing skills Moses may have developed years before as an Egyptian prince, we shouldn't be surprised if the writing falls a little short in describing what God told him on Mount Sinai about the creation of the universe and humankind.

"Second, we have a timing problem. After Moses received the Creation story on Sinai, days may have passed before he actually reduced it to writing. That makes for a likely divergence in what he was actually told and what he remembered at the time he finally recorded it. Third, we have a man in Moses who, even with the best of Egyptian science behind him, couldn't possibly have understood a literal statement of the Big Bang and evolution.

"So we have a prophet who starts out writing the most important document the world will ever know with meager writing skills and even less scientific acumen, after an unknown but deleterious time delay. What a disastrous combination, especially for the lawyer reviewing God's contract with the human race to determine if it's still binding three thousand years later.

"Think of James Madison, a man with considerable writing skills and much more recent, but perhaps not quite modern, scientific knowledge, drafting the US Constitution, and trying to do it so as not to leave any ambiguities. The Constitution certainly doesn't achieve that, especially in the areas it has in common with the Bible, like gay rights, abortion, even the teaching of Creationism vis-à-vis evolution. So how was Moses supposed to get it right with his limitations?"

"John," Caleb broke in, "I've gotten to the same place by a different route. If the Five Books of Moses had been written without human error or apparent inconsistencies, and with 100 percent scientific accuracy because either God wrote them or Moses took precise dictation, the world would have destroyed itself long ago with knowledge it wasn't ready for. Or if God arranged to have a 'perfect' Pentateuch hidden like the Dead Sea Scrolls for millennia until the world was ready for it, such an ancient text that was 100 percent scientifically accurate would drive the world into rigidly believing in aliens or God, neither approach being God's preference. But most significantly, if a divinely written Torah had been lost to the Jews from the day it was placed beside the Ark of the Covenant, in order for it not to prematurely deliver science to the world, the Jews would never have survived as a people, thereby contradicting those passages I mentioned yesterday committing God to the Jews' eternal preservation. The sole purpose of the Creation story is to establish God's ownership of the world and His right to promise what became the Land of Israel to the Jews."

"Thanks, Caleb," John said. "Now with Moses' deficiencies in mind, let's look at the Bible's first day of creation and search for wording that might be a proxy for a big nuclear bang. That's right: 'Let there be light!'"

"John, there's no need to convince us that the Creation story can be taken literally," Caleb said. "The truth is simply what you said at the outset: Moses screwed up in recording what God told him – his memory, his writing skills, his ability to comprehend the ultimate truths in science, things we still only speculate on, like the Unified Force. Haven't you ever read something you wrote years before, like a high school paper, only to come away thinking you could never have written such drivel? That's what makes us doubt, but, in fact, it's the very reason we should believe."

"The two of you have made some good points," Stitches said, "but evolution ain't nowhere in the Bible!"

"Okay," John replied, picking up one of the copies he'd passed around, "let's find evolution in the Creation story.

"On the sixth day of creation," he continued, "in Genesis 1:26–28, Moses records that after all other living things have been created, God creates man, male and female together – no rib, no Adam, no Eve, just the last step in the billion-year process for man to evolve from the primordial soup following the Big Bang. Remember, the first three biblical days of creation have no timeline: time as we know it begins on the fourth day. And then on the seventh day, God rested.

"But evolutionary man exercises his free will and fails to deliver the spiritual being God had hoped for. So after being disappointed an indeterminate number of years, God forms Adam from the dust of the earth as a second attempt at producing a spiritual being who will choose His will over free will. Note the Hebrew: Adam is 'formed,' but evolutionary man on the sixth day is 'created.' We're now at Genesis 2:8, in the Garden of Eden, a paradise on earth, and Eve comes into being from Adam's rib. Both Adam and Eve are isolated in the Garden, like in a test tube, void of evolved man, who's abounding outside the Garden."

"Not surprisingly, John," Tom said, "the interpretation you're espousing, which I've heard before as the Injection Theory, coincides with the end of the last ice age, almost six thousand years ago. My understanding of the theory is that it lays the foundations of language, writing skills, and analytical thinking at the supposed time of the Garden, primarily because they appear for the first time a short while later."

"You're ahead of me, Tom," John said, smiling broadly, "and you're stealing my thunder. So let's backtrack a bit and revisit Adam and Eve in the Garden. Along comes this wicked serpent, who convinces them to opt for expressing their free will with one bite of the forbidden fruit, and, voila: God is again disappointed and expels them from the Garden!

"All of a sudden Adam and Eve, the 'injected' children of God, as Tom put it, are on the outside looking in, stuck in the bushes with those less intellectually and spiritually developed evolutionary men and women. Adam and Eve have some children, murder happens, and Cain is forced to leave the clan. Now we come to Genesis 6:1–3, in which Moses says that the children of God – meaning Cain and Seth, the progeny of Adam and Eve – saw that the daughters of evolutionary man were fair, and they took them as wives. Where else did the women come from? Those marriages pollute the genetic material of Cain and Seth, and according to Moses, in verse 6:3, God says that man has now become evolved flesh and will be limited to a lifespan of 120 years, exactly what Moses lived to."

"That also happens to be the maximum target lifespan projected by our gerontologists for the human body," Caleb added.

"This was all before the Deluge," John went on, "and so as not to bore you with too much in support of evolutionary theory in the Bible, I'll conclude with one thought: when the Flood over four thousand years ago wiped out everybody but Noah's family, who became the forebears of today's human race, we ended up with our single genetic heritage – the hybrid from those intermarriages passed on through the Noah clan."

"Which, in a way, is what our very capable anthropologists keep uncovering," Tom said.

"And brings the Bible and modern science into total communion," John added, "even with a deficient Moses."

"Tom, as the only one with some expertise in this area," Joseph said, "does anything John's saying hold water?"

"I have a lesser problem with what John's been saying," he replied, "than with what Caleb said yesterday. To think that there's a divine contract that could deliver freedom from all disease is mind-boggling. But the Injection Theory has a beauty to it. Whether or not it's fact, and I doubt it is, it does reconcile Creationism and evolution through the women on Noah's Ark, a compression chamber making their mitochondrial DNA the sole link to the so-called Eve, our common evolutionary ancestor of eons ago."

"Even if the Bible is no practical joke like I was certain it was before tonight," Stitches said, "we're still a long ways from sayin' it's fact!"

"I'm with you, Stitches," Tom offered, "but I will give John his due with one piece of corroboration.

"One hundred thousand years ago, Neanderthal man appeared after a two-million-year reign by Homo habilis, our first toolmakers. Using John's timeline, both could have evolved during the first four days of Creation, before time as we know it began. Not bad for starters.

"Cro-Magnon man arrived about thirty-five thousand years ago and was so advanced that Neanderthal man quickly disappeared. It's an earlier facet of what I've established with my Caribbean Indian research. Well, anyway, after Cro-Magnon man appeared, we had the inception of the arts: musical instruments like the flute, cave art, and figurines. Even the sewing needle came of age about twenty-five thousand years ago.

"Now, what I said before about language, writing, and analytical skills arising at the end of the last ice age, about six thousand years ago, is prompting a growing academic persuasion in my field to play with the notion that a new order of mankind appeared out of nowhere and genetically introduced the capability for those absent skills in evolved mankind. On the Hebrew calendar, give or take a few hundred years, six thousand years ago is just about the time an Adam-and-Eve-type skill set appeared.

"The one additional corroboration, speculative as it is," Tom continued, "comes from the mathematical front. If we had had geometric population growth beginning with Cro-Magnon man, much less Homo habilis, we wouldn't be able to lie down today, it would be so crowded – even with all the wars, famines, and other natural disasters we know occurred.

"The mathematical model that gets us to today's world population, based on accepted growth progressions, targets a time a little over four thousand years ago as the starting point. You guessed it: the Flood, when the mitochondrial DNA of the Noah clan was all that humanly survived!"

"Before I forget this," Stitches said, "there was an article in the local paper the other day about the zoo here tryin' for over a year to get an ape to read. They were usin' the Bible as the readin' text, and just recently they had their first breakthrough: the ape looked up from his Bible two nights ago and asked, 'Am I my keeper's brother?'"

"Thanks for your support so far," John said joyously, "because it gets better from here. Let's turn to the footnotes in Tom's article, particularly the ones I've copied for you acknowledging the contributions of Father Conlin and the excerpt from the diary of Captain Charles Francis. More copies are on the table.

"Tom's research on Caribbean Indian civilizations documents rather thoroughly the differences in intelligence among them, which led to the Arawak domination of the Ciboney and the later Carib domination of the Arawaks.

"With the able assistance of a Jesuit priest, Father Conlin, who also happens to be an anthropologist with a concentration in Caribbean Indian cultures – perhaps the reason he's in San Juan – Tom not only compared the various tribes at the time of their conquests, but also in today's world whenever he could find a definitive tribal subculture. For example, Tom found – and correct me if I'm wrong, Tom – he found a strong Carib subculture but only a nominal Arawak one, confirming his premise that the intelligence differential that he'd documented as existing at the time of the Carib conquest of the Arawaks has indeed carried forward to today in areas of education, trade, professional standing, and public service.

"But Tom couldn't locate any Ciboney subculture and merely adopted Father Conlin's undocumented assertion, which appears in the first footnote I gave you, that the whole Ciboney nation – with the exception, perhaps, of its last chieftain – had died out. Tom doesn't say why he chose not to pursue the last Ciboney, but my guess, and correct me if I'm wrong, is that one Indian could not make a scientifically sound subculture anyway."

"It was that primarily, John," Tom said, "but there was also a lack of funds."

"There, you see," John said confidently, "we're still batting one hundred!"

"One thousand, John," Stitches inserted, "it's one thousand, and if you thought a hundred was perfect, now you're ten times better than that!"

"Thanks, Stitches," John said, adding, "you can't be better than perfect, although we do strive for it at times. This may be one of those times, if my next guess is correct."

"But let's also keep in mind, John," Stitches rejoined, "that you can be crazier than hell."

"If you say so, Stitches," John went on, "but I would like to turn to the other footnote I gave you copies of, the one quoting an entry, barely legible, in the diary of one Charles Francis, a nineteenth-century captain of the slave ship *Jason*. The diary was uncovered by Tom at the Library of Congress in Washington, DC. Let's read it together:

> On 16 September we sailed from the port San Juan. About an hour out, a storm hit, tormenting us for hours. When the blow died and the swell of the sea abated, we dropped anchor and awaked to daylight with a small party of Indians. The Indians lay away the morning, but in early afternoon they motioned for us to land, as if the time was appointed and we were expected. I myself relented to the beckoning island.
>
> The crew held at shore while I was led into the interior of the island by one of the Indians. We entered the hut of a young chieftain who spoke in broken Spanish, apparently carried from father to son over many generations. The chieftain called his people Ciboney, as if I should know the name, and it proved my only hint of where we were.
>
> We spent a few days in the bay repairing and restocking the ship for the voyage home. But when I told the chieftain that we were soon to sail, he tried to keep me there with a tale of a little man who lived on an islet out to sea. The chieftain was willing to take me there, but time was too dear and I remained only long enough to hear the whole of the tale.
>
> The young chieftain spoke quickly. Many years before, apparently some hundreds, the Ciboney tribe, but for the young son of its chieftain, was lost to island floods during a great storm. After years communing with his god, the surviving son set out for the closest inhabited island to take a woman to renew his nation. On his way, the youth met a gale and drifted in his canoe for nearly a fortnight until he came, half starved, to an islet on which he thought he saw life. There he encountered a little man and a fountain which fed the islet's barrenness with fresh water.

> Days passed without companionship, although the youth and the man remained constantly with each other. When the youth found the courage, he asked about the strange mark on the little man's face. The man raged at the heavens and ran off, straight into the water, not to be seen again. The youth took water from the fountain for many days at sea and left the islet the way he had come.
>
> Days out, his water exhausted, the youth was come upon by a great ship like the Jason, which took him aboard and threw him below with a prisoner who taught him Spanish to pass the time. To repay that attention the youth told the prisoner of the islet. The prisoner seized upon the tale of the Indian to set them free. The captain of the ship, on hearing of the fresh water fountain, put in at the nearest port to outfit his ship for the adventure in search of the islet, and the youth and prisoner slipped away unnoticed.

After John had finished reading aloud, Tom said, "I have no idea where you're going with that footnote, but it was cited solely to establish the baseline on outside influences, like the Spanish, on Ciboney intelligence. That's all it was intended for."

"Well, I see something else in it, Tom," John responded.

They stared at John, and his face turned frighteningly strange for a few seconds before a smile appeared.

"Isn't it obvious to all of you?" he asked.

They shook their heads in unison, and his eyes opened wide. They smiled and shook their heads again.

"The Ciboney chieftain, the one the Jesuit says may still be alive, is the same chieftain the diary says Captain Francis met in the early eighteen hundreds. That makes him about a hundred and sixty years old today, if he's still alive, of which I have no doubt. And you know what else?"

He paused and searched their blank faces. Again they shook their heads.

"That's right!" he exclaimed. "That little man with the strange mark on his face is our Cain! And what else?"

"The fountain!" Caleb blurted out.

"Yes, what about it?" John replied excitedly.

"It's the fabled Fountain of Youth!" Stitches interjected, clearly joking.

"Yeah," Tom followed, "and I suppose that Spanish captain who picked up the Indian youth was Ponce de León?"

"What, who?" John asked, grabbing a pencil.

"Ponce de León," Tom repeated, "a Spanish explorer who was known for his search around the Florida Keys for the Fountain of Youth." John asked for the spelling of the explorer's and fountain's names.

"And I suppose," Stitches said with a smirk, "that the Jesuit's Ciboney chieftain is not only Francis' chieftain but Ponce de León's too! That'd make the Ciboney closer to four hundred years old!"

"Stitches, you said it, not I, although that is really where I was going," John said. "But your attitude could use some improvement. This is important to me, and I'd like you to treat it that way – just as I do your reasons for being here. I asked you to humor an old man's fancy, not laugh at it. You don't have to accept my insights, but you should at least respect them, especially after what we've been through together."

"I'm truly sorry," Stitches said. "I owe you more than I could ever repay. I was just tryin' to prevent you from gettin' too far out on that limb. There may be very good reasons why findin' Cain is important to you, but to actually try to do it – which I think is where you're headin' – is preposterous! I don't want you to get hurt, that's all."

"Please, Stitches, read the footnotes and the Genesis verses on Cain again, with an open mind," John said, "and if you still think I'm absolutely wrong, even after we discuss the riddle – that there's not the slightest truth in any of it – I'll walk away, I promise, especially since you're the one who's going to finance my finding him. But keep in mind one other thing, Stitches. You're the one who connected the diary's fountain to the Fountain of Youth, something my German education never taught me. I was intending to suggest only that the fountain might be an outlet for the stream the Bible says fed the Tree of Life in the Garden of Eden, water that became an eternal life source for the Indian. There are streams that flow through oceans, and although I wouldn't say it myself, yes, that does make the Indian much older. I didn't know how much, however, because I didn't have Ponce de León in mind to fix a date for the first Ciboney encounter. If you now say it's 400 years, I have no objection.

"Now, about the riddle," John continued, "let's see how it fits before we throw everything out. Here, I've typed it as I remember it, just as I recited it to you last night. Take a copy."

Minutes passed, and only confusion reigned.

"I take it to mean," John said to break the silence, "that God remains the King of kings even as Cain, the eternal wanderer, seeks to seduce man into straying from God's law. Of course, that unhappy wanderer is none other than Satan incarnate, seeking his own supremacy as revenge for his original banishment from God's favor, but never succeeding – unless you adopt an alternative meaning."

"There are so many alternative readings," Tom offered, "that, even assuming some type of divine authorship, which I doubt, and assuming minimal translation problems from the original, which most certainly was not English, the likelihood of focusing on the right meaning is nearly impossible. And obviously, the riddle has importance only if Cain still lives. John, why don't you just tell us where you're going with all of this?"

"Wow!" Stitches exclaimed. "If we could catch Cain like they caught King Kong, we could stamp out evil. Can you imagine with Cain behind bars, assumin' we could keep him there, all of a sudden everyone loves everyone else, there'd be no crime, no war, no poverty, maybe even no death or disease – just like Caleb said."

"And much easier than getting all the Jews to toe the line on God's commandments," Joseph chimed in.

"Yeah," Caleb said drily, "why should we ask the Jews to earn God's blessings for all of us by observing His laws when we might be able to finesse the whole thing by caging Cain. Even better, let's just appoint a delegate like the Messiah to come and do it for us! It seems more and more that modern religion's sole purpose is to make it convenient for us to belong to whatever religion we're into. The goal, it seems, is to demand of us only what will keep the charity plates filled and the membership dues rolling in."

"How about bringing some sanity back into this," Tom cautioned. "If there's a living Cain, then there's God, and proving that God exists through finding Cain makes everything else inconsequential. But since there's no way you're going to capture a supernatural being, if one should exist, John, what you propose is futile – even if it were true!"

"Tom, do you have any idea what you just said? 'Cause I don't." Caleb remarked.

"Nope, not in the slightest," he answered, smiling, "but then how can any rational person still be sitting here listening to all this?"

"You know why I'm still here?" Caleb asked rhetorically. "Because if there's even the slightest chance that Cain still lives, I want to be a party to confirming his presence and proving the Pentateuch is truly a contract that's still valid. If anything can motivate the world to back my plan, it's finding Cain!"

"I wouldn't make light of John's objective," Tom cautioned, "but I won't be lending my name to its credibility either. So, John, take some advice from an old pro at guessing wrong and let this sleeping dog lie."

"I think with the right publicity it could be the practical joke of the twentieth century," Stitches asserted. "Count me in for financial support – I owe you that much, John – but if your purpose is to enlist some bodies in this adventure, you'll have to look elsewhere. I've got too many people in critical stages of care to go gallivantin' around the Caribbean lookin' for a new source of Perrier."

"How about you, Caleb?" John asked.

"On going with you?" Caleb said. John nodded. "Of course I will. It's right up my alley – what I'd call a message from heaven. My medical background may serve you well in Tom's stead, too, especially if you're looking for a scientific writer who can document the discovery and marshal the proof."

"I assume you won't ask me," Joseph said, "because of my age and physical condition. A smart choice: who needs an old codger around to screw up the works on such a remarkable adventure?"

"On the contrary, Joseph," John replied, "you're the one person who must go. I knew you were critical the minute I landed the connection between Cain, the footnotes, and the riddle."

"What do you need him for," Stitches said, "a kosher sacrifice?"

"Seriously, John," Joseph added, "I can't relate to things like this; God's existence doesn't interest me. Until last night in my hotel room, when I looked up a few of Caleb's references in the Bible there, I haven't touched one in almost fifty years. It's just not for me, John, sorry."

Everyone stood to go, all somewhat uneasy with John's likely disappointment. John, however, was far from dismayed. "Tom, I'll need Father Conlin's telephone number and address before you go," he said as if everything had been settled in his favor. "A letter of introduction would also be useful, to get us going with him until you can join us."

"Did I miss something?" Tom said. "A letter of introduction, an address, and a telephone number are all of me that's going with you, John. I'll mail them off as soon as I get home."

"It's out of our hands," John said. "Stitches is the only one who will do his part long distance; money can be wired. The contribution of everyone else requires their physical presence, I'm afraid. The minute we converged at the center, there was nothing that could keep us from this quest. I'm sorry, Tom. You can mail those things off like you say, but be assured, the rest will play itself out with you on board, whether you like it or not."

Chapter XI

An Abominable Ending

EARLY THE NEXT MORNING Caleb hastened past the visitors' lounge on his way to Mitch's room. No one was at the nurses' station when he approached, and without being screened, he entered her room as he and John had done the day before.

Mitch was asleep, so he sat next to her and began reading her the poetry he knew she'd love. Slowly, painfully, she awoke. She turned her head toward him and forced a smile to her lips, as if he'd spawned her first soothing awakening in days.

There seemed to be a freshness in the air as he read anew, and Mitch sighed deeply, coughed, winced, and smiled again. She reached feebly to elevate herself, and Caleb pressed the control at her side to achieve her desire.

"Shall I keep reading?" he asked timidly, hoping she would rather talk. But all she did was smile again.

It was slightly past noon when her condition halted his reading. The nursing staff's interruptions during the morning had been tolerable, but when he was told by a nurse to close the book on the day's visit, he sensed that he was concluding the last chapter of their life together as well. That noticeably depressed him.

Escaping to the lounge, Caleb was intent on pondering his world without Mitch. A thorough airing was not to be his, however, for on entering the lounge he spied a man he thought to be Jerry Watkins, and that sent him scurrying to the elevators.

A minute later he was in the cafeteria, but nothing there could quiet the turmoil within him, which was fostering a plethora of unkind images of Watkins. Mentally attacking his old college roommate without understanding why, he deserted the cafeteria for the same park bench on which he'd composed his note to Mitch.

The bench held him fast for a half hour, as if it still presented the promise of the prior day, but his mind was losing its focus on Mitch, and that grated on him. Jerry Watkins had begun occupying more and more of his thoughts where Mitch should have been, and suddenly he felt like he was abandoning her again.

Springing from the bench, Caleb raced to the hospital, and, ignoring the elevators, bounded up the stairs toward Mitch's floor. Winded on arriving in the lounge, he greeted Watkins with an awkward nod that was left unanswered due to the entrance of a nurse who promptly invited the immaculately dressed Watkins to follow her to Mitch's room.

Rationalizing that his late appearance had been the cause of the nurse's total disregard of his presence, Caleb pursued them. At Mitch's door, though, the nurse who had banished him from Mitch's room the day he'd arrived barred him again. With a disdainful glance at the victorious Watkins, Caleb abjectly withdrew along with a contingent of nurses and doctors, and watched the door close on Jerry and Mitch – alone.

Again he sought out the lounge, this time to ponder his true place in Mitch's life. Pacing aggressively while debating Mitch's reasons for rejecting him in favor of Watkins, he retraced all rumor about Mitch he had heard over the years but recalled no mention of Watkins. Beyond those rumors, he knew nothing of her life after he'd left it – and he'd never bothered, during the time long ago when they were together, to learn much about her life before he'd entered it. That had burdened him in recent years when he'd sought to locate her, especially when her alumni association had also lost track of her. As he now viewed the situation, Jerry Watkins had indeed captured a significant place in what Caleb now desired.

Instinctively, Caleb took a measure of himself in relation to the Watkins he'd just witnessed. His own appearance had, since his departure from medical practice, decayed appreciably. And Mitch's condition had lulled him into further disrepair. All he could do presently was straighten his wrinkled trousers and scrape at a coffee stain on his shirt. Even his own spit wouldn't absolve him.

One thing was quite clear to him: each passing minute without Watkins' return to the lounge was registering a further depletion of his standing in Mitch's life. An image of Watkins and Mitch began teasing him too, uncovering a long-buried jealousy. He was away at med school, in his second year, and Mitch was calling him for permission to go with Watkins to the Homecoming football game he couldn't attend – just the game, she had stressed, not the weekend. How could he refuse her in her senior year when she'd been faithful all along and he had not? How could he deny her a wish to socialize, especially with his harmless ex-roommate?

"Idiot!" he cried out into the empty lounge, for the image he was recalling so vividly was from a photograph Mitch had sent him right after that weekend: a picture of Watkins and her grinning broadly, obviously laughing at him.

He sat down, closed his eyes, and let his mind wander to the last weekend he and Mitch were together.

***

There was a brazen bond that linked two lovers who were about to part. One knew their irreconcilable fate on the weekend they last met, the other did not.

How do you defeat the glitter of a bond that's lost its courage? How do you cleave it cleanly without drawing the tears and heartache that might forever mar the executioner's hand and the victim's horizon?

Washington was cold that year in early April, his second there attending med school. He had seen her two weeks before in New York City, and she was surprised yet pleased by his desire to see her so soon again. Her graduation from college was near, perhaps near enough to foster in her thoughts of marriage in conclusion to a three-year courtship.

"Still cold?" she asked. They were lying fully clothed on his bed. A wool blanket covered their clenched bodies in his apartment's changeover from heating to cooling. How ironically parallel to their own bodies' fates.

"Uh huh. You?" he answered. She nodded and kissed him. He had been fighting his passion for her, but now he was excited. She always had him hard whenever they met after a lapse of time, even before they'd touch. Once, in New York City, he'd walked erect from the bus terminal to their hotel, with a raincoat opportunely in place. He was thinking of that now.

"Glad I'm here?" she asked. He nodded and kissed her. They had just returned from the train station, and were in bed already. She read him like a book and put a hand to his crotch. He thought to stop her, to avoid the hypocrisy that would accompany the break if he allowed her to continue, but he didn't. A prick for a head, he thought, as he gained his satisfaction.

They lay there afterward in a silent conflict of emotions. One week before his engagement to another, how could he? He began to force out words, to disturb the comfort of the silence and forewarn her that a break was imminent.

"Remember our first date, the falls, how you tackled me after?" he asked.

"How could I forget?"

"What were you thinking when I forced you to play with me that first time?"

"I don't remember, really." She twisted uncomfortably.

"You just said you couldn't forget."

"Except for that part." She smiled tensely. "It was enough for anyone to forget."

"There's got to be some memory, think," he said. He was seeding the dislike of him she'd felt that first night. He'd even expected, back then, that she'd never want to see him again.

"I thought you were crazy. I thought you had a screw loose."

"But you went out with me again."

"I know, I know. At the beginning of the fall semester, after you'd come back from your summer abroad and hadn't written like you'd promised, I asked myself what I'd bargained for in you. I couldn't put my finger on it – what kept me attracted to you – no matter how hard I tried. Maybe that's the magic of love everyone talks about. And I love you all the same."

She hugged and kissed him, lingeringly, and he recognized her desire for satisfaction. He would be good for her now, after his more urgent desire had been tempered, but he ignored her foreplay.

"Had you ever done that before?" he casually inquired. He sensed her trepidation.

"Done what?" She rolled to her back to insulate him from her pounding heart.

"Touched a boy before, you know?"

"No." It was whispered in an injured tone, and he pursued her like a wounded animal.

"There's nothing wrong with having done it," he offered slyly. "How could it be right for us yet wrong with anyone else?" To him there was logic to his words, but to her they made no sense.

"Why does it matter?" she asked anxiously. "I said no, didn't I?" She was pleading with him to let it be, but he was unwilling to recognize a flaw in himself – that her answer was more important to him for what she'd say than as an excuse to break up. He never knew her to lie, and he didn't let up.

"I just want to know. Everything you've done affects who you are, and that's important to me, to understand you completely."

Under other circumstances she would surely have said, "Bullshit!" and walked away. But that day something was pinning her to the question; was it marriage in the back of her mind?

"My brother Larry and I, we played 'doctor'," she said softly, and he thought that she must be putting him on. But then a childish innocence emerged in her whisper, "Do you still love me?" and he became convinced.

He proved human after all. Showering kisses on her childlike look, he made love to her with a wantonness never equaled in the joys of their lives.

* * *

Caleb broke out of his reverie and paced the lounge some more. Watkins hadn't yet returned from his visit with Mitch, and that continued to perturb him. Not only did it seem that Watkins, his animal roommate, had supplanted him in Mitch's life, but Caleb felt foolish for not having anticipated Jerry's involvement with her. He circled the lounge time and again, as if he were racing at a track, but his real purpose was to keep eyeing the lounge entrance for Jerry's return.

Totally frustrated, he sat down on the couch facing the entrance and again addressed the picture of Jerry and Mitch. He was beginning to suspect an affair between them while he was away at med school, but even that couldn't alleviate the guilt he carried. For above all else, after inviting Mitch down for the weekend to tell her it was over, he hadn't had the decency to do it, not even to forewarn her that a break was imminent. Or had he? He lay back on the couch and retraced the last day they were together.

* * *

That last day was hell for him.

They'd already coupled ten times over the weekend, oblivious to time, protection, and intents; yet fully rewarded in timing, comfort, and intensity. How fitting that there should be such perfection at the end; now there would be only one memory, denying all past imperfections, until his guilt from that which he was about to do would become truly insurmountable.

He attempted one other time, at the end of the weekend, to rupture his hold on her soul and dissolve that brazen bond. Perhaps he never meant to succeed, for he failed again to disengage the embrace of years so as to allow her at least the slightest warning which hindsight might support.

They had made love for the last time. It was Sunday morning, still cold and cuddly, and on their sides they were permitting each other the warmth of active bodies melting from each other – he still within her, but slowly, involuntarily withdrawing his life from hers. How ironic. "Remember how disappointed we were the first time we made love, mainly because Jerry barged in?" he said.

She nodded, secure in knowing no disappointment existed now.

"We were both pretty naive back then," he went on. "Can you imagine if our fumblings had kept us apart that fall? It almost did. I certainly was aloof. Boy, what we would have missed!" His penis left her then, and its timing made them gush with laughter.

"I still think of what we discussed back then; it still bothers me," he added. Her laughter ceased immediately, and she sat up.

"We'd better get ready," she said. "The train leaves in two hours, and I haven't packed yet." She was rolling off the bed, and he grabbed her waist.

"We've got time," he replied, brushing her lips with his. "I think we should be open with each other like we were before – about your touching other boys."

She sensed the danger without the purpose and sought to avoid it. "Does that mean it's open season on questions from both of us?" she countered. "Or are you just playing decoy?"

"What do you mean?" He understood exactly.

"I mean, we started this wonderful weekend – and except for the beginning and just now, it has been wonderful – with the same kind of question, like you're looking for something to fight about. Is it a decoy? Is something else driving this conversation?"

"Nothing but what I've said," he replied hastily, realizing the coward he was. What was holding him back? He owed her so much more. "Secrets kill relationships," he added.

"They destroy people too!" she retorted.

"I want everything about us out in the open, totally, and then we can either accept things as they are or walk away from making commitments."

"That's the strangest proposal I ever heard!" she said. "Don't you think we have commitments already, or have these last three years meant something else to you entirely?"

He knew it then, with a callousness he would fathom only years later, that her question was unanswerable – that for whatever reason at that time, he wanted to be protected, to keep her hanging till the very end, in case his engagement to another fell through.

"Dammit!" he exclaimed, and it stunned her. "I just want to know! I asked you once about the first time, about its not hurting, no blood; just give me a straight answer. If you'd answered me when I asked at the beginning, this wouldn't still be coming up!"

"You know the answer, we discussed it fully before! I told you my mistake in inserting the tampon, what more do you want? If I were down here a few days from now when I'll have my period, I could have given you a demonstration! But then you might not have invited me down!"

He turned away from her in his haste to dress, and she accepted the discussion's end. The decoy had surfaced and sunk; the tenuous forewarning would wither like a pimple on hindsight's tale.

* * *

Hours had passed amid Caleb's reminiscences, which sleep had all but overtaken. He was stretched out on the couch in a slumber stricken with a sense of doom, when Jerry Watkins returned from Mitch's room and glumly thrashed him awake.

Chapter XII

Jerry

"HELLO, OLD BUDDY!" Jerry Watkins shouted while attacking Caleb on the couch. He seemed to relish every jab he gave. "Where've you been all these years?" he added, equally loudly. "No alumni connections, no reunions, no nothing! We've missed you!"

"Who?" Caleb said, sitting up.

"Jerry Watkins, of course!" he shouted. "Your old college roommate, Jerry Watkins! Say hello, old buddy!"

"Hi, Jerry. No, I mean who's missed me, who's asked about me?"

"The guys, Caleb, the guys! Ed said you'd gotten too rich and famous for us, something about saving sick kids and getting medical honoraria, but I said, 'Never!' Ha Ha! Get it, Caleb?" Jerry slapped Caleb hard on the back. "You don't get it? Well, well, what I meant was that you could never be a gifted doctor! Ha Ha! Get it now? Remember how lousy you were in biology? Must have been another Caleb Call who got recognized, probably some doctor with a heart. That couldn't be you! Right, Caleb, right!" He slapped his back again.

"Sure, Jerry, anything you say. Well, nice seeing you again." Caleb stood and stepped away.

"Whaddya mean 'nice seeing you'?" he shot back. "I'm taking you to dinner tonight – our own class reunion! Whaddya say, old buddy? How's a nice, juicy steak and a baked potato sound – especially when you're dying to know what's going on between Mitch and me?"

"Sorry, Jerry, but I've got to see Mitch again, and I'm going to wait here as long as it takes!"

"No way, Cal, old pal! I was just kicked out of there myself, and no more visitors is the order! You've done a remarkable job in raising her spirits – and keeping her awake. But sleep's what she needs right now, doctor's orders, really!"

"I can't, Jerry. I really feel I should stick around just in case she wants to see me, at least for a few hours. I don't think she has much time."

Jerry walked over to Caleb, grabbed his arm, and pulled him toward the door. Caleb shook him off.

"It's Mitch's request that we talk, my dear fellow," Jerry said at last, "and we shan't fail her again! Dinner awaits!"

The restaurant was one that appealed to Caleb immediately, except for the staff instantly recognizing Jerry. That bothered him considerably, but he was too intrigued by Mitch's request to allow any thought of retreat. And with the surprisingly prompt delivery of numerous appetizers, Caleb succumbed hungrily to the evening before him.

"Two double scotches, Frank!" Jerry bellowed to the maitre d', and in seconds the drinks were there.

"You still favor scotch, don't you, Caleb?" he solicited to soften his overbearing presumption. Caleb nodded.

"I should have asked," he continued, "but I recall your saying that you picked up a preference for the finest scotch whiskey from your father, Peter, I believe, and I thought it might relieve the tension. Well, anyway, you said your father drank only the best, and here it is! And the best to you too!" He lifted his glass toward Caleb, who responded in kind.

With the clinking of glasses, Caleb said, "And the best to Mitch too!"

"Yes," Jerry said solemnly, "the best to Mitch too."

They both took full slugs, and the scotch settled in quickly. Caleb's earlier neuroses soon vanished. "What did Mitch say about our getting together?" he inquired.

"Nothing!" Jerry replied, adding softly, "I'm sorry."

"Nothing? But you said –"

"I said I'm sorry! Look, I just used Mitch to get you to join me; it's been a long time!"

Caleb rose and asked Jerry for his coat check, which Jerry delivered.

"How's Mitch?" the maitre d' hastened to ask.

Surprised by the query, Caleb halted his exit. "She's suffering terribly now," Jerry replied, loud enough for Caleb to hear. "Probably tonight."

Caleb's knees gave way, and he allowed himself the support of a chair. "I'm sorry you had to hear it that way, old buddy," Jerry said, walking over to Caleb and urging him back to his chair, "but that's the way it is. She's under heavy sedation and there's no need for either of us to be there. Regretfully, her life is in our hands right here. I'm sorry to keep baiting you, all of this was arranged – and Mitch did make that request.

"Did you know she cut back on her pain killers to an unbearable extent after she knew you were here. And when you were with her, despite the tremendous pain she felt without enough morphine, she pretended she was in no pain at all. She must've loved you one helluva lot to do that after all the grief you've given her. And she spent the better part of what probably will be her last few hours of conscious life delivering her last wishes to me, like you were some kind of messiah. I'll never understand it, not in a million years. And to think she got me to promise. Can you believe that?"

"Promise what?"

"She's fought a tough battle, Caleb, and this afternoon was the hardest part," Jerry went on, ignoring Caleb's query. "She got to say what she had to, there's no one braver, and I promised to deliver it. Maybe you think you deserve better, some personal rite of forgiveness from her directly, but let me tell you, old buddy, you deserve shit, and if it wasn't for that promise I made to her, I'd beat your fucking face in. So just drink all the free scotch you can and unwind. It's gonna be a long night, and after these next few days are over, I'd love never to see your fucking face again. But that may be impossible."

Cringing from his animosity, Caleb whispered, "What does she expect of me? What can I do?"

"Mr. Call," Jerry said, "unlike Mitch and the two of us, the night's still young. Let's have another scotch for old times' sake before we divvy up her treasures.

"You know she still treasures you, Caleb," he continued. "Or was it that silly note you gave her. Maybe that was it."

Again scotch was ordered, but this time the bottle was left at the table. "We both know you're still the impostor you once were," Jerry added. "She's always believed you loved her, even after what you did, but you and I know differently, don't we? Say, are you hungry?"

Caleb had lost his appetite to Jerry's dissection and shook his head vigorously.

"Two filets, medium rare!" Jerry announced to a nearby waiter. "And a double Caesar salad," he added.

Caleb was about to voice his objection when Jerry asked, "And what'll you have?"

That nudged a smile from Caleb. Watkins, he again realized, was still the same old Jerry, packaged a little differently perhaps, but still with the same old animal appetite – twice as big as everyone else's.

"What's so funny?" Jerry inquired.

"Nothing you'd understand," Caleb replied, "but I'll take half of what you're having." Jerry called to the waiter and gave the order. Then he stared at Caleb for quite a while.

"Jerry, old buddy," Caleb said, growing uncomfortable under Jerry's gaze, "what brings you here? Mitch and I were one thing, but you, you hardly knew her!"

"Caleb," Jerry said calmly, "you always were the fool. I had my faults, major ones sure, and you guys dumped on me enough to last a lifetime, but you had Mitch – a healthy, happy Mitch. You had her like no one else ever would, and you threw her away.

"It wouldn't have been so bad if only you had lost her by what you did," he went on, "but you destroyed her for everyone, and that's unforgivable. Your selfish, myopic needs, whatever they were, left her with a wound so large it never healed.

"For a while I'd hoped I could fill the void left by you, that she'd eventually come back to herself, but it never happened, always settling on you – you and what you did to her. She was so beautiful, so vibrant, so much a woman when you knew her, until you abandoned her to a *New York Times* engagement announcement from which she never recovered.

"Do you know I lived with you our senior year just to be near her? And as embarrassing as it was at the time, I still joyously remember the first time I met her – at the end of our junior year, bursting in on the two of you making love that day, just before you went off to Europe. She radiated even then, and I'll never forget it.

"You were so good for her when you were with her; you fueled a magical glow that made her blossom into an angel. I would stare at her every chance I got, never getting tired. But what you stole from her – from me, you bastard, from everyone by being the selfish shit you were – that, I can never forgive."

The truth of Jerry's grievance surfaced freely; Caleb couldn't contest his guilt. "Jerry, we're often driven by forces beyond our control," Caleb began. "I loved her then, I still do, no matter how abominably I acted, and I admit to it. All those things you just said, how I destroyed her life, I accept; it's haunted me to the point I had to find her to beg for her forgiveness. All I know, without having the slightest hint of what her life has been like, is that I've destroyed my life too!"

"Do you really want to know what her life was like?" Jerry responded. "I mean really want to understand the hell it was on account of you?"

"Yes," Caleb said softly, choking back his emotions. Then realizing how indifferent it must have sounded, he exclaimed, "Yes!"

"Are you sure you wouldn't rather remain ignorant," Jerry said, "just so you can keep feeling sorry for yourself? Do you really care, Caleb, or are you here merely to gain a pardon you don't deserve but which Mitch can't refuse? You know, I don't believe you really give a damn about Mitch or me, or anyone for that matter but yourself!"

"Bullshit!" Caleb rejoined. "You could never know the torment, the punishment, the abuse I've inflicted on myself all these years. I became a pediatric oncologist to atone for what I did. As unbelievable as it might sound, I chose the most emotionally draining and morally demanding practice I could find. And I totaled my marriage because of what I did to Mitch. I'll die with her, that I know, but you... honestly, my sense of you has always been as a spectator. Obviously it's more than that, maybe much more, but when I first heard you'd been visiting Mitch I couldn't believe it. I suspected you were here as a witness to the death of what could never be yours, someone you couldn't claim but who possessed you. Now I don't know what to think. In fact, just before you woke me in the lounge, my imagination was running wild trying to fix your place in Mitch's life."

There was a sprinkling of tears on Jerry's cheeks, and Jerry quickly wiped them as they fell. The silent outpouring made Caleb search the conversation for the seed of Jerry's travail. He sensed he was now responsible for that too.

"Damn you, Caleb!" Jerry said at last. "Don't ever say I didn't try. If I've been a spectator, it's only because she wouldn't let me into her private world. After you left, she shut herself off to the world; she had no desire for honest companionship or compassion, from the second she read about your engagement in the *Times*.

"Like a fool, I gave her the copy. I saw the chance to have her, and I couldn't wait to tell her. I lost all sense of reason in looking to benefit from a rebound. I thought she'd become mine just by my being there when the news hit, when she needed a shoulder to cry on. But she just stared at the announcement, and I sensed, even though I didn't comprehend it at the time, that I'd never have the place in her heart you did.

"I used to think she married me because –"

"She what? My God, Jerry, why didn't you tell me! But the names: Levy, Watkins. The nurses called her Ms. Levy. My investigator did too!"

"A divorce, Caleb," Jerry offered, "but only on paper. After the cancer recurred, she forced it on me to give me the chance for happiness she said I deserved and never had. Let's drop the subject, please."

"I'm sorry, I didn't mean to pry," Caleb said. "You were saying you thought she married you for some reason. What was it? At least tell me that."

"I used to think, maybe too often, that she married me…that she married me because…," he seemed unable to breathe, to exhale the reason, "because I had lived with you, that some part of you was in me because we'd shared a life together living in that apartment our junior and senior years, that at least she could have that part of you by marrying me. But I don't care, I really don't!

"God, I'd rather have her as I did, than not have her at all. I'd even rather have her wasted as she is now, but without the pain, than lose her forever."

Caleb stared at Jerry, his mouth agape. The intensity of Jerry's feelings was beyond anything he himself had ever known. Could he, he wondered, ever reach that level of commitment to anything?

"Let's eat!" Jerry declared, bringing Caleb back. He raised two fingers and the salads were brought.

"How about a special red vintage, Caleb?" he added. "I think we'll need it with the work ahead of us. Let's chase the sorrow with the wine and usher in the future with our repast. Get it, Caleb? Future, repast! If only we could relive the past, how different it would be!"

The wine came and Jerry approved it. "To the future," he said after the glasses were filled. Caleb gulped his down. The glasses were refilled, and again Jerry lofted two fingers. The filet mignon followed.

"Where do I begin?" Jerry lamented as the main course was cleared. "How do I tell someone I've hated for so many years the secrets of my life, things I may not even wish to admit to myself?" He signaled for another bottle of wine.

"I'll tell you one thing if I haven't already," he continued, totally oblivious to the other patrons. Caleb stared mechanically through an alcoholic fog that had clearly clouded his mind. "I hate your fucking guts! I only wish you were in that hospital bed instead of Mitch, or were dead and buried long before she came to this!"

Caleb grinned broadly in the ensuing silence, but there was a building unease with the conversation. It was driving his thoughts toward ending the meeting and returning to the hospital.

"I know where to begin," Jerry finally said. "I'll start with the first time I dated her, that Homecoming game, about six months before you deserted her in her senior year.

"Do you know – yes, I'll say it – I lived in your shadow for so long I never believed Mitch could like me for myself. That Homecoming game proved me wrong, though. She was alone, always so alone. Mostly, I guessed, because of your being away at med school. She was a gorgeous coed without a date, and there I was, a second-year graduate student who had never dated. And I convinced her to go with me to the football game, but only after she'd called you to get your permission. Can you believe that? Here's this exceptional girl, no, this magnificent woman, who's got so much to offer, and she's been locked into an isolation booth ever since the beginning of her junior year when you went off to med school.

"It drove me crazy to think she had to get your damned approval, especially when I suspected that you were playing the field down in Washington. Funny, though, when she said you said yes, I said to myself, 'There's a guy who trusts his girl and hasn't said a bad thing about his good old buddy Jerry.' And I even changed my thinking about your playing around on her down there while you tied her hands at school. But the cat eventually got out of the bag: you were banging everything you could get your hands on down there, and you latched onto my date with Mitch, as innocent as it was supposed to be, as a sort of quid pro quo. How else do you get engaged like you did, especially knowing you, without sleeping with the broad long before!"

"Mitch sent me a picture of the two of you at the game," Caleb said. "It's the only picture I have left of her back then – my wife made me toss the rest. If you'd like to see it, I'll send you a copy when I go home."

"What game?"

"The Homecoming game. Isn't that what you were talking about?"

Jerry nodded.

"Well, you guys looked great together," Caleb went on, "good enough that I remember feeling a bit jealous. I should have realized the two of you would hook up after I'd left the scene."

"You should have felt more than that," Jerry said. "You should have suspected that Mitch stayed with me that whole Saturday, not just at the game like she said. And we had a great time too; she liked me for myself even when we talked about you, and it seemed that, like you said, maybe we could get serious if you weren't in the picture. And ya know what?"

This time he stared at Caleb until Caleb sensed something awful was about to be said. Caleb sipped some wine.

"And you know what?" he repeated. "I almost made it with her that night."

Something in Caleb had begun to erupt even before those words were out. At first Caleb wanted to believe he hadn't heard right or that Jerry was exaggerating to get his goat. But then he recalled the picture of the two of them laughing at him, and, suddenly, he lunged across the table and shot a fist at Jerry's jaw.

Turning his head away before the blow hit, Jerry still caught Caleb's knuckles on the tip of his nose. Caleb, initially collapsing awkwardly on the table top, a dish flipping to the floor, recovered enough to return to his chair while Jerry tended his bloodied nose. Two waiters hastened to the table; Jerry waved them off. The bleeding subsided quickly, but the blow cut deeply in other ways.

"I guess the animal instinct carries pretty far," Jerry remarked.

"What does that mean?" Caleb demanded.

"Just that the game of dominion – an animal's carving out its territory – extends to us."

"I think I was reacting to the way you were tarnishing my memory of Mitch."

"I was hoping my words would sting, but not at the expense of my nose. Maybe what happened'll clear the air so we can get on with Mitch's wishes."

"I'm sorry for the way I reacted," Caleb replied. "It hurt the way you wanted – I just couldn't control myself."

"Let's make a deal then," Jerry offered. "I'll control my tongue if you control your self-pity. Mitch needs both of us pulling for her right now. Okay?"

"It's a deal."

"I'll be as sincere with you as I can," Jerry continued. "There'll be pain and sorrow for both of us in what I say, but everything said will have a purpose for Mitch. Nothing'll be said just to get your goat, I promise."

He extended his hand, and Caleb took it. Caleb pushed his wine glass to the center of the table and gulped some water. Jerry did the same.

"I saw Mitch infrequently during her junior year, the year after our graduation," Jerry began. "I guess you might have wondered why I kept our apartment, paying for it myself, my first two years in grad school, but it was only because Mitch liked the place so much with you. I was hoping she might drop by for old times' sake, so I spread the word that I was there, and she came by a few times. I guess that's one of the reasons I think she married me: for the part of me that was you.

"Well, anyway, I had begun taking care of myself and the apartment in expectation of her just dropping by. I was no longer the animal you and Ed called me behind my back, and all because of Mitch.

"So she dropped by those few times, not paying much attention to me and merely walking into your bedroom, which I had made mine with the same kind of lighting and such. The first time she came I was kind of unhappy about her not wanting to stay long enough to really get to know me for myself, so just to keep her there a little longer, I got up the nerve to ask her about that year's upcoming Homecoming football game. She seemed sort of interested, but begged off, suggesting maybe next year. And I didn't forget.

"When her senior year came, I asked again, and this time she was real excited about it. You can imagine a senior coed being tied down going on three years to one guy, two of them when he's not around at all, and I guess she figured you might approve if it was me. I never thought it would happen – originally didn't even ask for that reason – and yet it happened.

"It turned out to be a great weekend, and I baited you before about taking advantage of her, but all we did was have a few beers at the game and go back to my apartment for a dinner I had prepared just in case. She got sort of depressed being there without you, and she mentioned how little you wrote, while she wrote almost every day. Then she hinted at her fears about your seeing other girls, like maybe you were bragging to me, your old roommate, about it.

"So that's the scene, and I don't know how it started, but I gave her a kiss on the cheek, like I was just consoling her for being alone so much, and I threw in a few hugs too. It certainly meant much more to me than her.

"After that weekend, things went back to the way they'd been. She dropped by every now and then, and I got her to promise to come by more often. But then in the spring, your engagement was announced. I read about it by coincidence – a relative of mine had her announcement in the paper the same day – and I became a sly bastard like you. I said to myself, if Caleb can do that to Mitch, then I could do what I had in mind to you. Of course, I wasn't really doing anything to you, until maybe now that is, because you could hardly care about Mitch and me after what you were doing to her with the surprise engagement.

"So as the sly bastard I became, I decided Mitch had better learn the truth from me than from some coed at her dorm, who would just as soon stab her in the back as look at her. So I got her to come over on a pretext I won't discuss, made this fantastic dinner with all the works, and when she was a little tipsy from all the wine I gave her, I let the news out of the bag.

"We made love that night like the ricochet romances you hear about, and I've lived with the memory of that night all these years. Maybe it was you she made love to through me, and I reaped the benefit, but whatever derision I hurl at myself for the bastard I was that night, it's so readily overcome by the ecstasy of remembering what happened.

"Now, Dr. Caleb Call, if you'd like to haul off and deck me, be my guest." He held up his chin, and, almost affectionately, Caleb tapped the point of it.

Caleb, however, had become numb to the part of Mitch's past that wasn't really his. Involuntarily, his mind reverted to his last weekend with Mitch, just before his engagement, and how he hadn't softened the blow to her.

"My parents were true WASPs," Caleb confessed, "truer than most. I suppose it was because, as I recently discovered, there's some unacknowledged Jewish blood in the family on my father's side; the name Kallmanowitz was blotted out of the family tree some time ago. Anyway, my mother was rabidly anti-Semitic, and so I never told her about Mitch – although I told Mitch I had – but I did tell Tommy, my older brother. I knew he'd blab to my mother that I was dating a Jew to pay me back for being her favorite. I never intended initially to have an extended relationship with Mitch or any girl at the time, especially when her last name was Levy. It was to be a couple of dates and lots of sex. But over time I fell in love with her, really truly in love; yet I was afraid to disappoint my parents and get cut off from med school funding. So I told my brother, thinking I'd test the water and deny any feelings for Mitch if my mother reacted heatedly.

"I don't know for a fact that my brother ever told my mother, because there was only one time the subject of dating Jewish girls ever came up, and it was in an entirely different context. My mother was commenting about a friend's son dating a Jewess, as she called her, and my mother, prudish beyond your imagination, said a lot of things which boiled down to Jewish girls being good for only one thing before being tossed away – the stereotype I'd grown up with. But that conversation seemed to ease my problem, and as time passed, I became hooked. I felt I couldn't live without Mitch unless I did something totally irrational and horrendous, and that's what I did.

"I asked my brother about it a few years ago, when I was missing Mitch real bad, my marriage had collapsed, and I'd decided to look for her. We were at a basketball game, and without owning up to telling my mother, Tommy said that I'd done the right thing in not marrying Mitch for the same reasons my mother gave, but added as an afterthought that since sex in any marriage got boring soon enough even if it was fresh to start with, having had Mitch for almost three years would have made marriage to her a disaster anyway. Of course, marriage to my ex-wife, a 'fresher' woman, proved to be a disaster anyway!"

"We're digressing," Jerry interjected, somewhat disgusted. "We're beyond your engagement, and I'm seeing her regularly now. But she's seeing others too, like a peacock out of her cage. And I started hearing things about her, like her sleeping around and such, and she was putting on weight and couldn't seem to do anything about it. So I got her to visit the doctor for a pregnancy test, hoping she was, and hoping the baby was mine; from the calculations I made based on her due date, it came out to be me. She wouldn't admit it, but I was sure it was a result of the night she read about your engagement.

"I married her, which she wasn't too keen on at first, by convincing her that for the baby's sake it should be legitimate when born. But really I was trying to make an honest woman of her and keep her out of trouble with all the rumors that were going around. And, of course, I won't deny seizing the opportunity to claim her forever. I mean, I was sure I was the father, and we got along well together, so I took advantage of her wrestling with being pregnant by proposing a safe, easy, and permanent solution.

"We were married only a couple of months when the baby came, a bit early. She was a gorgeous little girl, five pounds, two ounces, and I figured the delivery would surely eradicate Mitch's constant depression. But she rejected the baby right away, and I thought, well, maybe if we named the baby for her brother, she'd take a motherly interest. Besides, I'd heard Jews named children after dead relatives, and that way her family would be more receptive to me – which they hadn't been till then."

"The Jews don't name babies after someone who died young," Caleb blurted out, then regretted having said it.

"I didn't know that, and wouldn't have known what else to do if I did," Jerry responded, "so I chose the name Leah. But it made no difference.

"Her periods of depression got deeper and longer, and we had the baby without any mothering, so I had to quit grad school with only a masters and try to make ends meet. Fortunately, Leah was born late enough in the year, way after Mitch's June graduation, and no one except family really knew the situation. She had no close friends anyway, but she demanded extreme secrecy, which I now think I understand, although back then I thought it was some sort of crazy psychosis. She wouldn't take the baby out for fear someone would see her and so on."

He smiled at Caleb, an expression Caleb took to signify the relief one feels at sharing some horrendous burden never disclosed before. So Caleb smiled back.

"Within the year, Mitch was in a sanitarium for the first of many breakdowns – she's been in and out of them more than she's been home – though that's the only one she's ever admitted to. Every time she'd come home she was like a new person, like in those years with you, and then she'd deteriorate and have to return.

"I debated constantly whether the good was worth the bad, and when I made the decision that bound me in cement, I never looked back. You see, one time when Mitch had just come home and was her old self again, she pleaded with me to put Leah in a boarding school. She was six at the time, and I agreed, even though she'd been the focus of my life until then. I thought that maybe with Lee gone, Mitch might be able to stay home. But it didn't happen that way.

"Mitch went back again, and with Leah gone, I invested all my energy into my business interests. My visits to Lee at school became less and less frequent, and she basically grew up on her own. Now she's a handsome young lady, a beauty like her mother, no thanks to me.

"She's also quite rambunctious and high strung, a real thoroughbred, only swifter and tougher I'd say. I've recently tried to repair the damage from our separation, and with Mitch's cancer being terminal, even Mitch pushed for a reconciliation between Leah and me. But Lee rejected me completely, I guess in the same way she sees me having rejected her. In fact, she told me only last week that even after Mitch dies, she'll continue to feel unwanted because there'll just be another woman I'll choose over her like I did Mitch."

He took a deep breath and stared at Caleb. "Caleb," he whispered, "Leah is your daughter; Mitch told me this afternoon."

Caleb swallowed hard and dropped his head to his hands.

"What do you expect of me?" he said at last.

"It's what Mitch expects, not me," Jerry replied. "I'm sure there were many reasons for her telling us now, none of which were told to me with the little strength she has. In time you might be able to piece together her reasoning, but right now custody is the thing."

"I don't think I can," Caleb murmured. "Please don't ask."

"What, Caleb? I couldn't hear."

"I would really like to, Jerry," Caleb said hesitantly. "You can't imagine the number of times in recent years I've thought that as reckless as we were back then with birth control, if Mitch had only gotten pregnant, I'd have done the right thing and married her despite my parents' objections. Then all of this might not have happened. So I would like to, but I can't. Are you sure of what you heard?"

"Yes, Caleb, even with Mitch's vocal difficulties, she said it, I heard it, I repeated it, she nodded. I'd never have told you if I had a chance of winning Leah back. As weak as Mitch is, and over my strong objection, she was quite adamant that this be done. And I suppose she's right in a way. If Leah can be tamed into reaching her full potential, she'll need a new father figure like you. And your pediatric training won't hurt."

"I meant are you sure I'm the father?"

"Yes, Caleb. Mitch anticipated your insecurity – maybe she was just cutting off my contesting it – but she said she missed her period a few days after your last weekend together in Washington. She said it just like that, then added something about your seeing each other in New York City the month before. Is that something you understand?"

The light weekday traffic in the restaurant was gone, and the hour was late. Caleb's silence became unnerving. Jerry repeated the question. Finally, Caleb nodded, weakly but clearly.

"I brought Leah back from school yesterday. She's home now, and she'll be going with me to see Mitch in the morning. Mitch has kept her away until now, until the end, and I think it's been for fear Lee might refuse to come. She's a real sensitive kid, if you can crack that shell of hers. You'll meet her in the morning, too."

"I don't know," Caleb murmured. "I just don't know. There are other plans, other obligations that might take me far from here. I've got to think it through tonight. Please."

"You can think all you want, Caleb, old buddy," Jerry retorted, "but be ready to take Leah under your wing tomorrow. You won't fail Mitch again, now will you?"

"Does Leah know about me?"

"No."

"Will you tell her?"

"Not unless Mitch can't tomorrow. I think Mitch has reserved it as her last act."

"Please make sure she does, if she can," Caleb said, putting Mitch's truthfulness to one last test. "It's important that Leah hears directly from Mitch that I'm her real father."

"I'll make sure."

"My God, I just don't know," Caleb whispered.

"There's no room for refusal, Caleb," Jerry declared. "Custody is settled, and there are other requests. Can we go on?"

"More?"

"Yes, more! Look, why don't we have some beer to chase our fears." He raised two fingers and spoke to a waiter who walked over. "We're through the hardest part," he went on, as the beers came, "let's not fail Mitch again."

Caleb wouldn't drink. He pushed his glass and bottle to the middle of the table and remarked, "I think the place is closing. Hadn't we better go?"

"I own the place," Jerry responded with pride, "and it closes when I do. Here's to your Leah." He lifted his glass while Caleb merely nodded.

"I mentioned Mitch's stays in sanitariums. I thought with her first breakdown that her problem rested solely in your rejection of her – although there were these horrid nightmares she'd have about her brother often enough. But Dr. Gordon, her last and best psychiatrist, concluded, as I understand it, that your rejection of her was the catalyst in her dissociative response to her brother's death. I'm telling you this for two reasons: the first is so you recognize your partial responsibility for all this, and the second, to rechannel whatever's in your head about skipping out on Leah."

"I'd never do that!" Caleb shot back. "And that professional analysis is way off. I'm responsible for a lot of Mitch's past misery, that I'll admit, but to tag me for her breakdowns is going too far. It was her brother's death alone. She was having nightmares even while we were together those three years. You should know! That time you barged in on us my last day at school junior year, when you met her for the first time, she'd just confessed the damned thing – her being unable to ease Larry's pain, her not being with him when he died. She said she constantly thought about what Larry was thinking when he died, about how she let him down by not being there. We never talked about it again – I guess I never wanted to – it was so disturbing to her. That was the cause of her breakdowns, not me!"

"Did you know she drove over him when he fell out?"

"Oh, my God, she never said! No, I didn't know! Only that she was dazed and couldn't find him until she heard his moaning and cries for help. My God, rode over him?"

"When she came home this past year for the last time, and a new drug therapy seemed to be working, she said Dr. Gordon almost had her convinced that she didn't intentionally kill her brother, but then, out of the blue, she added with a weird, knowing smile that she knew better. I couldn't believe what I heard and assumed she'd misspoken, but, anyway, he died quickly. There were no moans or cries for help; she never got out of the car before help came.

"She was trying in her own way to adapt to his death when you came along," Jerry continued. "She never told anyone at school what had happened to her and her brother over that spring break. In fact, she'd gone back to school against her parents' wishes – they'd wanted to keep her at home for the rest of the semester. The first time she told anyone about the accident was you that last day at school. Did you ever see a picture of him?"

Caleb shook his head.

"He had the strangest likeness to you, lots of similar features, like your light blue eyes, the way you'd always leave unshaven hairs in that deep cleft you have in your chin. Just remarkable. Well, it's my guess, unprofessionally of course, that you became part of how she came to terms with her grief.

"Please, Caleb, think about it as much as you want, but accept it as it is. Maybe that's where your exoneration comes from: knowing

Mitch used you as much as you used her, and accepting your responsibility for Leah."

There was a long silence after that. Caleb was clearly fighting the conclusions to which Jerry was directing him, and yet there was some solace in being the father of Mitch's child.

"Please, Caleb, understand all that she's asking," Jerry said, about to deliver her final request. "She's going through hell right now so she can leave this world knowing it's not the worse for her. She loved you, loved me, loved Leah, the only way she could. Remember all the happiness she brought us, and do what she's asking for her sake, if not for yours."

"Did she forgive me?"

"Yes," Jerry replied. "You'll hear it from her in the morning. She promised you that."

Caleb looked at his watch, seeing the paradox of time he was feeling reflected in its face; his impatience to see Mitch in the morning was tantamount to hastening her death. For Mitch's sake, Caleb wanted to fault the Levitical teaching that unlike the Talmud, in which the rabbis concocted a "world to come" to explain why bad things happened to good people, the Five Books of Moses revealed no such thing – no afterlife, no Messiah, no resurrection – just a right to a heaven on earth if the Jews submitted to God's will and followed His laws. But he couldn't fault the Levitical teaching, and that merely steeled his desire to see Mitch before she died.

"There's one more request before we're done," Jerry said on noting Caleb's sudden preoccupation with time. "It should help you realize her forgiveness. She wants you to write something for her."

"What? I'm not a writer!"

"Caleb, she's read every medical journal article you've written, including the two that you put out in German for that foreign pharmaceutical company. In fact, there was a time in the early stages of her cancer when she was thinking of contacting you for advice, but she backed off at the last minute.

"Look, we're digressing," Jerry added. "We were discussing what she wants you to write."

"Yes, I'm sorry."

"What she wants is for you to write her story, a history with more or less a medical touch, totally honest, accurate. She thinks it's important that others know about her problems, how she coped with them, and the help that's available. She's certain that there are thousands of people like her, crying for the help that might prevent the hell she's faced. She's released all of her medical records for your review and authorized access to all her psychiatric files and psychological profiles.

"I spent over four hours getting what little I've delivered to you tonight, and I'm spent. Unless you've got a pressing question, we should call it a night."

They rose from the table, took a few steps, and Caleb stopped. "Shouldn't I see Mitch before you and Leah?" he asked.

"That may, in fact, be better," Jerry replied. "That way Leah will meet you before she sees Mitch. And if Mitch dies tonight, you'll be there to help break it to her. I'm not sure how she'll take losing her mother and gaining a new father in the space of a few hours. We'll move our time with Mitch back to nine o'clock. You get to Mitch at eight and meet us in the lounge around eight forty-five."

They walked some more, and as Caleb's coat was handed to him, he asked, "How are things with you, Jerry? It must have been rough all these years."

"Things are as good as can be expected," he replied, somewhat warmed by a question about him and his suffering during the years with Mitch. "The financial burdens have pushed me to succeed; what else was there with Mitch and Lee away? Ironic isn't it, how lazy I might have been otherwise. I busted my ass to give them the best of everything – medical care, private schools – but I'm ending up with neither of them. Maybe my role was just to bring us all peace of mind.

"I guess that's why I got so upset when you called me a spectator. Sometimes I've thought of myself as a perennial visitor: to Mitch at the sanitarium and Leah at her boarding school. But when you add it all up, I guess it's okay to be a spectator as long as you're observing someone you love. What'll I have now, with both of my girls gone?"

"Sometimes I replay the past, never sure how good or bad it was," Caleb offered graciously. "When I learned you were here, my mind naturally shifted to memories of us. I like to think of those times as the good old days – Mitch, Ed, Sue, you, and me. Things were simple, relationships honest, and life was ahead of us. We didn't have to reconcile things all the time. And we did have some good times!"

"Yeah, Caleb, I remember the fun we had," Jerry responded. "I remember being down because I'd flunked some exam or didn't have a date again when you and Ed did. I remember the names you used to call me when I did masochistic things like letting the garbage pile up that spring break. Sure, those were the good old days with honest relationships, like the ones where you did nothing but spout lines for a single purpose. And yes, Caleb, life was ahead – like Mitch's."

"Jerry, I'm sorry, I didn't mean it that way. All I was trying to say was that maybe you were the only one to walk away from our past with your humanity intact. In fact, I was the animal we often claimed you were. I wish I could change the past for that alone, and maybe Mitch wouldn't be where she is today if I had been the person I am now."

"I think we'd better call it a night," Jerry said. "Your actions tomorrow with Mitch and Leah will make or break your past. Mitch'll confirm all the things I've said to you tonight to the best of her ability, but if you still intend to think things over and come to the hospital tomorrow looking for a way out, I'd rather have you give me a call. There's a lot of room to manipulate Mitch with the little strength she's got left, and we don't need to devastate Leah. I hope that's not what you have in mind."

"I don't understand what you're talking about," Caleb said. "I haven't anything of the sort in mind!"

"Let's not end the evening on a sour note," Jerry said. "It's purely a matter of understanding personalities."

"I think you owe me an explanation about what I supposedly have in mind, that I don't even know myself!"

"Caleb, I don't want to argue the point. All I'm suggesting is that you weren't too thrilled with the prospect of Leah coming into your life, and if you intend to talk Mitch out of it when she might not have the lucidity or strength to hold firm, do it so Lee doesn't get clobbered by it. If you're not in the lounge by nine, I'll assume you've run, and I'll give Leah the best excuse I can."

"I'd never do that!"

"I take it back, then," Jerry said, "but someone who seems so into the past may not have room for a new face in the future."

"I brought up the past to acknowledge some misdeeds and go on from there," Caleb said, "especially with all you've had to go through. I accept my responsibility for Leah. I plan to be at the hospital at eight, primarily to get a better idea of what Mitch wants me to write – a responsibility I also accept."

"I'll see you tomorrow then," Jerry said, walking Caleb to the door.

Caleb shook Jerry's hand and stood outside. The doorman soon had a taxi at the curb. "You never told me who won that Homecoming game," Caleb said as he stepped inside the cab. "You won Mitch, but who won the game?"

"We did, I think," Jerry said, holding the restaurant door open, "the only game we won all year!"

"What a lousy football team," Caleb shouted through the cab's window, "absolutely the worst!"

"Eight o'clock!" Jerry shouted back.

"Absolutely the worst!" was all Jerry could make out as the taxi pulled away.

Chapter XIII

Joseph and John

The same evening Caleb and Jerry were eating at Jerry's restaurant, Joseph arrived extremely troubled at John's apartment, after a long day of suffering at Goldie's bedside. His spirits had been declining throughout the day in step with Goldie's failing condition, but that wasn't the root of his unhappiness. John had become a constant source of comfort to Joseph in his deteriorating environment, and Joseph now believed John had, to put it bluntly, double-crossed him. It was only partially true.

He found John hunched over the kitchen table with a half dozen reference books on Caribbean history spread over it. That set Joseph off.

"I thought you should know, if you don't already," he said angrily, "that I promised Goldie this afternoon I'd go with you on your damned journey. You shouldn't have gone behind my back this morning before I got there, especially after I'd told you last night that I wasn't interested. You took advantage of her condition to get her to do your dirty work. It put me in a situation where I couldn't refuse.

"She was so taken with your pursuit of Cain and that stupid fountain that she wouldn't get off the subject the whole day. She'd go in and out of consciousness spouting your ridiculous theory when I wanted to talk to her about more important things. It wasn't right to wind her up like that when there's so little time left."

"It wasn't my doing," John said.

"You shouldn't have talked to her about it at all," Joseph argued, "certainly not when I wasn't there and already said I wasn't interested!"

"Please, let me explain," John broke in.

"And you had the nerve to tell her it was the perfect way to top off our wonderful lives, to make them truly worthwhile," Joseph ranted on. "Just because she's dwelling on the past a lot lately, on whether she's really made a difference in being here, doesn't give you the right to propose some asinine way of making her feel she won't fall into oblivion when she dies. You've been telling us all along that cancer in its final stage can dim the perspective you have on your life, and we were doing just fine guarding against it. So why'd you go and play on it, telling her there was something I could do to give her life more meaning when I've been telling her every day how much meaning she's already built into her life. She built real monuments to herself: our business, her charities! And now you've gone and made it seem like there's still more she needs to do. She's made things happen that'll affect people for generations to come, things that wouldn't and couldn't have happened without her. That's how she'll be remembered, not by some foolish journey that we might take!"

"Are you finished now?" John asked as Joseph's rage abated. "After all that we've been to each other, you should know I wouldn't do as you've said. So let me explain.

"I was passing Goldie's room early this morning, and, truthfully, I thought you'd have been there by then. I stopped in to say hello to both of you. Goldie was awake, staring at the ceiling, and you weren't there. I couldn't let her be alone like that when she's so eager to talk, to feel alive in the time she has left.

"We began discussing the session we had last night; you were the one who told her we were meeting for dinner at my place last night to continue the sessions we'd started the night before, and you were the one who told her about Caleb's view of the Torah. Well, she went right at it, kept digging about the session, like she does so well with her doctors until she's satisfied with an answer, and there it was: the journey to find Cain was out. I intended nothing by letting her know, except maybe to test the theory with her enormous perception.

"Honestly, I had accepted your decision not to go as final, but like I said last night, I think there's a greater power involved here. It's put us together for a reason, each with a contribution we may never truly comprehend, but on the journey regardless.

"Goldie grasped the significance of the fountain immediately, mentioning Ponce de León as quickly as Tom did. And since I remembered nothing from my German schooling on the topic, I borrowed these books from the hospital library to find out about Caribbean history. We are about to embark on a historic undertaking!"

"She always was a lover of history," Joseph said, smiling, "and her mind's always been like a computer in storing information and solving complex problems. If she could be with us, I'd be packed already – there'd be no chance of failure. I'm going to miss her so much!"

"Why not go then, for her sake?"

"I said I would, I promised her! But you should know, I think this whole thing is ridiculous, believing there's a five-thousand-year-old man we can capture. While Goldie slept, I replayed the whole of last night's conversation in my mind and there's no way it'll fly."

"That's because a modern, scientifically advanced civilization is trained to seek the answers to its problems in a laboratory," John replied. "But in a laboratory, as many new problems will arise as there are solutions. Look at genetic engineering and motherhood in an era of laboratory conception. How many virgin births do we need before there's the Second Coming? Perhaps that's why part of the solution to our problem is in a riddle.

"Can't you imagine how wonderful the world would become if the existence of God were proved through finding Cain?" John went on. "Just maybe, finding Cain will be the catalyst for Caleb's otherwise impossible dream of the Jews' full observance of God's law. Then, the lion and sheep could lie side by side, and maybe, just maybe, Caleb's world of health, peace, and prosperity would come to be, and put those laboratories out of business."

"But maybe, just maybe," Joseph mimicked, "like those Polish rabbis concluded, we shouldn't know for a fact that God exists."

"Maybe we shouldn't, but who are we to abandon what's been preordained for our therapy group? How about discussing it further over the leftovers from last night's spaghetti dinner?"

Chapter XIV

Jerry, Caleb, and Leah

THE NEXT DAY WAS WARM AND CLOUDLESS, instilling in Caleb the anticipation of a special day. After Caleb's dinner with Jerry Watkins the previous night, the opportunity presented by Leah's presence had nestled its way into his mind. Now he saw her as a vehicle of redemption, through which they both could be polished over time into the image of God, as he now longed to be. This was to be his day of past forgiveness and future promise, and his enthusiasm for seeing Mitch was already sparking a radiance in him that had been absent since he learned of Mitch's terminal condition.

It was 7:50 in the morning when Caleb arrived at the medical center. He'd walked from his hotel at a good pace, eager to spend some of the energy that came with his new potential; yet the walk animated him further, to the point that on entering the center, he detoured once again to the stairwell adjacent the elevator bank.

Mitch's floor was eerily quiet as the stairwell door opened. The visitors' lounge, directly across from the elevator bank and stairwell, was vacant, and noting the approach of eight o'clock on his watch, Caleb quickly strode toward Mitch's room. An elevator door opened behind him, and Jerry's voice overtook him. Caleb ignored it, however, pushed open Mitch's slightly ajar door, and stepped inside her room. When he focused on her bed, his countenance was eclipsed instantly.

It is impossible to describe the horror Caleb felt on seeing an empty, straightened bed. He had seen beds like that too often to assume any other meaning. And when a nurse entered seconds later in response to his anguished cries, she discovered him pounding on the bed with his fists. Instantly he fled.

With his eyes ablaze and face sunken, Caleb raced toward the stairwell by the elevators. Having anticipated the scene that was unfolding, Jerry was already stationed in the hallway to bar Caleb's way. And reacting promptly to Caleb's choice of egress, Jerry caught Caleb's arm as Caleb reached for the stairwell doorknob.

"Leah's waiting for you in the lounge!" Jerry said sternly, wrapping his arm around Caleb's back. "Don't forget your promise last night!"

Gradually loosening his grip, Jerry led Caleb toward her. "I'm okay now," Caleb remarked as they entered the lounge. "As much as I expected it, the suddenness of it still got to me. I'm sorry."

"Let's hope that's all it was," Jerry responded as they approached a young woman on the same couch Caleb had napped on. "You have responsibilities now, remember? I've notified the school that Leah won't be returning. I figure that with your being home writing Mitch's story, you'll become a perfect father in no time. Isn't that right, Caleb?"

Still too numb to comprehend Jerry's words but nodding anyway, Caleb turned toward the young woman who stood to face him.

"In that case, Dr. Caleb Call," Jerry continued, "I'd like you to meet your daughter, Leah Watkins. In due course, you and she may wish to change her surname to yours. I would have no objection."

With immeasurable trepidation, Caleb addressed Leah in the full light of the lounge. He was stunned by her similarity to her mother. "That's a pretty name," he stammered while reaching out awkwardly to hug her.

She wrinkled her nose, as if to accentuate the corniness of what had been said, and with the cutest smile, responded, "Just call me Lee, if you'd like."

Chapter XV

Isaac

"You see, Pa, the clock was wrong," Stitches said to Isaac. Stitches had just arrived on the farm after flying in from the medical center, and they were standing outside the shed. "Our Jo Jo's comin' home again one way or another. If a transplant operation doesn't happen by next week, she's comin' home to be with us. I'm goin' to fix the clock and get back its magic. Then I'm goin' to sell the machinery business and work the farm with you and Jo Jo like we used to. Tomorrow we'll start with the land over there, the land you got for Jo Jo and me when we got married. Pa, are you listenin'?"

"I'm listenin', Stitches, but the magic's gone from that clock forever, since our Becka died. My Jo Jo may be comin' home, but there's no gettin' back the magic, hers or the clock's."

"When we was young," Isaac went on, "time was free and plentiful, especially after you did the magic with it. It could go fast or slow or not at all 'cause we was the chaser. Now it's chasin' us. Time was part of the pleasure of bein' young, 'cause by its passin' you got where you was headin', even if not fast enough. If you set your mind to doin' a chore that was long in gettin' done, all you needed to do was keep at it, a little bit every day, and time would pass, there ain't no stoppin' it, to make sure you got it done. But, really, it's the devil hisself who 'ventioned time, especially the clock to tell where it's at, so that as you gets older, all it does is play with you – tease you today with hope, laugh at you tomorrow for hopin' at all."

"Pa, we'll talk about it later," Stitches said, "but now we've got to get Jo Jo's room ready for her homecomin'. She hasn't seen you since you stopped comin' to the center with me a month ago, and she can't wait to get here."

They walked into the farmhouse slowly. Except for electricity and plumbing, it hadn't changed much since the first time Stitches saw it. Jo Jo's room, their room before they bought a house in the best section of town to be nearer their machinery business, was off to the left. Isaac went right to the double bed he'd made for them as newlyweds and began tenderly stroking the headboard. He was humming too while Stitches checked the dresser drawers for space. That's when Stitches spied the clock, buried beneath the spare clothes he'd left there for the nights he stayed over.

He wound the clock hesitantly, expecting it to be over wound, but it began ticking. He turned the hands to match the time on his wristwatch, and as he passed the alarm setting, it rang out. He looked toward the bed where Isaac had been sitting, but Isaac was gone.

Rushing to search for him, Stitches promptly noted an open shed door and entered. The shed, too, hadn't changed from the first years he'd been there, except for storing some modern machinery Stitches had given Isaac on the pretext of testing it. The mound of dirt Isaac had used to test his original inventions was still there, but now, feverishly, Isaac was working at destroying it, alternately kicking and digging at it.

"Pa, what're you doin'?"

"I'z returnin' the earth to the earth," he replied. "It's been good to me for so long, I can't see no reason to leave it here as a reminder."

"Reminder of what?"

"What once was, son," Isaac replied. "There comes a time when things got to be put back in order so's you can meet your maker. This here is special earth from which all the good things in our life come. It was my beginnin' and will be my Jo Jo's end. We'll use it to bury her. I kept it here as the last reminder of what was. I used to come in here at night, when the house was sleepin', and use the magic of the clock to help with my 'ventionin'. I always thought I was chosen by my maker for deliverin' better things to the people 'round here, that there was somethin' special happenin' to me to set me apart from the ordinary. And that was the most wonderful feelin' ever happen to me, and I touch this earth whenever I want to remember."

"But there were so many other good things in your life after the years of 'ventionin','" Stitches argued. "There was our buyin' the land from the owner, there was the machinery business..."

"That's good if you still creatin' when your time come," Isaac interjected, "but that ain't for me now. I stopped climbin' the mountain years ago, and there ain't goin' ta be no Isaac soon neither."

"Stop talkin' that way, Pa! Jo Jo and I need you!"

"Stitches, remember for yourself so you don't let it get this way for you at my age. The only thing I ever done real good, that my spirit was in, was my 'ventionin'. It was so good to take my thinkin' and change things for the better, for me and the others 'round here. The 'ventionin' no one can take from me, no one can say was done by some other man. But my time of creatin' came and went so fast I didn't catch hold to enjoy it long enough, didn't ever think it might disappear so's I should cherish it till it was gone. Like that, it went!" He snapped his finger.

"It was my whole life in such a short time," he added, "the whole reason for my bein' on this earth, and this here earth feels so good to the touch, such a nice reminder of the chosen person I was."

"Pa, please don't talk that way!" Stitches said. "Look outside, look at the land, look at what you've made of yourself. You own it all! It was only Becka's gettin' sick that stole the 'ventionin' from you. You'll start up again as soon as Jo Jo and me come home."

"No, son, that ain't the way it was," Isaac said ruefully. "I never said nothin' 'bout this afore, but I stopped 'ventionin' long afore Becka took sick. There came a time I jus' couldn't climb no higher.

"Listen, now. Anybody can work the land. Anybody can be a peddler like you was way back. It's God's gift of skills in your body and mind that makes you different, chosen, in this world. When I used to 'vention somethin', I used to think of it first and then make the ideas into somethin' to touch, over and over till it was jus' right. I used to think I was special above all, the smartest body in the whole world, my little world here, doin' that. I didn't care nothin' 'bout other folk havin' more or livin' better. I loved everythin', liked myself, relied on me alone, and maybe I sometimes forgot that God give it all to me. But I felt I had control over my world, that nothin' could take it from me – not time and not God neither.

"You see, Stitches, I let other things get in the way of my 'ventionin' 'cause I couldn't do it no more. But I wouldn't admit it, 'cause I liked the stares of people at church and in town, so I covered it over with managin' the farm 'stead a creatin'. Now I comes to understand it, son. I jus' got to a place in 'ventionin' that needed a better mind than me. It was God's way o' punishin' me for thinkin' I done it on my own mind and might, not what He blessed me with.

"So don't say it's goin' to come back. As many times as I come in here to get it back, it never comes. Like in this whole world, you get only one speck o' time to be somebody, one chance to be chosen, and you gots to hang onto it while it's here, praisin' God for it, 'cause soon enough if you don't, if you comes ta thinkin' you do it on your own, it's gone forever – you reach your mountaintop and fall away."

"But you'll always be somebody, Pa," Stitches said. "I don't understand why you're so down on yourself."

"I was somebody, son, a long time ago. Now I'z jus' livin' off it. You have to be somebody movin' up in your head always. You can't live on reminders or coulda beens. When people tell me I done well, I think to myself I done well once, and now's only the rewards for that time. But the rewards are bitter if you know you're still fallin' from the mountaintop." He began kicking and digging at the dirt again.

"What about the clock, Pa?" Stitches asked, hoping to rejuvenate him. "You said last week it was broke, but it works fine. It started up again – so can you!"

"It's broke, son." He rested his arm on the handle of the shovel. "Maybe it works the way you know it to, but its magic is gone, gone back to its maker like my Jo Jo and me is gettin' ready to do."

Chapter XVI

Joseph and John

"Can you hear me, Goldie?" Joseph whispered to her in her room at the medical center. Her breathing was imperceptible, and he searched for a rise in the bedcovers. He looked around, took her cold, rigid hand, and started talking into her ear.

"I dreamed last night that I was cleaning out my old apartment," he said, "like I did before I moved in with you last year. All those decisions about what to keep and what to throw out. There was such a mess, and you made me trash most of it. It's getting that way again, but it's your apartment this time; it needs you. I'll drown in the mess I make of things if you're not around.

"Pa was in my dream too, his voice only. It came from the picture albums, which I looked at the last time I was home. There are no more loose photos like you always complained about. Some of the ones I put in the album were from long ago, the ones I had in my dresser drawer. You're beautiful in them. In the dream Pa said I broke up the family by starting my own business. He said I had no right to keep you to myself all these years. He said Ma is very upset you didn't marry. She wanted lots of grandchildren, and you were so pretty and smart. He said I stole you like I stole those roses from Mrs. Stern's flower box for Ma's birthday one year. Remember? Can you ever forgive me for keeping you to myself your whole life?

"There was a picture of Harry Finkelstein in my dresser. Remember him? How could you forget him? You deny it, but I'm sure you would have married him if the war hadn't come. We visited his grave in Europe the last time we were there – remember how you cried? You were holding hands with him in the picture. I think if I had known how deep your feelings for him were back then, I would have been very jealous. Even now I suspect there was much more to the relationship than you ever let on.

"Oh, Goldie, I miss you so much already. I'm sorry I didn't protect you more. I know you said this illness was just another test. You've always thrived on competition. Success to you meant being tested and making it!"

"Mr. Kallman, please," a nurse interrupted, tugging at his hand, "it's time to let go."

The nurse freed Goldie's hand from Joseph's, and Joseph became irate. He pushed the nurse aside, as he had done an hour earlier, took Goldie's hand again, and bending over her, whispered, "I love you, I always have, and I hope you've known it all along." He turned to the nurse and glared at her until she backed out of the room.

"I love you, Goldie," he declared as soon as the nurse was gone. "I should have told you more often, but I was sure you knew it. I –"

"Joseph," John whispered, pulling him away, "it's time. You told her the most important thing, that's what counts. Come back to my place, and rest while I initiate all the arrangements you've made to bring her back to New York. You've been here since early morning; I'll take care of everything else."

"I said it, I said it," Joseph mumbled as they walked down the corridor to the elevators. "She's with Harry now, like it should have been all along. You know we all have people waiting for us in the world to come."

"Yes, Joseph, she's there, at peace now."

"We have a family plot on Long Island; Ma and Pa are there waiting for her. But Harry's in Europe; that's where she is now. I have nothing left, no reason to live."

"You need some sleep, Joseph. You've been under a terrible strain these last few days. Tomorrow things won't be so bleak, you'll see."

At John's apartment, John quickly ushered Joseph into his bedroom. Urging him onto his bed, John stripped him of his shoes and pants, covered him with a blanket, and drew the drapes. Joseph merely stared at the ceiling.

John remained with him, watching Joseph's vacant gaze, until an overwhelming emotion drove John from the room. He bolted the front door and paced the living room. When John peered into the bedroom, Joseph was still staring at the ceiling.

"Joseph, close your eyes," John whispered, taking his hand.

Joseph blinked and closed them. "She was my strength," he said softly. "I feel so alone."

"You can rely on me now, Joseph. I'll be your strength."

John hesitated before resuming, "I was reading a book on the South Pacific, and I want to tell you about it – about the islands there, the warm winds blowing off clear waters. Think of yourself as a child there, crying in your mother's arms because you are troubled in some inexpressible way. Your sister Goldie is hiding nearby watching her mother comfort you.

"Your mother is gently massaging you, which prompts your sister to sneak closer. Your mother does not see her, although she has no interest in secrecy. As your mother continues to massage you, your crying turns into a whimper.

"Goldie is staring at your mother's touch, which has begun to draw all your energy toward the center of your body. Your sister's eyes are wide with wonder, and your mother is smiling, as your body becomes increasingly stimulated. She cradles you in her arms now and brings her face down to your body, kissing it softly where she had been massaging you before. Your energy is flowing uncontrollably toward your center as your mother's lips and tongue continue to draw it there. Suddenly you stiffen and shudder, then become deeply tired, and fall asleep without the pain that had made you cry." Joseph, too, soon stiffened and shuddered, and fell asleep.

Joseph awoke the next morning at peace with Goldie's death. John had been asleep on the living room sofa, but snapped awake on hearing Joseph lock the bathroom door. When Joseph finally arrived in the kitchen after an extended shower, John had coffee perking, pancakes on a serving tray, and some hot oatmeal sitting on the stove, all items Joseph had praised at John's breakfast three days earlier.

"How are you this morning?" John asked, searching Joseph's demeanor for any reaction to their recent encounter.

Avoiding eye contact, Joseph replied caustically, "I slept well, considering."

"You have a plane to catch in six hours," John advised, changing the subject. "Everything's been arranged for Goldie's funeral tomorrow afternoon. I wish I could be there, but a new group starts tomorrow afternoon. I also have certain things to do to prepare for our journey to the Caribbean, and Father Conlin appears to be the best place to start – we'll go once you've settled everything in New York."

"I can handle things from here on," Joseph said, "but I'm not sure I should be going off to the Caribbean so soon after Goldie's death."

"It's what she wanted, Joseph," John countered. "If you put it off today with one excuse, you'll find another to put it off tomorrow. Believe me, Joseph. Right after your days of mourning are over, we should go."

"I know what I need, John," Joseph rejoined, "and you're not going to control what I do! Cain isn't going anywhere; your riddle says he's got all the time in the world!"

"And you've got all the time you need, Joseph," John replied. "You're no good to either of us if you don't really want to be down there. Keep in mind though: we're not talking about gallivanting through the Caribbean for the fun of it. Goldie understood that. It's a very demanding mission we're on, with very important consequences if we succeed. So you decide when you're ready, and that's when we'll go."

Chapter XVII

Tom

A FEW DAYS AFTER RETURNING to Boston, and in response to a pointed reminder from John on the telephone, Tom sent this note:

> *Dear John,*
>
> *As a follow-up to our recent conversations, I have given your pursuit of Cain the further consideration you requested. My conclusion remains the same: I should not accompany you and Joseph in your search even if Caleb now cannot. I am, therefore, enclosing a letter of introduction to Father Conlin, along with his address and telephone number, as I promised. He should definitely be your first contact in the Caribbean, so mark your initial destination as San Juan. Just give him my best and tell him I would have been along but for the press of university business – he'll understand. The complexity of your analysis on Cain's eternal nature may have already convinced you not to disclose more of your purpose to anyone than you need to. I often find that helpful in my own research.*
>
> *If you need anything from me while you're down there, perhaps just a third opinion on a find, don't hesitate to call. I do have other contacts, but none as good as Father Conlin.*
>
> *Thanks again for the thought-provoking sessions we had together at the medical center. Please do keep in touch. As*

things progress both here and there, we might find it in all our best interests to have me with you on your final approach.

Good luck and good sailing!
Sincerely,
Tom

Chapter XVIII

Caleb

On the morning John was to fly to Puerto Rico, a secretary at the medical center reached him at the airport with this cryptic message from Caleb:

> *Can't seem to reach you at home or work. Massive change in my plans with Leah. Will meet you in San Juan in two days and explain. Leave your hotel name, telephone number, and address on my answering machine if you don't reach me directly before you go.*

Chapter XIX

Father Conlin

APART FROM A SLIGHT DELAY IN THE MORNING FLIGHT from New York, Joseph's rendezvous with John in San Juan went as planned, two days after John himself had arrived in Puerto Rico.

Joseph's time in the air was spent constantly watching white, billowy clouds that lay like a blanket on his past. The clouds made him realize that his current life was very much like them – a bank of fond memories, not a life lived in the present – and unlike those who lived life to the end, he was quite content to be approaching seventy-three, his life basically behind him. It was as if his life – or any life for that matter – was truly the test Goldie said it was, becoming bearable, possibly even enjoyable, only after it had been weathered into old age, only after the fear of not making it, of being cheated out of a full life, was over.

Goldie had said as much on her deathbed: she wouldn't trade the many years she'd had of good health and fortune – even if scathed at times by unbearable trauma – for a new one, a fresh one that would again subject her to the whims of future unknowns. And yet she loved to be tested, and had demanded that Joseph, her twin in body if not in spirit, accompany John on a final test, a last gauntlet, to seek Cain and the fabled Fountain of Youth, to make their lives truly worthwhile.

At the designated gate, John was waiting impatiently for Joseph's flight to arrive. And when the two men saw each other for the first time in almost two weeks, they embraced awkwardly in a symbolic union of their fates.

During the taxi ride into San Juan, there was conversation about Joseph's days of mourning, Caleb's cryptic reversal, and John's lack of success in seeing Father Conlin, who had been disembarking in San Juan at the same time Joseph had been lifting off in New York. Pleading Goldie's interest in Cain, John convinced Joseph to bypass a restful day at the hotel in favor of a trip into Old San Juan to attempt a visit with the Jesuit priest before he disappeared again.

Dropped outside the Jesuit enclave, they were met by a flood of children as school let out. Not knowing how long the exodus would last, John grabbed Joseph's arm and began wading through the sea of students. At last John was able to grasp the doorknob of the one huge double door that was not in use. With a twist and yank of both his hands, the door slowly opened.

"Keep that door closed!" a man's voice thundered from within.

John instantly released the doorknob, but the door kept swinging open, pinning both men against the metal railing behind them. Joseph was embarrassed and uneasy in this strange, Catholic world, but John seemed as confident and assertive as ever. As soon as the rush of children eased to a trickle, he pushed Joseph across the entranceway, which was closing again under the enormous weight of the double doors. Once inside, they faced a lone man in priestly garb who, displaying a crowning crop of grey hair, was standing at the end of a lengthy hallway. He looked quite ordinary, almost incapable of the earlier outburst, and Joseph relaxed a bit.

"I'm sorry to have yelled like that," the priest said as John and Joseph approached, "but that second door is kept closed to keep the children from running down those stone steps. They've been responsible for many a bad scrape, even with that second door closed. The name's Conlin." He extended his hand to each of them and added, "I'm the headmaster of that brood you just saw, and all this brick and mortar. What can I do for you?"

"Hello, I'm so very pleased to meet you," John said. "I'm John Hauser and this is Joseph Kallman. We've been trying to see you these past few days to ask a question or two. I called your secretary and left a message about Tom Petersson's letter of introduction. Well, here it is. May we have a minute of your time?"

Father Conlin took the letter and read it quickly. "Well, I'll be!" he exclaimed as he folded it and put it in his pocket. "Surely you may have a minute! How is he? It's been over a year since we last spoke."

"He lost his brother recently, to a fall," John replied. "That's how we met: at the hospital. I'm a psychiatric social worker there. Otherwise he's fine."

"I'm sorry to hear that," the priest said. "I was about to take him to task for not having written – not even to send me a courtesy copy of the article he authored with my help. If I hadn't my own subscription, I wouldn't have learned how far beyond our investigations he went with his theory. Now, I'll have to limit my call to him to an expression of sympathy when I'd rather have argued about the article and my attributions in those footnotes."

"We have just a couple of questions if you don't mind," John said.

"I don't have the pleasure of assisting many Americans down here, and Tom was a joy – his work was right up my alley – although I disagree with his conclusions. You sound like a Midwesterner with German origins, am I right?"

John nodded.

"I come from Maryland, myself," the priest went on. He was staring at John as he spoke, a searing gaze, and it unsettled Joseph. "How may I assist you?"

"Tom told us you were the expert on the Ciboney Indians," John said, beads of sweat suddenly appearing on his forehead. "He admires you greatly, and you should be flattered by those footnotes. They're what brought us here."

The Jesuit was still staring at John when, abruptly, he turned and marched farther down the hall, stopped, bid the two men follow him, and then backtracked into his office. He pointed to two wooden chairs opposite his desk, and they sat down in tandem, Joseph sitting only after watching John for any ritual he might have to follow in a priest's presence.

"Now that we've exhausted introductions and the small talk," Father Conlin said, "how might I truly help you? I assume Tom mentioned that the Ciboney tribe is gone from the face of this earth. But that's another story. Please, tell me specifically what questions you have in mind."

"What we'd really like," John responded, "is for you to recount all that you told Tom about the Ciboney for that footnote mentioning the possibility of a still surviving chieftain. Tom and you chose not to pursue that Ciboney, but we would like to judge for ourselves."

"That would take days I don't have," the priest replied. "I gave the time to Dr. Petersson because I knew his credentials and thought his project worthwhile," he continued, "but I don't know anything about the two of you or your purpose here."

"That would take as much time as you say you don't have," John remarked. "For the little we need, perhaps you might tell us merely what you know about that last Ciboney chieftain. For that we would be forever grateful."

"I'll give you what you need," the Jesuit responded, "and then, perhaps, you'll favor me with your true purpose here."

"Thank you," John said.

"The Ciboney were a peaceful, nomadic people," Father Conlin began, "who originally lived on Cuba and Hispaniola, the latter now comprising Haiti and the Dominican Republic. But the Arawaks came, even before the Spaniards set foot in the Americas, and pushed their more peaceful brothers into the sea. The Ciboney were forced to split into bands of lesser numbers to escape the Arawak onslaught, and they became either forest or canoe nomads depending on where they fled. But that wasn't their end, sad to say, because the Caribs and Spaniards hit them harder than the Arawaks ever did, and in fact nearly exterminated them.

"There was one band, though, that seemed to multiply from out of nowhere, and they were the Ciboney of St. Thomas, who were forced by the Danes in the mid-seventeenth century to flee to one of the smaller islands of the Virgin Islands chain. The rest about the chieftain is mostly hearsay, of which I've never seen solid proof. It was told to me by a Protestant missionary, who supposedly had it from the chieftain himself – but I doubt that completely, well, almost completely.

"It seems that the band of Ciboney that left St. Thomas flourished into the early nineteenth century and then disappeared – some epidemic, I would presume – leaving only its young chieftain alive. But the Ciboney who told the missionary these things about ten years ago was, by his own admission, the same young chieftain who was the sole survivor of whatever vanquished his people. Yet the time lapse between the time of the epidemic and ten years ago makes the rest of the tale better left unsaid. You see, I've turned those numbers over in my mind more often than I care to think, and the chieftain, if alive today, would be over one hundred fifty years old.

"The missionary, however, described the chieftain who told him these things as at most forty, and that alone throws the whole thing out. As a matter of fact," Father Conlin concluded, shaking his head and smiling, "I don't know that it was even worth the time relating such suspect information."

"Everything you have told us so far will be quite useful," John said enthusiastically, "but we're still missing the piece we came for. We're after the Ciboney chieftain to interview him. Do you have any idea where he might be found?"

"What on earth for?"

"For research on aging," John replied. "At the medical center, he would easily take the prize for being the oldest man on earth. So please, let us be the judge of his veracity, assuming we can locate him. We're certainly willing to put time and money into finding him."

Again the Jesuit deliberated. "The Ciboney chieftain had sought out the missionary to gain assistance in locating a ship that sailed these waters in the early nineteenth century," Father Conlin offered. "The ship was named the *Jason*, and apparently went down somewhere near St. Thomas. Its captain had supposedly stolen a powerful religious object from the Ciboney after a storm forced the ship to anchor off the island. At the time, I unprofessionally belittled that Indian's polytheistic culture. I assumed that whatever icon the chieftain was after, if it ever existed at all, was probably some artifact or totem that the good captain carried off as a souvenir. I just couldn't see the Ciboney god of thunder, or whichever god the object represented, coming down and decimating the people for its loss, or sinking the *Jason* for its captain's theft.

"Well, anyway, I regret those perceptions now, primarily because they kept me from pursuing the man as a good scientist should have. In anthropological research, the first thing you learn is to hunt every lead down to its rightful end, even the hoax you believe from the outset is out there to embarrass you. And therefore, gentlemen, I must confess, if I had it to relive, I'd go after that Ciboney and put the supernatural to rest. So be my guest, if that's your true intention, and hunt him down like I should have."

"That is what we intend," John acknowledged, "and if you were embarking on such a search now, where would you start, if I might ask?"

Hesitating only momentarily, the priest said, more to himself than them, "With the captain of the freighter I use to transport me between islands. I disembarked this morning after visiting St. Thomas, and you'll find him here until this evening, on the wharf down the way. He too is searching the Caribbean for answers to questions he chooses to disclose only in half truths. If you hurry, you will find someone much like yourselves."

"May we have the ship's name, the captain's name, and precisely where they both may be found?" Joseph asked, eager to play an active role with the change in their fortunes.

"Certainly, if you promise to keep me in touch with any success." His visitors nodded, and the priest transcribed the information. "Who knows," he added somewhat cynically, "maybe that Indian really is a century and a half old. But I think you'll end up as I began, walking away from it in silence, a hoax for sure, keeping it dead and buried like those pitiful Ciboney."

He rose from his desk and walked to the door of his office. Thoughtfully gazing one last time at John as he approached the priest with his hand extended, the Jesuit offered the two men good wishes, and watched them push through one of the huge double doors to the outside.

Chapter XX

Captain Bakchos

"Captain Bakchos?" John inquired as the captain relaxed in the forwarding office of the San Juan wharf. The two men had gone directly there after leaving Father Conlin, and Joseph had been as eager as John despite the draining effects of his earlier flight.

The captain nodded, and John continued, "Father Conlin, a frequent passenger of yours, suggested you might be able to help us shed some light on this part of the Atlantic waters. We're doing a research paper on the North Atlantic and Caribbean Sea, and he claimed that if anyone could enhance our efforts with some unusual information, you would be the one. Things like fresh water fountains springing forth from barren islets and such would be just the thing."

"Please excuse our eagerness," Joseph interjected. "This is John Hauser and I'm Joseph Kallman."

"Yes, excuse my bad manners," John said, shaking the captain's hand. The captain had remained seated, and motioned the two men to be seated with him around his table.

"You are interested in the Bermuda Triangle, I take it," the captain said with a heavy Greek accent. "Most of my passengers find it fascinating with all that has been written on it lately, and I wonder if that is not really what you wish to know. Am I right?"

Joseph shook his head. "No, sir," he said, intending to drop John's deception and get to the point. "We've read a considerable amount on that already. To be more specific, have you ever heard of a ship called the *Jason* that sank off the Virgin Islands in the early eighteen hundreds, or an island inhabited by Ciboney Indians, an islet with a fountain, or the whereabouts of a Ciboney chieftain?"

"That is much to recall," Captain Bakchos said, "including the stories of Jason and Colchis! Yes, there are many interesting things concerning the North Atlantic, even from the days of Plato, and the most intriguing is that of Atlantis and Eden. Is that what you wish to hear?"

John and Joseph looked at each other, and John winked at Joseph to bury his frustration and let the man speak. The captain did, and as he spoke about Atlantis and Eden, the two strangers strained to hear what they hoped was not just the ramblings of a sea captain caught in a false, mythological past.

Plato, he told them, was the first to dream of a lost continent beyond the Pillars of Hercules. With growing intensity, the captain proceeded to tell his own belief, shared by his father, his father's father, and still older generations of his family, all Greek seamen of the North Atlantic, each adding experiences of his time to those who came before. The sum of all these generations led to the captain's present-day belief that the stories were not myths of the North Atlantic, but solid convictions that needed only one further piece of tangible evidence to make them whole.

"And what I have told you," he said, standing to end the conversation, "you may think is more myth than fact. But the truth is within reach, and I believe in it completely. That is why I took this – how do you call it? Ah, yes, this commission, a few years ago. I can search for that missing piece and work at the same time. I will prove the truth, you will see."

"Even if there is such a place," Joseph commented, standing as well, "how can your sailing here find anything new? You sail in charted waters, and it's highly unlikely you'll run into your Atlantis on your island hopping."

The captain said nothing and walked to the door.

"Captain, please tell us," Joseph continued, following him to the door, "we'll keep your confidence. What other evidence are you seeking?"

The captain turned to him, studied his face, and then looked at John, who had remained seated and motionless. He walked back to the chairs and, sitting again, whispered, "I cannot tell you all, but I can tell you one thing more that relates to something you mentioned earlier, and is the sole reason I have said as much as I have. It comes from my family many generations back, and it is part of the final proof.

"It says in the Bible that a river went out from Eden to water the Garden. Who believes today in such nonsense? But we all know there was an ancient flood like the one in the Bible – it has been scientifically shown – and it was that flood that sank Eden and my Atlantis, to keep the Garden and its omniscience and eternal life buried forever out of man's reach. That river still flows through the Garden, however, and like the maiden Arethousa, it runs under the Atlantic and surfaces in a fountain on one of these islets. When I find that fountain, it will prove it all – that it is as I have said."

"How do you know to look in these islands?" Joseph asked. "Doesn't it seem likely that you would have heard of such a fountain by now? Doesn't that prove your assumption wrong?"

Captain Bakchos considered his words carefully. "The Bahamas and Antilles have so many barren islets and cays on which man has never set foot that I doubt I alone could ever visit all of them to check. The islet need not be large to harbor a fountain of fresh water, and dunes and crags can easily hide it from view. But I know it is there.

"Scientific studies of the Atlantic Ocean's floor have established the existence of the Mid-Atlantic Ridge and its rift valley, the valley through which that Eden river flows. And the Gulf Stream Drift separates from the main Gulf Stream over the valley, turning south and following it in this direction. Yes, it is here all right, my Arethousa, and I will find it. Of that you can be sure!"

He stood again, feeling relieved. John, who suddenly seemed extremely agitated, stood too, gazed into the captain's eyes, and was about to speak when the captain was intercepted by his first mate, who spoke to him at length in Greek. John could not endure the interruption, however. He grabbed the captain's elbow and pulled him aside.

"I am afraid you do not understand," the captain rebuked him sternly. "I must return to shipboard duties. I am sorry, but I told you more than I should have already. You, on the other hand, have shared nothing with me. There is no more that I have that you would understand. Thank you for your patience in listening, but I must get back to my ship!"

"No, you don't understand!" John called after him as he walked off with his mate. "I want to make it right, to offer you a piece of information, from one believer to another."

The captain turned around.

"You have convinced us that you know what is out there," John went on, "and perhaps we can help each other. I mention this for that purpose. I have been told, and you may know this already, that there is something at the islet with the fountain. Do you understand what I'm saying?"

The captain's face flushed, and he leaned against the door. "You know of the sea serpent?" he muttered. "Is it true? Is all I have told you true? Who are you that you should know these things? Only my family is aware – who are you?"

John was staring incredulously at the captain. Joseph, who had risen and was a step away from John, had to find a chair to steady himself. "We're just two passengers on your ship," John stammered, "who have an interest in these things as well. That's all. We know no more than what you have told us, but that doesn't matter. I think we have all learned to believe more strongly in what we are after because of what was said here. And for that we should be grateful. Perhaps sometime before we arrive in St. Thomas tomorrow, we shall have the opportunity for another conversation. And if not, may we wish you good luck on your search for the – what was your fountain called?"

"Arethousa," the captain mechanically replied.

"Yes, we'll remember that," John said. "Well, we too must be going. Thank you for the interesting conversation, and hopefully we'll see each other before St. Thomas."

Captain Bakchos did not immediately return to his ship after the conversation ended. Rather, he watched the two men book passage for three to St. Thomas for that night's now fully booked sailing, doubling up in the only two cabins left. Puzzled, he sat down and reviewed all that had just happened, how a chance meeting of lost souls had rebuilt his enthusiasm previously lost to doubt.

A sense of urgency soon overtook him, and he reveled in how his family's folly had just blossomed into renewed promise. He sensed he would encounter the fountain shortly, and having known of the sunken *Jason* from his father's accounts, he readily discerned his next task: to thoroughly investigate his newest clue, the Ciboney chieftain.

Chapter XXI

Leah

"If I were the Caleb Call of five years ago," Caleb said on greeting John and Joseph in John's San Juan hotel room, "I'd have a drink."

"Is that because of the trip here?" John asked. "Or the situation with Leah at home?"

"Both!"

"Which do you want to tell us about first?" Joseph chimed in, smiling at Caleb's humor in misfortune. "We've got till nine tonight before we have to be on board the *Argo*."

"The what?" Caleb exclaimed.

"The freighter we're taking tonight to St. Thomas on the next leg of our quest," John said. "That's why we left that message at the front desk about coming up here before checking in. If you need to shower or nap, my room's available. Use it as you would yours. Now, about Leah: What happened to bring you here? We don't have to hear about the trip down."

"When I studied the Book of Genesis, I empathized with the Patriarch Jacob more than any other Old Testament character," Caleb began. "I was constantly amazed at the scope and depth of the deceptions that defined his life. To think that the founding book of a religion would discredit its patriarchs so thoroughly is amazing. And yet that fact rises above all others to convince me that the Pentateuch is nothing but the gospel truth. No writer like Moses, nor any redactor they say wrote it, who was intent on creating a religion through revelation, would so discredit his ancestors, the religion's founding fathers, and still expect to gain adherents. Who would want to become a member of a religious clan that had Jacob, someone worthy of so little respect for much of his life, as a patriarch? And yet I'd be tempted to convert – still might, even after Mitch's death – if the Jews would shun their personal gods and return to the God of their Torah.

"After Leah, and especially with the coincidence of names, I'm seeing my life more and more like Jacob's. It's been fraught with deceptions, wrong turns, and unfulfilled promises. And again like Jacob, this late in life I'm going to turn things around."

"So what happened with Leah?" John asked again. "The last time we spoke, when you advised that you wouldn't be going with us, you were so excited about your new life with her. What went so wrong?"

"In truth, John, the events of the last few days are confusing as hell, and I'd rather not talk about them right now. How'd it go with Father Conlin?"

"I won't let you off that easily on the subject of Leah," John countered. "Better to put it on the table now than let it eat us alive on our trip while you try to sort it out."

"Father Conlin's on the table now, John, not Leah, at least for the moment."

"Everything's on target," Joseph said, "in fact, better than I'd ever expected. I'm getting a feeling that John may be right about this search being preordained. In any event, since we're at a stalemate on what topic's on the table, and I haven't had a minute's rest since I arrived today – I didn't check in either – I'm going to take a shower and rest before dinner. From my one experience on a cruise ship, there may not be much sleep for me tonight."

"We'll discuss Father Conlin over dinner," John said, as Joseph disappeared into the bathroom with his shaving kit. "I'm hoping the captain of the *Argo* leads us to our next level of discovery before we get to St. Thomas. So far he's tossed us a few crumbs, but my guess is there's more. That's why we're on the boat, in case you're wondering, certainly not to go to St. Thomas. You'll know everything we do by the time dinner's over. And without Joseph here, what better time is there to discuss the harsh realities of what Leah brought you. Just stretch yourself out on the couch and let go."

"It's a long story," Caleb said resignedly. "Sometimes I wonder if I've intentionally made my life miserable, making everyone I touch suffer at my hand in order to punish myself in return. When I had Leah with me, my mind was a constant battlefield: I wanted to enjoy her as the flesh and blood I never had, and yet I wanted to escape her grasp and the good I might do."

"That's a fear we all have in situations like yours, Caleb, of not measuring up to our own or others' expectations," John said. "From what you told me on the phone the other day, you seemed to fear the possibility that a week or a month from now, Leah might demand that she be given back to Jerry, the roommate you loved to hate. That could make anyone want to escape, especially someone like you, who's so fertile with feelings of relationship failure anyway."

"No, John," Caleb said, "escape wasn't the issue. Believe me, I did what had to be done. I haven't been known for doing the right thing – sacrificing my own self-interests for the good of others – but then again, I'm not the same person I was a few years ago. We always wonder why we're put through hell if there's a just and merciful God – the 'Why me?' syndrome – when we think we're basically good people. The shocks of these last two weeks with Mitch, Jerry, and Leah, they have to mean something; life just can't be all chance. There's got to be a way of bringing God actively back into the equation to halt all the chaos. Which leads me to conclude that for some unknown reason I'm being tested, put through hell so that I can finally embrace the atonement that leads to true redemption. I did what I did for Jerry's and Leah's sakes, not my own."

"Cleansing the soul before feeding it," John said, "is always the better order."

"But, still, I have doubts that I did the right thing," Caleb went on. "Judge for yourself."

✻ ✻ ✻

Our farewell to Mitch was informal and hasty, as if we hardly knew her: her ashes were all that was left of the beauty I once knew. For me at the memorial service, there were expanding pressures of parenthood, which frustrated my honest emotion at every turn. Jerry was clearly despondent, but I suspected it was more because of his impending loss of Leah than of the void Mitch herself was leaving in his life. Leah was distant but not indifferent to what was going on, as if her mother's death and her new parentage were sweeping her from a feeling of not belonging or caring, to a sense of adventure with me. The latter emotion became quickly apparent when we left the city, and she expressed no regrets at leaving Jerry behind.

The car ride east with Leah began a four-day odyssey that I will attempt to explain as I go. From the second we were alone in the rental car packed with her immediate needs, Leah was eager to explore her new relationship with me.

"Can I drive?" she said as soon as we'd pulled away.

"No," I said, "and you're taking advantage of my tender age as a father. You're just fifteen, right?"

"Almost sixteen," she replied, "and I've driven before. My father, I mean Jerry, let me drive whenever we were alone, from the time I was ten!"

"Sorry," I said, "I'm not Jerry."

"Then you're strict?" she asked.

"As strict as you force me to be," I replied. "Don't forget, I've never been responsible for a teenager before."

"Would you hit me if I got you mad?" she asked. "Jerry never did."

"I think you'd better stop comparing me to Jerry," I chuckled, "or you'll find out pretty quick whether I hit when I'm mad."

She looked at me and smiled. "At least you have a sense of humor," she said. "Jerry never did." She giggled and added, "Just kidding, I promise I won't mention the name Jerry ever again."

We were silent for some time, and I was thinking how nice it was to have her company when she said, "How long is the ride? It's getting dark."

"About six hours," I said. "We'll stop for dinner in an hour or so to break up the trip. Hungry?"

"No, sleepy," she responded. "I think I'll crawl in the back on top of my clothes and nap. You won't mind ironing them for me if they get wrinkled, right?"

"Sure," I snickered, "but you might find it more comfortable reclining the seat. Your clothes definitely would."

"No, the back's fine; it's always been my place," she said. "You sure you won't miss me? Jerry always used to say that long-distance driving was a nightmare without someone to talk to. He said he loved to ride with me up to school but hated the ride back alone. When he said that I'd think it was such bull. What he really meant was that he was glad in going 'cause he would soon be rid of me, but didn't like the trip back 'cause he had nothing to look forward to. Anyway, you want me up here?"

"No, get some sleep," I answered. "It's been a rough few days. Sure you don't want to just put your seat back?"

"No, thanks," she said. "I'm used to the back seat, especially in going places I'm not sure I'll like." She squeezed between the bucket seats to the back.

But her absence didn't diminish her presence, if you know what I mean. Although I wanted to begin mentally outlining the book I would write for Mitch, my mind kept reverting to Leah. I questioned my paternity, but came away believing Mitch wouldn't have lied; she never did in the years I knew her. I debated my responsibility for Leah and decided I would try my damnedest to make it work. There was also a pleasant feeling which I believe began emerging soon after Leah had put Jerry down as a father and friend. Then again, maybe I was just starting to see her as my salvation from an improvident life, or even as the seed of my redemption for what I'd done to Mitch.

"Hi," came her voice, toward the front seat. Her head came next followed by her body.

"Good sleep?" I inquired.

"No," she said. "I kept thinking about something that's been on my mind since Jerry told me about you. I'm afraid to ask 'cause you'll say it's none of my business or I'm too young to know. Say, do you have a piece of gum?"

"No. And come on," I said calmly, though I was anything but calm, "let's talk about whatever's on your mind. We've got to start out very open with each other if we're going to make a real father-daughter team. We have the best thing going for us right now: clean slates. You don't know me, and I don't know you. So spill your problem, and we'll attack it without any preconceived notions. We'll just see where it takes us. Okay?"

"You're sure now?" she asked.

"Yes, I'm sure," I replied.

"Well, then, about you and Mitch," she said. "I'd like to know why the two of you split. No, not really that, though I'd like to know it. What I'd really like to know is…is…is if I'm a bastard?"

"A what!" I exclaimed, cringing.

"A bastard," she said louder, "you know, illegit!"

"Of course not!" I bellowed, struggling ineffectively to refine an answer. Then I said, "I want you to know that I'll never lie to you. That approach held up well over the years in my medical practice, especially with young adults like yourself, who always seemed to know the truth anyway, no matter what their parents sought to hide. So it's the truth you'll get, now and forever. And in this case, I wasn't married to your mother when you were conceived, if that's what you mean. But your mother was married to Jerry at the time you were born, so you're not what you thought you might be even under the worst circumstance. 'Bastard' isn't a word you should be using anyway."

"Being illegitimate wouldn't be so bad," she commented, "and I wouldn't be upset by it."

"What are you talking about, young lady?" I asked. "I just said you weren't!"

"Oh, nothing," she answered. "Forget I said it."

"No!" I said. "If it was important enough to raise earlier, it's important enough to finish now. I said we had to be honest with each other. Well, it's a two-way street. So what do you mean?"

"Oh, just that it'd be okay at school if I was illegitimate, that's all," she answered. "We used to sit around and dream up neat natural parents, as if we were adopted or illegitimate. Some of us were, you know."

"Uh huh, and how do I fit in as a newly discovered natural parent?" I asked.

"I don't think you'd rate a 'neat,'" she said. "That's for movie stars and such, but you'd be okay, I guess. You don't seem very exciting, even though I always thought doctors had lots of money and could buy all the excitement they wanted. What happened to you?"

"I'm slow and steady, just what a fifteen-year-old needs," I said.

"Sixteen!" she shot back. "At school I want to be sixteen, okay?"

"All right, sixteen," I said, "except to the principal."

"You're going to put me in a public school?" she asked.

A restaurant came up on the right. "Yes," I said, as I pulled off the interstate. "The high school's down the street from where we'll live, and it's academically excellent from everything I've heard. You'll have a clean slate there too, so make the most of it. And that means thinking seriously about whether you really want to start out lying to everyone about being sixteen."

Leah maneuvered across the bucket seats after we parked, and grasped my hand. "I'll think about it," she said, and I felt terrific.

Dinner was a joy. I began to see my features in her face as she sat across from me. She smiled often with the small talk of a youngster returning home from a vacation, and I listened attentively. She was just like her mother in her mannerisms, and I thought how foolish I had been to consider running from her at the hospital.

"I've always called Jerry, 'Jerry,'" she said as we returned to the car, "never 'Dad' or 'Daddy' like my friends call their fathers. I wonder now if my mother made that happen because she knew you were out there all along." She paused for a moment. "So you're going to be 'Dad.' Okay, Dad?"

I began to chuckle at the turn of events, but she pressed me for an answer. "Great!" I exclaimed. "I love it!"

"Dad," she said softly, "why did you and Mom break up? It must have been something real explosive for her not to mention you my whole life, even to Jerry when she thought I wasn't listening. I really can't recall a single time she ever mentioned you."

"It's very difficult to explain," I said, "and you deserve an honest, complete answer. Can you accept for now that your mother asked me to write a book about her life, and I intend to include a full explanation of the impact our breaking up had on it? In fact, while you were sleeping in the back before, I started mentally outlining the book, and I figure the part you're interested in will get my first attention. It's the one part I won't have to research. When I've drafted the story of how we met and how we parted, you'll be the first to read it. How's that?"

"But if you've thought it through already," she said, "why can't you tell me like it's going to be written? We've got plenty of time."

"Because it won't be entirely honest until it stares back at me from the paper and makes me admit things I'd rather forget," I said. "If we do it now, you'll miss all the juicy parts. Besides, it'll be better for you to read it before discussing it. Okay?"

"I guess," she answered, "but it still would be nice to know now."

"I promise it'll be written as soon as we're settled," I said. "The minute you're back in school, I'll be at my typewriter banging it out. Just a little patience, okay?"

"Okay, but remember, I'm no kid when it comes to understanding things," she advised. "You don't have to soft-pedal the sex and stuff. I'm as experienced as Mitch was at my age, except I know more about birth control than she did."

My body tensed instantly, and my mind collapsed. "I know I'm being a bit shocking," she went on to break the heavy silence, "but I'm trying my best to be as open with you as you said I should." I couldn't think straight. "Well, as long as you're not going to say anything, I might as well say it all: I need more birth control pills, and my mother isn't here to get them for me."

With those few words, my emerging parenthood was shattered. If Jerry had been there, I would have returned her immediately. Leah needed a mother, not me. "We'll talk about the pills later," I said at last, "after you've gotten settled into your new school environment. There'll be a thousand new faces for you to meet in the next month, and I hope you'll take advantage of this chance to change things that you didn't like about yourself before. Fresh paint, so to speak."

"But my body'll be the same," she argued. "I need those pills!"

"Why don't you hold off dating for a month or so," I said, "as a favor to me – at least until you're settled and know what's to be expected of you in school. It'll be a waste if you blow this opportunity to get a fresh start no matter how great things were before. We all need second chances; you're mine."

"The pills give me the confidence I need to be my own person!" she declared.

"Bull!" I shot back, and the tone of my voice startled her. "Whose person would you be otherwise?"

"They put me in control, that's all," she replied. "Look, I don't have sex very often, and I'm really very sensible about the whole thing. Mom, I mean Mitch, saw to that; we were very close about it. In fact, it's probably the only thing we were close about. Hey, I'm not promiscuous, if that's what you're worried about. I don't sleep around!"

"Just so you don't see sex as an escape," I said. "You don't want to be running into some boy's arms merely because we have a little argument."

"You don't have to worry, if that's your big concern," she said. "I'm a bit more mature than that!"

"Boy, you sure are full of surprises," I said. "I've read about teenage sex, but it never hits home until you have a conversation like this. I knew I had a lot of growing up to do with you helping me along, but I never thought I'd grow old so fast. You're way ahead of me."

She smiled.

"Just keep in mind that self-respect and confidence go hand in hand," I continued, "and self-respect means that you like yourself: who you are, what you are, and what you do. I just hope that with your taking the pill, you're not creating a greater chance of doing something you'll regret. Because if that happens, it's your self-respect that gets clobbered, and the pill will have done you in, confidence and all. Besides, I thought with all the recent concerns about sexually transmitted diseases, chastity was the 'in' thing."

"Dad, Mitch said it all," she responded. "She also agreed that if I was to have sex for spite, I was better off being on the pill than off it. So I'm on it, and the way those things work, I'm not supposed to stop."

"Okay, you win," I said, patting her hand. "All I'll ever ask is that you think things through before jumping into anything, and that you keep talking openly to me like you're doing now. Remember, I'm a doctor too. We shouldn't ever let ourselves get so angry or frustrated with each other that we stop talking. Okay?"

"It's a deal," she said. "I think I'll try for that nap again. Thanks for understanding. I'll show you the label when we get to your place so you can see what I'm on."

"One thing more before you close your eyes," I said as she climbed to the back. "You said your mother was as experienced as you at your age, except for birth control. Where'd you get that?"

"She told me last summer when she came home for the last time, and I was about to go off to another sleepaway camp," she said. "Jerry had gone on a business trip, and we had a fight as usual. I teased her about my being pregnant – I said it because I was mad about not having an older brother at school to keep the other boys from teasing me. My best friend's brother does that for her, maybe too much – he's such a hunk! Well, I said I had no one to protect me like that, and she told me a few things."

"Like what?" I asked.

"Like I told you," she answered, "like about having sex and not knowing about birth control."

"Do you think she might have said it just to get you to open up?" I asked.

"No," she said. "One thing about Mom was, she never lied to me – to anyone, Jerry included – that I know about. I think she felt it might be her last chance with me with the cancer coming back, and she wanted to do her motherly thing on sex education before she died. She also told me some weird story about her brother, Larry, who I'm named after.

"He died very young in a car accident, if you didn't know. I knew it was true from the way she cried while telling me. I'd never seen her that way before. Yeah, there were things in what she said that were too awful to be a lie."

"Like what?" I asked. "I'd like to understand, for the book I'm writing."

"I'm afraid I can't say," she said. "She swore me to secrecy, not even to tell Jerry."

"But she's gone now," I said, "and it would be a big help with the book. It's your mother's request that I'm fulfilling, and I think you and Jerry and her doctors are the sources I'm supposed to use to fill the voids. How about it?"

She considered my request for a long time. "I'll tell you what," she said at last. "When I get to read how and why you broke up, I'll tell you all she told me. But not before. I'd like to have a pretty good reason to break my promise. Boy, I'm tired. Is it okay for me to go to sleep now?"

Knowing I had already mentally composed much of my part of the bargain, I said, "Sure," and began to imagine all sorts of things.

Chapter XXII

Caleb and Jerry

"That was the easy part," Caleb said to John, as Joseph returned from the shower. "You can already taste the souring of what I'd hoped would be my redemption."

"Joseph, you're going to take a nap now?" John asked, as Joseph sat down.

"I was thinking of it before the shower, but the shower seems to have woken me up. My stomach's growling too, so maybe we should go and eat."

"Let's give it another half hour while Caleb finishes his story," John replied. "That way we can limit our dinner conversation to discussing Cain. The two don't mix."

"Then maybe I will lie down for a while," Joseph said. "The last time Goldie and I went on a cruise, she slept like a log, while the ship's rocking kept me awake all night. I can't swim, and that doesn't make for a safe feeling on a boat. Just get me up when it's time for dinner."

"Caleb," John said as Joseph went into the bedroom, "why don't you continue where you left off."

* * *

Four days after I'd left him, Jerry drove up to get Leah. She knew nothing of this reversal, and was at her first day of school when Jerry arrived.

The events that led to Jerry's appearance were quite upsetting to me. I hadn't disclosed them to him on the telephone, except to tell him that he was Leah's father. And he responded to the urgency of my request much as I'd expected: by driving through the night.

"You're the father, not me!" was the first thing he said on walking through my door. "Mitch never lied!"

"She could never know a hundred percent in a situation like that," I said calmly, hoping to quiet him. "She told us the truth as she knew it, but this test doesn't lie."

"What test?" he demanded, clearly exhausted.

"Look," I said, "why don't you take your coat off and relax. We've got a few hours before Leah gets home from school, and we'd better have our act together by then, or she'll get clobbered worse than she should."

"Just tell me what test you took, dammit!" he shouted.

"I won't say another word," I declared, "until you calm down."

"Okay," he said softly, "what test?"

"We had DNA blood tests," I replied. "It's new and still experimental, but foolproof."

"So Leah must know," he said.

"No, her blood test was done as part of the workup for her school physical. The DNA tests were done as a favor to me."

"Are you sure it's incontrovertible?" Jerry asked.

"Yes, I'm sure," I replied.

"Then I should be tested too!" Jerry said.

"Jerry, slow down!" I said. "It's not available to the public, I can't ask the lab for another favor so soon, and you can't get results that fast anyway. Besides, if it turned out that neither of us was the father, what would we do then? The important thing right now is that I'm not the father. Leah belongs in her old surroundings, with her old friends, not here. We can explain the situation any way you like, maybe even tell her that the blood test results showed you were the father, not me."

"But that would be a lie!" Jerry yelled. "We don't do that in our family. Besides, what if she knows about those things from something she's read or heard? Those soap operas on television have all sorts of educational tidbits like that. She'd feel totally rejected!" He stared me in the eye and added, "Are you sure this isn't just another attempt on your part to avoid Mitch's last wish, like I know you wanted to do back at the hospital? I wouldn't put it past you to have fabricated this whole thing!"

"It's the truth, Jerry!" I asserted. "I think Mitch hated both of us, maybe you more than me, because of the things she perceived we did to her. I know the horrendous thing I did to her, so I deserve whatever she's throwing my way, but you, you've borne the brunt of her misery all these years. What score would she want to settle with you?"

"You're right about the lack of options," Jerry said, ignoring my assault on Mitch. "If you're not the father, it doesn't matter who is. I'm the one on the birth certificate; I'm the one who's signed on the dotted line for the duration. I love Leah too much to hurt her, so let's spend the rest of the time before she comes home figuring out how best to ease the blow. Her life's on the line, and we'd better not pull any punches. Tell me everything that went on between the two of you since you left me."

"The conversation we had during the ride here had its ups and downs," I began. "It started the minute we did, and after a few minutes of minor testing, we got into the heavier stuff, like her needing a renewal of her prescription for birth control pills. Did you know she takes them?"

Jerry's forehead wrinkled drastically as he broadcast his disbelief. Shaking his head mechanically, he said, in the same shocked and depressed tone I must have had when learning it from her, "What are you trying to do, destroy everything? You've got your mind set on kicking her out, and now you feed me these lies about her, this birth control crap, just to buy my silence. Do you really think I won't talk to her about these last few days on the way back?"

"Jerry, I'm telling you so you *will* ask her about things like that!" I said. "She was going to show me the label so I could renew it, but she never did, and I didn't ask. Maybe she still has enough pills, but there can be problems if they're not taken continuously. So now you know."

"You sonuvabitch!" he shouted. "You're making her life out to be as much of a hell in fifteen years as her mother's was in over twice as long! What else is up your sleeve, Caleb?"

"It's got its roots – this whole nightmare has its roots – in Mitch's brother's sexual abuse of Mitch from the time she was twelve or thirteen," I said quickly, to get it all on the table. "When Mitch drove over him after he'd fallen out of the car, it was intentional. She really did kill him like she said to me that last school day my junior year, and hinted to you when she came home that last time from the sanitarium. All the pieces to the puzzle fit with that hidden event in her life. Things she said when I was with her those three years, things I'm sure you'll recall as the fact of it sinks in. Remember, she told you to get me to write the story of her tragedy. But there's no story in her cancer by itself, and there's no story in her bouts with depression without uncovering the cause. Leah was given that piece to the puzzle, which she herself couldn't understand, but which someone like me could if I had access. And Mitch's paternity assertion, which she might truly have believed, gave her the opportunity to put Leah and that piece of information in my custody."

"Incest? Murder! You shit!" Jerry cried out. He was livid.

"Did you know," I said to cut him off, "that the car swerved and Larry fell out, not because she wanted to avoid an oncoming truck as she told me, but to avoid his grabbing her as she drove?"

"Why, you sonuvabitch!" he screamed. "I told you a week ago I thought you and her brother had joint responsibility for her hell! But not this!"

"You didn't let me finish before!" I shouted back. "I said Leah is on the pill, and I mean it! She –"

"You're wrong, Caleb!" Jerry broke in again. "I would have known about contraceptives. She was just testing you – you said she never showed you the label! You've always been a gullible bastard!"

"Cut it out, Jerry! This is getting us nowhere fast," I said. "Leah'll be home soon, and either you want to know what's been going on or you don't, but she's sexually active – I know that personally!"

"You what?" he shouted. "What the hell does that mean?"

"She came into my bed last night and wanted sex!" I retorted. "That's what it means!"

"I'd like to smash that fucking face of yours!" he raged.

"Yeah, a lot of good that'd do," I said. "What better way to solve our problem. Jerry, listen to me! She knows I'm not her real father and that's why she came into my bed. Yesterday, while I was at the doctor's office getting the blood test results, she read the stuff I was writing about Mitch and me – our time together, from beginning to end – and there were things in it that might have caused her to do what she did."

"You really hate being her father, don't you?" he said.

"Jesus, Jerry, it's all the truth!" I said. "I think she's already anticipating going back with you. You'll see, there'll be no squabble when we tell her."

"And what if there is?" he argued. "What then?"

"She still goes back with you," I said. "Jerry, please understand. I'm not her real father, and what's happened these last few days will convince you, as it has me, that she belongs with you. And as for not wanting her, I'll admit I'm somewhat relieved at her going back with you. But I regret it too. I really enjoyed her companionship, even with the aggravation. I think I really wanted something of Mitch and me to live on in her. So you can sit on your high horse all you want debating my motives, but you'll have to put yourself in my shoes before you can doubt them. I married horribly just to escape Mitch, the Jewess, and please my mother; I never had kids because I couldn't stand myself, so I buried myself in my work; and I got divorced about the same time I left my medical practice to finally give myself the chance to find out who I really was. That's when I began focusing on locating Mitch, as part of my own self-discovery.

"So initially I was thrilled to get Leah," I went on, "partly because I never had kids, but principally because I could have Mitch through her – she's so much like her. So my acceptance of the situation was really growing. I mean, after getting divorced you become a creature of habit just to preserve your sanity, and unexpected intrusions into your life become hazardous.

"Think of it, Jerry – a teenager like Leah popping into your life from nowhere, and without the benefit of getting the request directly from Mitch. For a while, after hearing about her birth control pills, I suspected you'd concocted Mitch's last request just to deliver a time bomb. Don't scream, just try to see where I'm coming from. You'd said Leah was undisciplined and wouldn't accept you as a father, so here comes good ol' Caleb Call, instant father, to take her off your hands."

"Watch it, Caleb!" Jerry said. "I'm willing to listen, but don't start insinuating!"

"I'm not, Jerry, please," I replied. "I'm just trying to let you know my state of mind – how I wanted her but didn't, the plusses and minuses in it for me. Let's face it, I could have walked away from it all in the hospital, and there was no law on this earth that could've held me there. But I stayed and accepted her. I just want to put to rest all your suspicions that I'm abandoning her. She is yours!"

"Okay, okay!" he responded. "Get on with it! If she's mine, I want her, and I want to know everything that happened!"

* * *

"So I told Jerry everything that had been said that first day in the car on the way to my place – what I told you earlier, John – and then added the things that happened after that."

"And what happened?" John asked. "Don't stop now."

* * *

Well, the night that I eventually called Jerry to come and get her, Leah came into my room, crawled into my bed without my permission, and announced that she'd read what I'd written on Mitch and me. After gauging my reaction, she added that she was ready to deliver her side of the deal we'd struck in the car – she'd tell me all that Mitch had sworn her to secrecy on. And then, as casually as an old gunslinger, she blew me away when she snuggled next to me and cooed, "And because you were so disappointed Mitch wasn't a virgin the first time you made love, I'll deliver that too."

"What?" Jerry exclaimed when I told him that. "Is that it? Is that what makes you think she's sexually active? Come on, Caleb! And you're a doctor too!"

"No, that's not it, Jerry!" I said. "She also told me the story about Larry abusing Mitch, which is what I started to tell you before. When Leah mentioned to Mitch that having an older brother would protect her from aggressive boys, she got straight to the heart of Mitch's issues. With her remission over, she bled right there for her daughter. Whether it was her love for Leah or just something inside her that finally snapped from Leah's comment, we'll never know. What we do know is that Mitch was nearly hysterical in recounting to Leah the horrors of having an older brother. That's why Mitch never wanted another child – you may know this already – because she feared the prospect of a brother, even a younger brother, for Leah."

Jerry walked to a window and looked down to the street. "The subject of other children never came up," he said at last. "I never thought about it. Either I was so thrilled having Mitch with me after her stay at a sanitarium or she was deteriorating again to the point where she couldn't function. I had Lee, who I always believed was mine, so it wasn't like there were no children in my life."

There was a long, awkward silence, and I became hopeful that the ordeal was over. "Let's keep going," Jerry suddenly said. "If we're going to do the right thing with Lee, I've got to know all Mitch told her and all that happened last night. Go ahead, Caleb, please."

"I think I'm done," I said softly.

"No, you were saying Mitch didn't want a brother for Lee," he said. "You were getting to Mitch and Larry."

"Oh, yes, that's right, Mitch and Larry," I repeated, taking a deep breath. "According to Leah, Mitch said her brother forced her to have sex with him just before her thirteenth birthday, and that it continued until he died in March of her freshman year at college. So much for the supposedly low statistics on Jews and incest, despite how much emphasis the Bible puts on it as a prohibition.

"Mitch said she thought she was pregnant by him that spring, that in her situation there was no such thing as birth control, much less pills for it, and that she'd never see Leah suffer like she did from the fear of pregnancy. She went on to describe what happened on that fateful ride home after Larry picked her up at school spring break."

"You try to be with them all the time because they fight constantly when you're not there," Jerry remarked wistfully. "The restaurant business was perfect for that. Ironic, isn't it. The one conversation between them that I miss because I'm out of town is the one that would be the most devastating, and produce a legacy we all have to live with. Damn!" He clapped his hands like an explosion. "There's so much I have to do to make things right, so much!"

"There'll be plenty of time for that, Jerry," I said. "The important thing is not to add to Leah's trauma by what we're about to do. Jerry, are you listening?"

Jerry's eyes shot vacantly toward me. "I said we've got to find a way to make Leah's return to you a smooth one," I repeated. "We can't add to her problems with a new rejection, but if it's to be taken that way by her, it's better now than later. So let's discuss the way to break it to her. She'll be home from school in less than an hour."

Still Jerry didn't respond. "Jerry, dammit!" I yelled. "We don't have the time to ponder last year or last week!" I walked to him and nudged him. "Look, I probably read more into what she said than was meant. Okay, so you're disappointed in not having been there. But by offering to make up for Mitch, maybe she was admitting she's still a virgin, right?"

"Tell me the rest, Caleb," he said, nodding slightly at my last comment. "I should hear it all."

"There's no point," I replied quickly. "I've said enough already."

"Finish it!" he ordered. "I can't make the mistake again of not knowing all that's happened!"

"Okay," I sighed, "I understand."

"It was around ten last night. I had gone to bed early, even before Leah, I think, because I'd gotten up at dawn to write, and was intending the same schedule the next morning. This is exactly how it happened.

"She crawled into my bed and snuggled up next to me. Instantly I was awake and tripping the switch on the night table lamp.

"What's the matter?" I asked.

"I came in to keep you company," she said, "to make up for my mother."

"Just like that she says it," I remarked to Jerry, "and I have no idea what she's talking about. Then we get to her reading what I wrote and her apologizing for doing it without asking. By now I'm getting uncomfortable with her being in the bed because those pieces I wrote were sort of explicit, and then she says she wants to make love to me, to make up for Mitch's not being a virgin.

"Well, I just about hit the ceiling," I went on, "literally exploded, told her in no uncertain terms to get back to her room and that we'd talk about it in the morning before school. I was just afraid of saying something I'd regret if I let the rage in me get out. But she starts crying and changes her tack."

"I just want to make things right for what my mother is doing to you," she said.

"What do you mean?" I asked.

"Making you take me as if you're my father," she replied.

"But I am your father," I said. "I'm sorry it happened this way, but I am."

"No," she said, "you're not. Let's make love instead of arguing."

"Stop with the cute talk!" I shouted, even more upset. "What do you mean, I'm not your father?"

She said nothing and slowly moved toward me to kiss me.

"Stop it!" I shouted and jumped from the bed to my desk chair. "Tell me why I'm not your father," I said reasonably calmly. "Leah, please talk to me."

"Will you make love to me if I tell you?" she asked.

"We'll talk about that later," I said, "but first tell me why I'm not your father."

"Don't you see! She made love to you that last time right before her period was due. You can't get pregnant then. So I couldn't be your daughter – but I could be yours in other ways. You're the best looking man I've ever seen in real life, maybe even in the movies too!"

"Before, after, middle," I said hastily to camouflage my embarrassment at her last remark. "What difference does it make? It could be mere forgetfulness on her part. You know how time can change one's memory. I only hope my own writing is fifty percent accurate!"

"Except that my mother was very careful in how she said it," she countered. "She specifically said it was dangerous to have sex at any time without protection, even though she'd never gotten pregnant from intercourse around her period! Now why would she be so specific if not to tell me something she wanted me to eventually tell you?"

"And what was that?" I asked.

"From your writing, it's easy," she said. "She was shattered by what you did to her – the suddenness of your engagement after having been so intimate the week before – and I was her revenge. She never cared about me all that much anyway, but she probably didn't want you to find out so soon after taking custody of me, thinking I would never read your writing right away, or that you wouldn't start your writing so soon. If it had been a month from now – after we'd cemented a relationship and I'd settled into my new school – you'd be stuck with me, and she'd have her best victory yet in those games you played on each other. You called them 'put-ons' or 'finesses,' like you feared she was doing on that last day of school your junior year when she told you about running over Larry, and then you made love to her for the first time. But from what you wrote, your hating yourself for what you did was probably revenge enough."

"That's a lot of insight for a young lady," I said. "But how do I know you're not making all this up so you can go back to Jerry and your private school?"

"I don't want to go back!" she said. "That's why I'm telling you this, that's why I'm here! She hated me, Jerry hates me! You'd have found out about her revenge – maybe from her psychiatrist – and sent me back anyway. This way, before we establish a father-daughter relationship, I could become your lover and not have to go back!"

She began sobbing, and I sat on the bed to cradle her in my arms. "I'm not going to send you back," I whispered.

"It's always happened to me, ever since I can remember," she sobbed. "Different people taking care of me, boarding schools, away camps."

"Are you feeling sorry for yourself?" I asked sarcastically. She looked at me and wiped her tears away. "At least give me a chance," I said. "So far it's been fun, even if I'm not an exciting doctor. And we do have a fresh start, both of us, so go to sleep in your bed and get ready to knock 'em dead tomorrow. Okay?"

"Okay," she said.

"Well," I said to Jerry, "that's it."

"Then that seals it, Caleb," he responded.

"We'd better start packing for her," I said.

"Caleb, you've misunderstood," he said. "I meant there's no way she's going back with me, not after what she said about my hating her, not even if she's mine, not when she said she doesn't want to."

"It'll be disastrous if she stays, Jerry!" I screamed. "I didn't have to be truthful just now and tell it like it was! But I thought it was best that you know before I returned her to your care. I stayed up long after she left the room debating what to do before deciding to call you. You can argue about what last night means till you're blue in the face, but one thing's clear: I can't handle her no matter how hard I try. Returning her to you is the only way to send a message to her that we care. It's not by keeping her here. It's by giving her strong discipline and lots of love, things you can do now that Mitch is gone. And that's a pediatrician's advice."

"Caleb, it won't work," he replied. "She's rejected me totally. Mitch wanted it this way, and I don't know for sure that I'm the father, even if Lee's story suggests that you're not."

"Then there's one thing more you should know," I murmured. "It's why she can't stay."

"I couldn't hear," Jerry commented. "Repeat what you said!"

"I thought you knowing she was yours would be enough," I said, "and understanding how manipulative she is would make you discount her negative comments about you and Mitch. Then again, maybe you want your freedom – we know how that would erode with Leah in your charge. Hell, I've gone through that debate myself. So if you must know, she can't stay because I'm afraid of the physical relationship that might result. I know she's not mine; I know she's on the pill; I know she's as much a knockout as Mitch was when Mitch was my nineteen-year-old college steady. She's got her looks and mannerisms, and a forty-year-old has-been like me can easily imagine the delectable taste of a sixteen-year-old virgin like her, especially in an era when STDs keep us celibate. You know me, Jerry, how much of an animal I am – you've said it often enough. If you leave her here, it'll be playing with fire!"

"Come off it, Caleb!" Jerry said. "You want me to believe that Dr. Caleb Call, renowned pediatric oncologist, can't keep his hands off children? Talk about manipulating people, Cal ol' boy, the only thing that might keep you and Lee from making a go of it is that you're so much alike. So don't play your games with me, Caleb – I'm off. I'd better get going before Lee comes home and wonders why I'm really here."

Catching his arm, I pleaded, "Jerry, I don't know about father-daughter relationships like you. It's not incest with Leah and me, not even an age difference when she's spouting Lolita, and I see a midlife crisis in the offing. Come on, Jerry, use your head if not your heart.

She has no place here with me. You're the better material for a father. Can't you understand what I'm saying?"

"Of course I can, Caleb," he rejoined. "It's the same bullshit I heard twenty years ago! Maybe Mitch did hate me, and that could explain why we're beating ourselves up like this. Maybe not. But I promised her that you'd look after Leah, and you will. I'll call in a few days to see how things are going. Ta ta!" He walked to the door.

"Jerry, a minute more, please!" I pleaded. "I can't be a good father, the kind you can be, because I'm a self-centered bastard. I can't change in a week or two from what I've been!"

"Yes, you can, Caleb!" he shot back. "I've seen you change colors in seconds – sure you can change for her!"

Jerry opened the door and began walking down the hallway to the elevators. I ran after him and blocked his way as an elevator door opened. "Jerry, I need something else to redeem myself! Leah's not it! There's no legal obligation for me to be her father – you're on the birth certificate! I'm certain once it's done, it'll be the right thing, for you and her. You said she was your whole life once; let her be it again, for your sake as well as hers!"

"Caleb, you're crazy!" he shouted, pushing his way past me into the elevator. I followed him.

"Jerry, don't make me say this!" I cried out. He held the elevator doors from closing and looked at me with dread. "We didn't just talk last night like I said we did," I whispered. "She had a nightie on, it was draped off one shoulder, she did it so suggestively while she talked of being my lover, leaving it that way and bending over time and again to expose bare flesh, bare... I couldn't help myself. I got hard, I wanted her, and it *will* happen if she stays."

We stood motionless. I felt nauseous. I wanted Jerry to hit me, but he remained Jerry, reorganizing his plans.

"Leah will be home in a few minutes," he said as we walked back to my apartment. "We don't want to disappoint her. Just let me do the talking."

Chapter XXIII

The *Argo* at Sea

WHILE JOHN BRIEFED CALEB over dinner, Joseph was immersed in the ocean of possibilities that awaited them in their pursuit of Cain. He was pulled from that meditation, however, when John abruptly rose from the dinner table to announce that they would leave immediately for the *Argo* to check if a third cabin had become available on the ship. And as Joseph followed John from the restaurant, one conclusion comforted him among the many possibilities: after another conversation with Captain Bakchos in the morning, he would, upon arrival at their hotel in St. Thomas, phone Tom Petersson, who had asked to be kept informed, to get the benefit of his thoughts on what they had achieved so far.

"You should keep in mind, Joseph," John offered, when Joseph mentioned his intention in the taxi to the wharf, "that the supernatural is at work here in everything that's happening. So Tom will join us whether or not you call him. But remember, the riddle casts doubt on who's pulling the strings:

> *"If God made Cain to e'er walk the earth*
> *He [God] surely watched Satan's birth.*
> . . . .
> *But shouldst Cain the earth walk still,*
> *he [Cain or Satan] surely shall make reign his*
> *[Satan's] will.'*

"That's the reading I'm leaning towards the more we move forward. At times, the sense of evil lurking in our midst overwhelms me. It sort of forces me to distance myself from the rest of you, whether consciously or not. Fortunately, I haven't felt that way too often so far."

"That's reassuring, John," Caleb remarked as they came to the wharf, "that is, as long as I'm not the one that has to sleep in the same cabin with you tonight." They laughed as they entered the forwarding office to secure a third cabin for Caleb. None was available.

"You should know, Caleb," Joseph said, pulling him aside as they boarded the *Argo*, "that for personal reasons I'm sure he understands, John and I can't room together. So if another room doesn't open up before we sail, and two of us have to stay together, it won't be John and me. And Goldie always complained that I snore up a storm, if that bothers you."

John and Joseph had arranged for adjacent cabins, and while they awaited a steward's delivery of their luggage, Joseph stood at the doorway to John's cabin, watching Caleb and John explore their room. "You know," Joseph said as John and Caleb stretched out on their lower berths, "Goldie's illness really threw all the control I had of my life right out the window. At the end she said I'd lived a good, long life, like her, so the rest could be gambled away on something as foolish as this trip. Frankly, I thought we'd end up sitting on a beach somewhere laughing at ourselves. But now, finding Cain seems to be taking on a life of its own, as John said it would. It doesn't seem foolish at all anymore – and all I wish is that Goldie was here to help if things go wrong."

A steward delivered their luggage, and Joseph retreated to his room to unpack his immediate needs. Anticipating an arrival in Charlotte Amalie around eight in the morning and a leisurely breakfast on board to allow for another meeting with Captain Bakchos, Joseph retired for the night. By midnight he was deeply asleep, snoring away, and totally unaware of the ship's departure. Caleb lay in bed, wide awake, debating what might follow from his companions' efforts that day. Waiting for the ship's rolling motion to lull him to sleep, he drifted into a lazy slumber even before the *Argo*'s engines began powering the boat out of port. John, on the other hand, never had trouble falling asleep, only staying that way, for too often nightmares of unremembered memories and unrecallable dreams would visit him. Tonight would be no exception.

After an hour at sea, the *Argo*'s rhythmic hum gradually turned into thunderous heavings of its bow into water. As the magnitude of the ship's pitch began testing the ship's design, cabinets and doors lost their magnetic holds, and the earlier meek sounds of the woodwork gave way to loud, eerie moans. Caleb bolted upright at an alarming crash of the desk chair into the bathroom door, and for some horrifying seconds, he couldn't remember where he was. His breathing and heart were racing uncontrollably, and his stomach was knotting in cadence with the groans of the engine room. Picturing a swollen sea awaiting the slightest error of the captain, Caleb frantically held to a bedpost and turned on his reading light to help ward off flying objects. Searching for John in the dim light, he was shocked to find him still in bed, outwardly oblivious to the storm's fury. His eyes tightly shut, his body rolling yet mostly covered, John showed his discomfort only by the sweat of the nightmare that was securing his sleep.

The *Argo* began shaking spasmodically as waves of unyielding strength smacked randomly at its hull. Caleb tried not to panic. He lifted himself from the bed to lock the desk chair in the bathroom to guard John and himself from its destructive path, but he was violently hurled back onto his bed by a monstrous roll of the ship. The chair rebounded off the wall and struck John's arm, which was protruding off the bed. Responding to his own distress, Caleb sought to flee the cabin's cramped quarters by fighting his way to the door.

Another roll of the ship, however, threw Caleb back. John flew from his bed toward Caleb's feet, his forehead glancing off Caleb's bed frame on the way. Rising in pain and spinning in the dim light, John cried out for the motion to cease. By then, Caleb had again reached the door, and he was attempting to grasp the key in it to unlock it and free himself, just as a lurch of the ship catapulted him and John against the opposite wall. The two men sank to the floor after impact, but Caleb wouldn't lie still despite his injuries. He began clawing his way toward where he'd dropped the key, raging at it for eluding him, banging his head and limbs against chair and bed, beseeching God to bring calm.

The key was lost, and Caleb stood to take revenge on the door and chair. He lifted the chair, teetered toward the door, and swung the chair at it with savage fury. But the distance was too great, bringing only a glancing blow. He righted himself, this time closer, raised the chair again, reared back, and was poised to deal the door a massive blow when Captain Bakchos's soothing voice, firm yet calm, issued from the speaker system. Caleb slumped to the floor.

John had remained on the floor after crumpling there from his collision with the wall. He lay there now, oblivious to everything about him, sweating profusely and increasingly writhing in pain. Caleb crawled to him, to aid him, and kneeling over him, observed diabolical contortions of his face. Suddenly John's eyes opened wide, glassy and unseeing, and in German, he addressed the Gestapo regarding the fate of a Jewish lad in the Church's custody.

Caleb shook him vigorously, but John merely smiled back grotesquely, and, looking beyond Caleb, recounted an obscene episode which culminated in the lad's belated acquiescence. Finally struggling to sit up, John added, again in German and with a horrid laugh, "There is another to take his place!" Caleb retreated in disgust, and without his support, John's torso rotated to the floor.

By five in the morning, the sea and Caleb finally returned to states of calm. Caleb had decided just before dozing that he wasn't sure what John's admissions really meant, and would let them lie without confrontation. But unlike Caleb, the *Argo* was not at peace with the sea. The *Argo*'s prow was cutting swiftly through calmer waters, heading unmercifully toward St. Thomas in response to the captain's demands on the engine room to recover lost time and distance off course.

Chapter XXIV

Arriving in St. Thomas

THE DAY WAS ALREADY WARM, and the bright sun in a cloudless sky was clearly touting St. Thomas's unconditional guarantee against rain. It was a pleasant contrast to the experience John and Caleb had shared during the night; Joseph had slept through the whole ordeal.

There was another positive note that morning. As the three were seated for breakfast, a waiter delivered an invitation from the captain for John and Joseph to join him in a tour of the ship's bridge.

"Maybe he's in here?" John said as they entered the wheelhouse after breakfast.

"Let's check that room," Joseph said when the wheelhouse proved vacant. Caleb poked his head into the adjacent chartroom as John squeezed past him. The chartroom was filled with detailed maps spread over mahogany tables, but no captain. Just as John turned to leave, Captain Bakchos bellowed from beneath a table, where he was retrieving a fallen drafting triangle, "Stay, Mr. Hauser, if it is the Ciboney you are after!"

Joseph and Caleb quickly entered the chartroom, and the captain hesitated. A silence engulfed them. "This is Dr. Caleb Call, who joined us late yesterday in our research effort," John offered, and the captain smiled.

As the two shook hands, Captain Bakchos said, "And what kind of doctor are you, Dr. Call?"

"A medical doctor," Caleb replied.

"Before the call of the sea, I, too, was a medical doctor," the captain offered, "a neurologist specializing in the comatose.

203

"I asked you here," he went on, "because your interest in these waters justifies a tour of the bridge. My ship has delivered you through extremely rough seas, of which we had no forewarning. That is as it often happens, or we surely would have waited out the storm in San Juan. I hope you are not the worse for it."

The three passengers smiled. "No, we're okay," Joseph said as John touched his bruised forehead, "and we thank you for inviting us here."

The captain motioned them into the wheelhouse and explained its operation. He returned with them to the chartroom and strode over to a map on the table under which he'd recovered the triangle. Picking the triangle up again and touching a vertex to St. Thomas's position on the map, he said, "This will be interesting for some, more so for others – if it is the Ciboney you are after."

"Yes, Captain," Joseph responded, "we have an interest in the Ciboney."

"I do not understand its connection with what we discussed yesterday," the captain went on, "but you did mention that name alongside the *Jason*, and that ship I do know. Is there a connection, Mr. Kallman?"

"None that we know of," John broke in. "It was for our research project, as I mentioned. It would be very useful to prove a point about the differences in intelligence of certain Caribbean Indian tribes. The Ciboney are one of those tribes. What can you tell us about the Ciboney?"

"Please tell me first what you know of the *Jason*," the captain said, smiling, "if, in fact, it is the same *Jason* I have in mind."

"Certainly, Captain," John answered. "The *Jason* was the ship of Captain Charles Francis. Do you know of him?"

"Ah, Captain Francis, of course! And what do you know of him, may I ask?"

"We learned of him in our research on the Caribbean slave trade, when we were seeking to evaluate the effect of foreign influences on Indian intelligence," John responded. "It seems that Francis found out about the islet with the fountain early in the eighteen hundreds, but lost the *Jason* on one of his runs. Francis survived, along with his diary, and we read a few of the more legible pages concerning the islet. What information do you have?"

Captain Bakchos hesitated, studying the three men for a long time. Finally he said, "A distant great-grandfather of mine was on the ship that rescued Captain Francis after the *Jason* went down. Francis told my great-grandfather about the islet, and a later grandfather of mine sighted the sea serpent, confirming what Captain Francis had said."

"And where was the sighting?" Caleb excitedly asked. "Can you point it out on the map? It would be of tremendous help in locating the islet."

"I am sorry," he responded, "but I cannot tell you that. It is all I have left of the stories handed down to me that I have not disclosed to you. I am willing to say, though, that I have searched where I was told, as my fathers did before me, and I have seen neither the fountain nor the serpent."

"Then why do you still believe?" Joseph asked, clearly depressed by the turn of events. "Have you read the Francis diary?"

"No, I have not."

"Wasn't it with him when he was rescued?" Joseph probed further. "Didn't your great-grandfather see it?"

"You have brought up by coincidence the one thing that makes me disbelieve," the captain replied. "It is the seed of my never-ending pain and doubt.

"As I have been told, Captain Francis did have a diary with him, the only item found in his possession. But it had no reference to anything dealing with the islet – no fountain, no serpent. And although, unlike you, I have never seen the diary, it is that inconsistency that continually questions my sanity in searching further."

"But we know for a fact that the diary mentions the islet and fountain, even a Ciboney youth who came upon it," Caleb said, resisting John's nudges to keep quiet.

"Ah, so the Ciboney Indians are a pivotal part of this story," the captain asserted with eyes suddenly sparkling.

"Yes," John said ambivalently, "but only to attest to the introduction of foreign influences on the Ciboney."

"That does not matter," the captain rejoined. "There is a connection now, unlike what your prior answers led me to believe."

"Maybe Captain Francis recorded the story of the islet after he returned to America," Joseph remarked.

"Perhaps," the captain replied, "but only if the *Jason* went down so soon after Captain Francis learned of the islet that he had no time to record it."

"In any case, Captain, may we at least benefit from your knowledge of the Ciboney?" Joseph added. "For that we would be forever grateful."

"I should not favor you with that, after your own previous insincerities," the captain remarked, "but because Dr. Call was honest among you, I shall not disappoint him.

"You mentioned the *Jason* and the Ciboney yesterday in Dr. Call's absence, and I thought, when you went to book passage on my ship, that there surely was a connection which could be gleaned today in trading information. Fortunately, Dr. Call's presence has rewarded me in that regard, and I shall return his favor.

"When yesterday I decided to tell you of Atlantis and Eden, I sought to share the burden of doubt I face daily. But first I tested your purpose and sincerity by discussing Colchis as a garbling of your word Ciboney. I wanted to be sure that you would not mock me for not having information about the Ciboney, after I had bared so much of my soul. And when I saw the despair on your faces at my mention of Colchis, I knew you were in fact sincere in your search for the islet."

"Go on, Captain," John urged, "about the Ciboney. I ask your pardon for misleading you, but what connection do you make about them because of Dr. Call?"

"It is an odd coincidence, as this whole episode appears to be," he said, "but I was listening, as I always do, to the news of my next port before I arrive, and this morning I heard about an Indian the radio called the last full-blooded Ciboney. It seems that he lost a friend to sharks yesterday while diving off the coast near here. That is all I know. The name caught my ear immediately because you had mentioned it yesterday, but until Dr. Call's admission, I had no manner of making a connection. I am as grateful as you must be for a new piece of information that reinforces our searches. Might there be something else to offer?"

"No, Captain," Joseph said firmly, "and I apologize too. If we come across something that will help you, we shall be more eager next time to reveal it."

"And I will do the same. My time will arrive, of that you can be sure."

The three visitors hastily departed the ship, and the captain remained on the bridge only long enough to watch them pile into a taxi on their way into town.

Chapter XXV

In St. Thomas

IN RESPONSE TO THEIR REQUEST, the taxi driver delivered them to a first class hotel right off the water in Charlotte Amalie. Rooms were available, and after checking in, John and Caleb debated the merits of going from marina to marina to try to locate the Ciboney of the news story. Joseph, pleading his age, disappeared into his room just as Caleb thought of a more logical approach to the search. Pulling John into the same taxi that had brought them there, Caleb directed the driver to the main police station.

The young officer to whom they were referred greeted them pleasantly and invited them to sit at his desk while he sought information on the shark attack.

"You're in luck," he said on returning with a newspaper. "We're not the authority involved in the investigation, but today's morning newspaper has a thorough article on it with all the relevant names and places. Here you go." He handed Caleb the paper, and added, "If you cannot find him at the marina, check the marina's office for his address." Cordially inviting Caleb and John to return if they were unsuccessful with what he'd given them, the officer wished them good luck and sent them on their way.

The marina reminded Caleb of his New England youth, except that the water here was much clearer, warmer, and more inviting. As John and he hastened toward slip 24, Caleb peered over the edge of the wooden walkway and spotted schools of minnows darting among the piles. John, however, was panting from the exertion, gulping clean, warm air as sweat dripped from his forehead to his shirt. His eyes were racing ahead to espy the state of the slip and allow him some leisure if the slip were empty. But the walkway ended without slip 24, and the two trekked back to an opposite walkway a distance off.

This time, though, John was able to anticipate the right slip, and he slowed markedly when Caleb confirmed from afar that the slip was unoccupied. Immediately, they sought to convert their first disappointment into success by seeking the Indian's residential address from the marina's office.

The view from their taxi in ascending the mountain overlooking Charlotte Amalie was magnificent, as each breathtaking scene became another, even more spectacular one. Soon they had climbed high above the city below and had rounded the mountain to the other side of the island. There, their driver stopped and turned to them, saying, "You wanna see Drake's Seat?"

Caleb looked at John, who looked at his watch, neither understanding what the driver had said in his lilting English. They were about to decline when the driver turned off the motor while still on the road and scooted out to open the back door for them. They got out reluctantly and followed the driver to a stone seat above the roadway, where they could view the wide expanse of Magens Bay below.

Caleb was overcome by the beauty; not so, John. A cloud seemed to be suspended over an unnamed cay out to sea, dropping a majestic band of rainbow colors to the tranquil land and sea below. "You know, John," Caleb said, "that rainbow represents an undertaking by God at the time of the Deluge not to destroy all living things ever again by flood. And you know, I could easily believe that this, too, is God's holy mountain. With that cloud hovering over that cay over there, why it's primeval – like we're in the midst of Creation."

Nodding to Caleb and the driver, John prodded them back to the car. A distance down the mountain, still overlooking Magens Bay, the taxi turned onto a dirt road and stopped. Ahead was a wooden shack in evident disrepair. The door was unlocked, and readily opened to reveal a single, empty room that obviously had not been visited in days.

"We'll head back to the hotel, eat lunch, and get some rest before trying the marina again," Caleb suggested. "We probably shouldn't have come up here anyway. With the slip empty, the man's most likely out on his boat diving again. Still, the view for me was definitely worth the trip!"

John didn't respond, and Caleb added, "Let's head back to the hotel, collect Joseph for lunch, and shoot for the marina after a short nap. That way we'll avoid any possibility of missing the Indian when he comes in from diving. I'd hate to have to make this trip after dark if we miss him at the marina."

John followed Caleb to the car, and the taxi dropped them at the hotel. Unknown to them, at the time they were visiting the Indian's mountain retreat, Captain Bakchos was concluding a search of the island's marinas for the Ciboney. He'd been following his newest clue; yet he hadn't had their foresight to check with the police to condense his effort. And typical of his quest's misfortunes, Captain Bakchos had found the right marina and the Indian's empty slip an hour after Caleb and John had. But the call of shipboard duties cut short his intention of waiting until the Ciboney returned, just before John and Caleb, with Joseph now in tow, advanced in late afternoon on the Indian's watery abode.

Chapter XXVI

Taino

WHEN JOHN AND CALEB RETURNED EMPTY-HANDED from their search for the Ciboney, Joseph was eagerly awaiting them in the hotel lobby. He had telephoned Tom Petersson to share the results of their conversations with Father Conlin and Captain Bakchos, and was quite excited to report Tom's closing comment: he would join them on the search for Cain if they found the Indian.

At a quarter to five in the afternoon, the three of them stood in front of the hotel debating the walking distance to the marina. Caleb, of course, was in favor of a hike; John, recalling his enervating efforts earlier in the day, opted for a cab; and Joseph, having decided from the first to avoid the heat, sided with John. A taxi screeching to a halt at their feet resolved the issue, for their morning driver was again behind the wheel.

"The marina now, Mistah?" he said, pushing open the front and rear passenger doors from within.

"Yes, to the marina," John said, leading the way in.

The taxi whisked them to their destination in minutes, this time delivering them to the right walkway for the Indian's slip. Over an hour later, Joseph and John were sitting on the walkway and Caleb was leaning against a pile in front of the empty slip, when Caleb spotted a speck on the red horizon and brought their discouraging discussion on alternative search plans to an encouraging close.

John and Joseph stood, joining Caleb in debating the likelihood of the Indian being aboard, until they could make out a small sailboat with its sails down, apparently running in the calm waters under the power of an outboard motor. There was only one visible occupant, they concluded, although Caleb thought someone could be within the cabin of the boat.

At last the boat had been maneuvered through the marina to slip 24, and Caleb caught the line thrown to him by the sole occupant, who obviously had assumed that anyone standing where Caleb was would be willing to help. Caleb quickly tied his end to a metal anchor at the foot of the pile he'd been leaning against, and rose to confront the man who embodied all of their hopes.

"Are you the person in the shark attack?" Caleb asked even before the Indian had alit.

"Yes, I am that," the man replied while tying down the boat. "Why do you wish to know?"

"We have some questions we'd like to ask, if you don't mind," Joseph answered, then introduced each of them. "And what is your name?"

"I told the authorities everything about the incident," the man said, somewhat vexed. "That is where you will get your answers. Please, let me be about my business; I have much on my mind."

He jumped to the walkway to check Caleb's mooring, and even in the twilight, none could miss the man's gruesome scars. Wherever there was exposed skin, they saw scar tissue – not just evidence of nicks and scrapes, but also the cicatrices of deep gashes – all the result, Caleb surmised, of wounds that had healed without the benefit of stitches. It made Joseph turn from the man, who rose from adjusting Caleb's knot to stand with his hands on his hips facing John.

The last full-blooded Ciboney Indian, as the radio had called him, although slightly hunched, stood taller than any of them, and fit neither the description of the man in Father Conlin's story nor that of any other man they could possibly have imagined. And yet his thick, straight black hair and heavily scarred face still presented rugged, dark, almost handsome features, while his lean, muscular body was flawed only by his marred skin and the bent of his back. It took the three visitors several moments to accept what they were seeing and speak, but the Indian was used to stares. He stood quietly, attributing a growing significance to this meeting as the seconds passed, facing John eye to eye and waiting for the questions to continue.

"We're pursuing a rather bizarre story to its conclusion," John said at last, "and you happen to be one of the missing pieces, you and the Ciboney people, that is. You are of that tribe?"

The Indian nodded.

"We have much to tell you and much to learn," John went on. "May we have a few minutes of your time?"

The Indian nodded again, and John quickly narrated what they had read in Tom's article and been told by Father Conlin, what was in Captain Francis' diary, and what they knew of the riddle and Cain. Nonetheless, he was reluctant to give his competition any benefit, and so he refrained from mentioning Captain Bakchos. Instead, he ended with a straightforward plea: "Can you help us find the islet?"

The Ciboney fidgeted throughout John's account, yet faced him eye to eye, and when the narration was done, he merely smiled, revealing decayed and missing teeth, while pondering his answer. Finally the Indian resolved what was troubling him, and he invited his three visitors to sit with him on his boat. He moved with the fluidity of youth in boarding the boat and in arranging canvas folding chairs brought up from the cabin while the three watched from the walkway, bringing into question the visitors' earlier hopes of finding an ancient man.

Joseph accepted the Indian's offer without conferring with his comrades, and they followed Joseph onto the boat. None of them, however, displayed the pervasive enthusiasm that was earlier manifest, and they merely sat down and studied the Indian's face anew.

"You have said many things which relate no doubt to my ancestors," the Ciboney offered cautiously, "and there are many questions I would like to ask you, as you would me. But before we ask the many little ones that try one's patience, may I ask one big one?"

The visitors squirmed in their seats. They squinted their eyes to behold the Indian better in the scant twilight, and the Indian responded by lighting a kerosene lantern he retrieved from the cabin. "Please do," Joseph said, as the light brightened their faces.

"Do you know where the islet is, where your little man can be found?" he asked. "We should start from there."

The three guests were uniformly stunned, and the Indian noticed. "Is it somewhere near here?" he added. "Or possibly to the north in the area of Bermuda? Certainly you know!"

Joseph gradually found some relief to counter his disappointment, for he concluded from the Indian's query that there would be no dangerous, final leg of the trip. John, on the other hand, immediately sensed premeditation and brewing conflict with the Indian. Only Caleb's spirits continued their decline as the Indian's query unfolded.

With negative answers coming from Joseph, who was debating whether they should even stay, the Indian suddenly said quite cheerily, "Shall I take it that you are seeking the answer from me?"

"Yes," Caleb responded.

"That is good," the Indian replied, "for if you will tell me again, please, your interest in this little man – why you seek him – I may choose to help you. Surely your interest is not for the reason you gave before – that he is mentioned in the diary and may be the biblical Cain. I too can count the centuries involved and question your motives."

"We believe that by finding him and proving he is Cain, we can validate the existence of God," John said, taking up the Indian's challenge.

"We also believe that the fountain is a special one," Joseph added, "the subject of a fascinating myth. It is understood to deliver eternal youth to anyone who might drink of its waters, like the little man... and perhaps even you."

"I see," the Indian said without the slightest reaction. "Then you may yet have your fountain and your little man. But first, may I ask those little questions, the ones that may try your patience at first but in the end will become quite enlightening?"

Joseph and Caleb looked at each other and shrugged, confused but willing to let the Indian proceed. John, however, stood abruptly and said, "You don't seem to be as knowledgeable as we had hoped. Perhaps we are too caught up in our research to realize how foolish it is. Thank you for your time, but I believe we should pursue other avenues."

The Indian turned from John and watched Joseph and Caleb huddle in quiet debate. There followed a subdued argument, agitated by waves lapping at the boat's hull as the wind picked up. His guests' indecision finally prompted the Indian to stand and confront John again, eye to eye.

"I think you will be of a different mind after we have gone further," he said, pointing to John's vacant chair. "Please be as patient with my questions as I will be with yours."

Caleb stood and put his arm around John's shoulders. Pressuring him to sit, Caleb told the Ciboney to continue.

The Indian rained personal questions on the three men, mostly directed at uncovering some unwelcome motive but never discerning more than what had been said nor less than the desire of three disenfranchised men to find meaning in their lives. The Indian accepted it all and floated one last question: "Do you have two thousand dollars?"

Joseph gasped and Caleb was aghast. John smiled at his prescience and his companions' agony. He stood again, this time pulling Joseph up with him. "He's not our man," John said to Caleb, who remained seated, while John pushed Joseph toward the walkway.

"Let's go back to the hotel, Caleb," Joseph said in passing him, "and treat the remainder of our stay on St. Thomas as a well-deserved vacation. We've earned it!"

Caleb was adrift even more than before. He feared, like Joseph, that they were being conned by a man they had sought for the ultimate truth. His stomach was knotting, and he was nursing such a heavy internal conflict that he didn't notice the Indian extending his hands and grasping Caleb's constantly cold ones. Instantly, the burning warmth of the Indian flowed into him, and Caleb's mind and body totally dismissed all the doubts he'd started to nurture about what they were after.

"Yes, we have the money!" he shouted, and as soon as he'd said it he felt the vast darkness of the sea and sky swallow his sanity.

At the same time, the moon broke from behind a dense bank of clouds, illuminating John's outrage at Caleb's response. "Not with Stitches' money!" John declared.

"Not with mine either!" Joseph added.

"Then with mine!" Caleb retorted. "Just let the man talk!"

"That is good," the Indian whispered, as if his guests' doubts had been fully resolved. "For you have attended to my problems as I will yours. Let me tell you why the money is important, and then I will tell you a story that will quash your lingering fears."

Joseph eased free of John's hold and returned to his seat in response to the Indian's muted voice. John, however, stepped to the walkway to face the moon and threw a ghostly shadow over the three seated men.

"I have been diving near here," the Indian continued, "for a treasure, like the missionary said, that is very important to my people, of whom I am the only full-blood left. I cannot do anything with your islet until I have secured that treasure. I need to replenish equipment lost to the sharks, which, I realized today while diving alone, I could not succeed without. And I must keep my boat, which the marina will seize tomorrow if I do not pay all my arrearages.

"That will require most of the money," he added. "As well, we will need some of those funds afterward to outfit the boat for your journey, which will be much more demanding than sailing in these local waters. If this is acceptable to you, you may have your fountain and little man, and I, my people's treasure."

Caleb chose not to look at Joseph or discuss the proposition with him. He sensed that if he did, Joseph would surely calculate some fraud in the Indian's offer and reject it flatly. So he stayed focused on the Ciboney and was about to voice his concurrence when Joseph said, "Yes, it is acceptable," and patted Caleb's arm.

"You will have to follow closely then," the Indian began, drawing Joseph and Caleb instinctively closer, while putting John out of earshot, "because the story I will tell you of my ancestors, some of which you already have heard, stretches over many generations."

* * *

Taino – that is what they called him – was born into the Ciboney centuries ago, the first son of the tribal chieftain on this island, now St. Thomas, well before the Danes and Americans knew of it.

From the time Taino was to attain manhood and achieve his rightful place in the tribe, he would not hunt for pleasure or food, being fully satisfied by the vegetation that abounded here. The rites of manhood that he shunned made him an outcast as he matured, and his mother, fearing he would come to harm, commanded Taino to flee to the central mountain – what you see rising in the distance behind your friend John – where no man dared set foot. Rather than becoming one of the Ciboneys' human sacrifices to the god Ochinkos as his mother foresaw, Taino was left to grow up in the solitude of that mountain, the holy place of Ochinkos, who, as the Ciboney god of the earth, would become Taino's sole companion.

And as he communed with Ochinkos, Ochinkos became his one and only God, for night and day, for the natural and supernatural, the earth, the sea, the rain, the wind, for everything. Taino loved Ochinkos as no other had before him, and he called upon His blessings wherever he roamed on that mountain until he asked for blessings no more. Taino had come to accept Ochinkos as his divine Master, the Creator of all things, and he realized that to ask for blessings was not to believe, but to seek proof of his God's existence; and he did believe, so constantly and completely, in his God.

After many moons, at what would be his eighteenth birthday in your time, a lifetime, sadly, for the Ciboney youth who were sacrificed each new moon at that age, Ochinkos appeared to Taino in a dream, and

Taino saw a tree rising to the heavens toward a brilliance descending from above. And midway in descent, the brilliance touched the tree, and a branch of the tree fell to the ground where Taino lay. And the brilliance spoke to him in his dream, saying, "I have separated you from your people to be for you your one and only God. You have come to understand that I am above all things; there is none that I am. Take hold of the branch that lies before you, and it shall be to you a staff. Neither profane it with any tool nor hold to it so fast as to worship it. It will be an everlasting sign between me and you of the covenant I am making with you this day. As long as you obey My commandments, which I will soon reveal to you, I will protect you, and all the peoples of the earth shall be blessed through you."

When Taino awoke, there was a branch at his feet, and he took it as a staff, as he had been commanded to do. He descended the mountain with the staff to bring his people the words he had heard, but his way was impeded by a sudden, extended storm from which he took refuge in a cave, thereby escaping the floodwaters ravaging the lowlands.

When the storm abated, Taino continued down the mountain and found his village washed out to sea. Again he dreamed, and Ochinkos began many moons of intermittent revelation, an additional lifetime and a half, until Taino was fully conversant in His ways. At the end of this period, he was commanded to make a canoe, single masted with sails of reed matting, and set out with his staff for the nearest island inhabited by Ciboney, to find himself a woman. Your Francis diary and Father Conlin have told you the rest.

* * *

Caleb and Joseph sat in silence for minutes after the Indian had finished. Immersed in Ciboney history, they replayed in their minds what the Ciboney had said as the air turned cooler with the rising wind and sundown. Compounding the silence, the Indian cupped his hands in an awkward gesture over his eyes, blocking out all trace of the real world from his immediate concentration of heart and mind on his God.

But the wind kept hardening, disturbing the water's calm and their silence, and the small waves began jostling the boat between tugs of the lines mooring it to the walkway. The Indian's thoughts returned to his companions, and he suggested that they go below or visit the hotel where his guests were staying to finish the conversation.

"The chill and motion will make it uncomfortable for all of us shortly," he explained. "My cabin may be too cramped to accommodate us this day, and we should understand everything we expect of one another before we confirm our commitments. So there is still some discussion to be had I would think."

Caleb was the first off, joining John before turning to assist Joseph. The Indian led them from the marina, John lagging behind, and with back street shortcuts lopping extensive footage off the acutely curved waterfront, they were back in their hotel in almost less time than it had taken in the taxi. Or so it seemed to Joseph. But to Caleb, who had a loaded question to ask the Indian, the trip was far too long.

Quickly volunteering his room with the hope that John and Joseph might excuse themselves due to the lateness of the evening, and leave the Indian to him alone, Caleb ended up settling all of them into his suite's parlor room. Its walls were cluttered with land- and seascapes of the Virgin Islands chain, one, in fact, picturing the marina from which they'd just come.

Immediately upon their seating themselves, Caleb preempted the conversation by saying, "You have told us much to complete our understanding of the Ciboney nation, but there are still grave secrets you have not shared with us. One of these, if answered, would relieve much of our apprehension in proceeding. May I ask it of you?" The Indian nodded.

"What has to be retrieved from the wreck of the *Jason* that keeps us from leaving for the islet immediately?"

As Caleb asked it, he focused totally on the Indian, who was sitting directly opposite him. Clearly as interested in how the Indian physically reacted as in the response itself, Caleb saw nothing of note, and added, "Couldn't you continue your diving for it after we return?"

"I am afraid I cannot tell you what you ask, what the treasure is that I have admitted is down there," the Indian said coldly. "It should suffice that I have made the admission, which confirms what the missionary reported to your Father Conlin. The treasure is something I must have with me for your journey to succeed. If you cannot accept that my diving must come first, I must regrettably decline helping you."

"Are you afraid that we cannot be trusted?" Caleb said. "That if you tell us and yet fail to retrieve it, we'll know what and where it is and pursue it on our own?"

"Yes," the Ciboney replied, showing the first signs of discomfort.

"But we know it is the *Jason* over which you're diving," Caleb went on, "and that ship we can locate independently of you if we choose. We also know that the treasure is the religious object mentioned to the missionary. So isn't it obvious from the story you just told us about Taino that the religious object you are seeking is the staff?"

The Indian flinched. "Yes, it is that!" he cried out. "I know precisely where it is on the *Jason*, and I must have it to begin again, to fulfill what my God seeks of me."

"Well, now that we've all been totally open," Joseph said, smiling at the thought of what Tom Petersson would now think, "we can all trust each other and go out there tomorrow and get the staff!" The Indian smiled without relaxing.

"May I ask two more questions?" Caleb said, wondering whether the staff alone could prove the existence of God without their risking a trip to the islet.

"Yes," the Ciboney replied, "I have nothing else to hide."

"The first, then, is, how did the staff get on the *Jason* when it was given as an eternal sign for your ancestor alone?" Caleb said. "And the second is, if the staff was on the *Jason*, why did it go down? Are you sure it is the same staff as the one received from your God by your ancestor?"

"It is man who reaps the benefit of the staff," the Indian responded with some irritation, "not things like ships! Your Captain Francis stole the staff without comprehending its significance. The ship sank; yet Francis lived, the only survivor of the wreck. He lost my people's treasure, maybe forever, but he survived. There is much that cannot be explained in human terms of what has happened to my people since the loss of the staff, and much to do if you wish to accomplish what you have set out to do. I will take you to the islet although I have no purpose there myself, but only because you will first help me retrieve the staff. Is that our agreement?"

"Yes," Joseph said, cutting off Caleb as he was about to ask another question, "you have our agreement. We must, however, have some guarantee that the staff won't be your sole objective, that you will take us to the islet even after you have the staff again in hand."

"And if I were intending to deceive you," the Indian said, "would I be so foolish as to admit it now?"

"Would you agree to give us the staff if you refuse to go forward – and put it in writing?" Joseph responded.

"If the staff is as I say it is," the Indian said, "then no power can take it from me if I remain faithful to my God. Please be assured nonetheless: trust is like faith – we must feel it in our hearts at times even though our minds are advising otherwise."

"Another question, please?" Caleb inquired.

"There will be much time on the trip to the islet for questions," the Ciboney countered. Caleb's face sank. "We have a long day ahead tomorrow, but perhaps there is time for just this one question."

"Do you have written laws given to you by your God to govern how you live, perhaps something Taino received during his original stay on the mountain?" Caleb asked. "In other words, does your people have a written record of your God's revelation to Taino?"

"That answer is no, but it may not be complete," the Ciboney said. "From the first contacts of my people with European missionaries seeking our souls' salvation, we noted the many similarities between our oral laws and the written laws of your Bible. And as we studied with the missionaries with a view to understanding what these possible enemies of our own people were about, my people came to adopt many of those written laws as our own, except for one alteration that I deemed consistent anyway: our people remained vegetarians, as was ordained on your Bible's sixth day of Creation even though later changed, and animal sacrifice was forbidden."

"That is absolutely fascinating!" Caleb exclaimed.

"Then we are agreed?" the Ciboney asked, standing.

"Yes!" Caleb said exuberantly, standing to offer his hand. The burning warmth was still there.

"What time shall we meet at the marina?" Joseph asked, joining them. "Is eight too early?"

"I will be there all night," the Indian said, "and sunrise would be later than I would like."

"Sunrise it is," Caleb said as Joseph reluctantly agreed.

"Can any of you dive?" the Indian asked, grasping the doorknob to let himself out.

"No, not in the slightest," Caleb said, speaking for them all, "but I'm quite ready to learn if you'll promise to keep the sharks away. I didn't come this far to end up as fish food."

"Then bring your best pairs of sunglasses," he said to Joseph and Caleb, who were walking him to the elevator while John went to his room. "There's not time enough for diving instruction, and the sharks get very hungry out there. Just be there to let me know the minute something dangerous appears."

"Don't worry on my account," Joseph said, touching his glasses.

"Thank you," the Indian said as the elevator door opened.

Caleb barred the door's closing. "I must ask before you go, what name are we to call you?"

"Taino," he said, and the door closed on his broad grin.

Chapter XXVII

Diving Deep for the Staff

AS IF STEALTHILY STALKING ITS PREY, the morning sun crept through a broken slat in the window shutters of Caleb's hotel room. It soon pounced on his dream-weary eyes, forcing him awake. But it wasn't until a phone call from Joseph demanded his presence in the lobby that he moved from his bed. Cursing his failed wake-up call, Caleb dressed and raced downstairs, where he was pulled by Joseph into a waiting taxi without the breakfast his regimen craved.

The marina was not nearly in the state of rest that the hotel and streets were. Slips were already vacant or emptying, and Taino was pacing the walkway to his sloop when his benefactors arrived. While John remained distant, Joseph and Caleb boarded with Taino, took the cups of coffee he offered, and sat with him on the folding chairs of the prior evening. Caleb eagerly addressed the sweet rolls Taino placed before him.

"Are you ready for your first sailing lesson?" Taino asked, trying to jump start the day.

"Certainly," Joseph replied, reaching for his third roll of the morning.

"That is good," Taino said. "Let us sit for the moment, finish what I have brought, and greet the new day. If you had been here as we agreed, you would have experienced a spectacular sunrise."

Grabbing his second roll, Caleb sat back to judge the day. Birds filled the sky. With wondrous dives and constant screeching, they monopolized everyone's attention. John silently joined the group.

Taino's eyes were the first to stray from the sky. Studying his three benefactors, John particularly, he concluded that they would be, at best, adequate financial backers for achieving his needs, and, at worst, a crew wholly unprepared for the rigors of retrieving the staff and seeking the islet.

Joseph was next to divert his eyes, probably because he sensed Taino's gaze on him, and he focused on Taino's face. Pondering a complexion that suggested a prize fighter who'd been hurt much too often, he debated the impending relationships among them in an attempt at gaining control over what he feared would be an unmanageable enterprise. But when Taino's eyes glanced back at his, Joseph returned to watching the birds in flight.

John had one desire when he looked at Taino: to fix his age. At that morning's hotel breakfast, which Caleb had slept through, John had learned from Joseph what he had missed in the prior evening's discussions. Now John's primary clue to Taino's age had become the very name Taino, dating from the Ciboney tribe's earliest days, and it was currently teasing him. He stared at the Indian's dark brown eyes to reflect on the origins of his scar-marred face, and concluded that the Indian, whether mortal or not, was due a full measure of respect. Those eyes were broadcasting a much more assured knowledge of man, he thought, than did Taino's dark, ravaged body, etched like a roadmap through Ciboney history.

Caleb, during a restless night of sleep, had gone way beyond both Joseph and John in his acceptance of Taino's promise. While the birds distracted him only from food, he remained comfortable in Taino's hands.

Putting his empty cup down, Taino stood to prompt the others. Joseph and Caleb followed, leaving John to nurse his coffee and reflect.

"I think we had better start if I am to dive today," Taino said. "I am that close that with new equipment, I will surely have the staff by sundown. First, though, a sailing lesson is in order until the shops open. We will begin with terms and work our way gradually into the real thing. You will support me from above during my diving today, and spell me at the helm on our voyage to the islet. There are no divers among you, but are we fortunate enough to have a sailor? I will teach you what I can, but nothing prepares for the sea like experience."

"I have some experience," Caleb said. "I grew up on the water, sailed off a marina something like this, but never really fell in love with it, probably my father's pushing too hard. Anyway, I haven't been at the helm of a sloop like this for a good twenty years."

"It does not matter," Taino rejoiced. "I now have a mate. Let us begin!"

The terms came easier than the dry runs, but as Taino paced them through the twenty-six-foot keel sloop, enthusiasm prevailed. Taino talked safety constantly while demonstrating how to rig the boat. He discussed basic sailing maneuvers with, against, and across the wind before starting the outboard motor with Joseph at his side and bringing the sloop beyond the still waters of the marina. There, he assembled the mess of sails and ropes with his crew's hands.

Suddenly the air filled the sails and began driving the sloop out of the bay. And as they hit open sea, the boat hooked onto the wind, racing with refreshing abandon across choppier water. Calling his crew into active duty, Taino threw the full weight of helmsman's chores on each of them, first in jibing, next in coming about, and lastly in tacking a course into the wind.

It was midmorning by the time Joseph and Caleb brought the sloop back in. Taino had explained more than his crew could absorb – more than Caleb ever knew – expanding, as they entered marina waters, on hazard situations like man overboard, right of way, and abrupt changes in weather conditions. Caleb jumped to the walkway and moored the boat, smiling with true pleasure when Taino alighted, viewed the knot, and walked on without touching it.

While John remained aboard, Joseph and Caleb followed Taino to a group of shops right off the marina. In one, Taino replenished his diving gear and satisfied his crew's other needs. In others, he obtained lunch to go and paid his outstanding marina fees.

Returning to the slip, Taino once again maneuvered the sloop out of the marina. While his benefactors ate, and without a single instrument reading, he brought the boat a half hour later to anchor near a small red ball bobbing in the open sea.

Detailing surface responsibilities to those who would listen, Taino suited up and tied a lifeline to himself, which he demonstrated as their means of communication in certain hazard situations. Fascinated more by the method than the goal, Joseph and Caleb voiced their understanding of their responsibilities and watched Taino tumble from the boat, his three-cylinder lungs plunging him quickly out of sight.

The bubbles soon disappeared, and Joseph became concerned despite the Indian's earlier forewarning. Tugging on the lifeline, he received Taino's response and reported to Caleb, "He's all right. It must be just as he said – he's under something that's dispersing the bubbles."

Chuckling at his overly zealous action, Joseph, joined by Caleb and at times John, resumed his watch for the ominous signs from sky and sea that might deliver Taino and them into harm's way. Nothing was evident, though, and they maintained a constant vigil.

Suddenly, a dorsal fin broke water, and Joseph screamed, "Shark!" Watching it lazily circle the boat twice and disappear, Joseph signaled Taino, who replied. Again they settled back into pleasant uneventfulness.

The day aged agreeably into late afternoon, interrupted solely by Taino's intermittent surfacing to take care of various needs before going under again. The weather continued sunny and cool, calming in its own right, as a gentle breeze kept the anchorline taut and dispersed the sun's heat. Still, the boat sat quietly on the water, like a cactus on desert sands.

The three on board were increasingly bored by the disuse of their newly acquired talents, but only John subliminally entreated the unexpected. Gradually it came.

Joseph spotted a shark, which like the first, lazily circled the boat. By the time Taino had responded to Joseph's signal, however, Caleb had yelled that there were dozens more. Joseph signaled again, but the water kept yielding sharks of different sizes, shapes, and colors, and Joseph despaired at keeping Taino informed because of the multitude.

The shark-infested waters started churning, making waves that rocked the boat and splashed the crew with bloodied foam spuming from the cannibalism of frenzied sharks. John moved to the mast to hold on.

"Let's send a signal that we're moving!" John shouted above the din of manufactured waves. "We've got to get out of here before they turn the boat over!"

"No!" Caleb rejoined. "He's our only hope in getting back alive! We don't know where the hell we are, and if we force him to surface, he'll be eaten alive."

"We'll manage for a bit longer, and then move," Joseph added, attempting to placate John. But John would have none of it, and he demanded once more that they leave immediately.

"Look, Joseph, the rope!" John yelled after another few minutes had passed. "He's tugging on it to tell us to pull him up!"

"It's the sharks, John!" Caleb retorted. "Just calm down! You haven't been involved since we found the Indian, so don't start barking orders when you haven't heard half the things he's told us. I'm as scared as you are, but it doesn't help the situation to panic. We'll give him a few more minutes and move if it gets worse. That's all that Joseph and I will promise. Just go back to being your indifferent self. Right now that's about the only way you could be helpful."

The thrashing continued, becoming more tumultuous as shark maimed shark, and their blood turned the sea redder. Soon there came a loud pounding from under the boat at the keel, and it vibrated every inch of their bodies, while testing Joseph's and Caleb's convictions to stay.

"Augh!" Joseph screamed as a shark almost joined them in the boat.

"They're trying to get us!" John shouted. "I can feel it! The boat will sink if they crash through the bottom, and what good will we be to the Indian then! Let's go!"

He raced for the anchor while directing Joseph to start the motor. But Caleb was right with him.

"No," Caleb shouted, pulling him down. "Not yet!"

John struggled ineffectually, and, staring at the diabolical contortions of John's face witnessed once before, Caleb vehemently added, "We aren't leaving here until his end of the lifeline comes up empty!"

"Then let's cut it!" John urged, struggling to rise. "They want him, not us!"

Joseph held fast at the stern even when he saw the others scuffling. Although he was at the motor, he made no attempt to start it. "Just a few minutes more, John, please!" he shouted to mediate without chancing moving forward. "Okay?"

Solely with the intent of extricating himself from Caleb's grasp, John ceased struggling. And when Caleb finally let him go, he hastily positioned himself amidships on the starboard side and resumed staring with unbridled awe at the red sea. Caleb inched toward Joseph, who was crouching at the helm, but as he moved aft on the port side, Caleb had to grab the cabin bulkhead and hold it dearly to counter a surprising increase in the boat's roll.

Suddenly the red sea was inundated with pale blobs that looked like disjointed bones: arms and legs and ribs and skulls, with streaks of what appeared to be tissue and hair, bobbing and sinking before rising again with the sharks' frenzy. And then there was no weight on the lifeline, no resistance, and Joseph screamed it as he slipped and fell in reaching for the outboard motor.

Caleb was at the anchor in an instant, without even waiting for Joseph to pull in the line and confirm that Taino wasn't merely swimming with Joseph's tugs. He began weighing anchor just as he saw a chewed-through braid of the anchorline attract another shark. As the shark did its work, leaving the anchor to the sea, the boat lurched and John grabbed the boom to keep from being knocked overboard. Caleb, half expecting the boat's movement, had dropped the anchorline just as it was severed, and laid himself on the deck to avoid being catapulted into the sea. Still, he was thrust against the cabin bulkhead and dizzily crawled toward the helm.

Joseph was unable to start the motor, and yielded his fruitless effort to a frozen gaze at sharks ripping the pale blobs and turning, sucking, spitting, and tearing at them and each other. Taino's empty lifeline was still in his hand.

Caleb shoved him, to break his paralysis, but all he got was a vacant stare. He pulled Joseph from the motor and was about to prime it when John beseeched Joseph to go in after the Indian, to save him. Joseph glared at John, and threw up on the cushioned runner along the stern.

The sloop was now floating free and shifting randomly in the turbulence, which seemed to follow the boat. Joseph got up just as Caleb started the outboard, slipped on his own vomit, and anxiously stood again, cocking his head to hear what he thought were calls from Goldie off in the distance. He raised himself awkwardly, and holding onto the cabin doorframe, searched the sea for Goldie's distant voice, coming to him above the din of frenzied sharks and an accelerating motor.

When Joseph began shouting and waving to Goldie, Caleb raised himself from the outboard to scan the sea, and as he did so, he sighted a huge silver object, reflecting in the sun's declining rays. John also followed Joseph's gaze, and when he saw the silver mass, he screamed, "Serpent!"

Arms were flailing in the water, and a long, slender, tentacle-like object could be seen. Caleb sat down and turned the boat toward the object despite John's remonstrations. And as they closed in on it, a human voice indeed seemed to rise from the water.

"Taino! Taino!" Joseph shouted back gleefully. "We're over here! I see you! We're over here!" Joseph looked at Caleb, who was nursing the boat through waters still brimming with sharks, and he watched in horror as countless sharks circled Taino's bleeding body. As the sloop closed in on Taino, a barnacle-laden wooden pole could be seen in his hand.

"Joseph, throw him a life preserver!" Caleb instructed after shutting down the motor.

Fearful of hitting and enraging the sharks, Joseph delayed his toss of the preserver. John had no such reservation, however. He reached for one and was about to fling it when Taino yelled to him to tie it down first and then throw it near him without hitting him. John reluctantly tethered it, then hurled the disc toward Taino with such force that it hit the pole, flipping it free. Instantly, Taino lunged for the pole, as if bounding from an invisible floor, and he retrieved it off a shark's back. That's when Caleb first saw the deep gash at Taino's left shoulder, spilling blood through his wetsuit.

"Pull me in slowly," Taino said, and John heeded the direction.

Gradually Taino reached the boat, and he steadied himself along the hull. Dozens of sharks followed him without attacking, almost like a pack of sniffing dogs, and others began circling the boat or diving under it, bringing renewed thudding at the keel in a replay of what had transpired earlier.

Time seemed frozen while Taino maintained himself mostly in the water at the sloop's starboard side. Finally, he pitched the preserver on board, and with his left hand anchoring him to the hull and the pole in his right hand, he swung his right arm fully over the side and lifted himself so that the pole dangled above the deck. Hanging there, he then unfastened the harness for the three silver cylinders with his left hand, and Caleb pulled them up as Taino disengaged. Taino now rotated his left arm over the side, waited a few seconds, and took a deep breath.

Taino seemed to be intentionally taunting the sharks for his crew's benefit. Blood was still flowing from the gash in his left shoulder down his left arm onto the deck and down the back of his wetsuit into the water. He lowered himself slightly so that his legs were fully in the water, and Joseph, Caleb, and John became mesmerized by the juxtaposition of man and beast, like Daniel in the lions' den, awaiting catastrophe at any moment.

The Indian searched the water intently, and when there seemed to Caleb to be the most danger, he dropped the pole to the deck and with both hands working together, vaulted his body over the side of the boat, spilling himself with a thud at John's feet. At the same moment, in a spectacular denouement, two sharks went after his left leg as it lagged behind the right in streaking from the water. The sharks rose to a height that allowed them to face John, who was staring at them, and in midair, each with its mouth agape and rows of razor-sharp teeth at the ready, snapped their jaws on each other as Taino's leg disappeared into the boat. In what seemed like slow motion, the sharks faded from the pinnacles of their leaps, each torn by the other's teeth, further reddening the sea. More thrashing came, but with Taino aboard, his crew felt safe once more.

"Here it is," Taino exulted, retaking the pole in his hand, "the staff through which Ochinkos may favor the renewal of my people!"

Joseph, Caleb, and John studied the staff. Despite Taino's dazzling performance in the water, they all still believed they were witnessing no more than a water-logged wooden pole from which no aura emanated, not even the slightest spark for their ripe imaginations, which had been rife with expectation. At that moment Caleb finally understood how the Israelites had worshipped the Golden Calf so soon after God had revealed Himself on Sinai, so soon after He had directly and verbally forbidden their worshipping graven images. That biblical conundrum was the source of Caleb's constant doubts about the validity of Moses' books. He couldn't envision witnessing the divine smoke and fire, the thunder and lightening, and the voice of God conveying the Ten Commandments – yes, the voice of God – and not believing wholeheartedly and forever in God and His laws, never again to forget the Covenant. Yet the Israelites did quickly forget – perhaps never even having understood the magnitude of what they'd witnessed – just as he, Caleb, was now apparently doing with the staff. For no matter how much he had just witnessed and wanted to believe that the pole was the staff with the status the Indian spoke of, it was too much a leap of faith for him to accept without more, especially when he was of such lowly spiritual origins – much like the Israelites at the time of the Exodus.

Caleb suddenly became uncomfortable in the presence of the staff. Having denied its status, he felt it teasing him, and so he decided to address the gash in Taino's shoulder and went below to retrieve a first-aid kit. Returning in haste, he cautioned Taino, "That gash'll need a few stitches when we get back to St. Thomas. You'd better lie down on the runner over here while I peel away the wetsuit and clean and dress the wound. Just tell us how to bring the boat in, and we'll do the rest."

"There is no need to worry about my condition," he replied. "You have seen all the scars I have; my body heals itself well. No doctor can do the job as well as nature. Just tape the skin tightly together, and I will be as good as new in no time. Well, maybe not as good as new – with one more tear to define the sorrow of my life."

"Are you sure?" Caleb asked, extremely curious but unwilling to open up another supernatural issue he wasn't ready to digest. "I've never seen anything that deep and wide that didn't require a suture of some kind."

"Just put some gauze on the wound and tape it tightly closed; that will be all I need," Taino responded. "Let us cut me out of this wetsuit, and we will discuss your journey to the islet as we bring the sloop in."

"That was some experience back there," Joseph said. "I've never seen anything so scary, so vicious. What happened to bring those sharks to such a frenzy? We really panicked when your lifeline came up empty."

"I was afraid of your reaction when I cut the line," Taino replied, "but it was the only way to safeguard the staff after I had seized it in Captain Francis's cabin. As many sharks as were roaming the surface with you, there were hundreds more below. So I decided to let the bodies out of the hold in order to divert the sharks while I made my escape."

"Bodies? No, Taino!" Caleb exclaimed. "I saw things that could have been skeleton parts, but bodies? Really?" Joseph hurriedly leaned over the side and retched toward the water.

"Do you want to know?" Taino asked as Joseph returned. Joseph and Caleb looked at each other and at John, who was again sitting off by himself, this time staring at remnants of sharks. "Do you?" he demanded when the response he'd expected hadn't come. Joseph nodded feebly, Caleb more vigorously.

Hoisting the sails at Taino's instruction, they had the sloop heading home in a stiff downwind as the sundown brought an increasing chill and darkness to the three men gathered at the helm. Caleb went below for four rain slickers and dropped one with John before delivering the rest.

"The *Jason* was a slave ship," Taino began when all had dressed to beat back the sprays of water and cold air, "and your Charles Francis was its captain. What you saw in the water today, which his diary may have told you, were the remains of slaves locked in the hold of the ship for delivery to your country. They went down with the ship after it had made an emergency stop for repairs and supplies off my people's island. I know of it from my ancestors, just as I know of the islet, the little man, and the fountain – and how to get there.

"The *Jason* required so much in food supplies and fresh water after a storm had driven it off course that when it put in at our island, my people soon suspected what the cargo was. Yes, one hundred sixty years ago, my people suspected the *Jason*'s cargo, as I did today. When the sharks blocked my way from Francis's quarters after I had the staff – though with the staff in hand I feared them not – I knew it was a sign from Ochinkos not to leave until I had raised the dead. It was right for their remains to finally be free, and proper to my purpose of retrieving the staff. Thank you for your help, and I apologize for instilling fear."

Joseph went below to escape the chill and was immediately joined by John, while Caleb became the helmsman under Taino's watchful eye. There were some striking omissions in the Indian's stories of the prior night and today, and that irked Caleb. Alone now with Taino, he hastily sought to address them. "How," he asked, "had Francis obtained the staff? Why are you only now pursuing it? And why, from such a multitude, are you the only Ciboney left, when your God had promised long ago, way before the *Jason* came, to protect your ancestor and through him bless the peoples of the world?"

Taino smiled and pondered but said nothing. As the sloop approached the marina, however, he informed Caleb that there would be a right time to disclose those things, but it was not then. He had one more trip to make before they'd embark for the islet, and when he returned, all would be told.

Taino directed Caleb to drop the sails and start the outboard motor, which Caleb did. Taino took control then and brought the sloop in, while Caleb went below for Joseph and John.

By the time everyone was on the walkway, Taino was ready to tender final instructions on their preparations for the trip to the islet. They would spend the next two days stocking the boat with the list of essentials he gave Caleb. They would also be responsible for making over the cabin into an improved cooking area and sleeping quarters for two. They would rotate shifts in the kitchen, at the helm, and in bed. "And while you are diligently employed outfitting the boat," he said as they walked to the street, "I will be performing the most critical activity in assuring the success of our trip: I will be communing with my God on His holy mountain."

Chapter XXVIII

Tom

"You're not just saying this to get me down there?" Tom Petersson asked Joseph, who was fulfilling his commitment to Tom to telephone him if they found the Indian.

"Nope," Joseph said smugly. "If you'd rather not come, we'll understand."

"And you say you recovered the staff today, and it kept the sharks from mauling him?"

"This call's costing me, Tom," Joseph said. "I don't need to waste my nickels repeating myself for your benefit. If you'd like to call back, we can spend all the time you want, but that is what I said."

"Why aren't you celebrating, then?" he asked.

"If you'd gotten as sick and scared as I did today," Joseph replied, "the only thing you'd be interested in doing when you got back, as Stitches would say, is washing out your underwear. Besides, I haven't had a bite since lunch and lost that meal on the boat, so I'm starved."

"I want to believe you, Joseph, but...is Caleb or John around?"

"Caleb's here. Why don't you just get your flight information and return the call. Then you can talk to Caleb for as long as you want. We'll be out all day tomorrow outfitting the boat."

"May I talk to Caleb for just a minute, Joseph? Please."

Caleb took the phone and greeted Tom with "I told you so."

"Caleb, don't crap around, please," Tom broke in. "Just give me your best shot on what's going on. Use your scientific head, not your spiritual one, okay?"

"After today, Tom, I have only one voice," Caleb said, "and it's going to tell you exactly what Joseph said with one additional thought.

As difficult as it might be for you to believe, I'm convinced that something supernatural is at play here. What, I don't know, but maybe things have gotten so screwed up on earth – Sodom and Gomorrah revisited – that after promising never to flood the earth again, God's trying out a combination of non-flood ways, some new, some old, to make us rethink why we're here, starting with a nondescript staff parting a shark-bloodied red sea. Maybe then we find Cain, and the world will buy my idea to nurture the Jews back to their roots so we all can share in God's blessings. Who knows: if the staff does its work and Cain lives, then God exists. And it follows, readily enough, that the Jews do indeed have a contract that can deliver a second Eden. Anyway, Joseph's nudging me to tell you that your minute's up. So don't protect your ass too long on this, or you might find yourself out to sea when the ship comes in."

"The least I should do is come down tomorrow so I can talk to the Indian and check out the staff when he returns," Tom said, thinking out loud. "You say he'll be back in two days?"

"That's right," Caleb replied, "after we've stocked the boat. And make sure you bring your wallet. There are no free rides on this roller coaster, especially if we're stocking tomorrow for a fifth crewman!"

Joseph took the phone. "I'm glad you're coming," he said. "It makes John's original prediction correct, about the four of us being destined to go, and Stitches financing John's share. Good to have you aboard – it makes me think I'm not so crazy after all!"

"Don't get too comfortable with my coming down, Joseph," Tom responded. "Even if I make it down, I may not stick around if the Indian doesn't satisfy me. And, truthfully, I might not even make it down. I have to rearrange a helluva lot to free up just the next two days, and it might take the next two days just to free up a week if I'm going to the islet. So you keep plugging along as if I'm coming – I'll pay my share – and I'll surprise you at your hotel tomorrow night if I do make it down. If the staff did what you say, that alone will put Joseph and Goldie Kallman in the history books."

"The staff did what I said, Tom. You'll see."

Caleb grabbed the phone. "What are you doing, Tom, with this 'coming, not coming' crap!" he shouted. "All you're doing is playing both sides of the fence: you're insinuating yourself into the rewards if something good happens and protecting your ass from any fallout if we end up making fools of ourselves. You know, for a supposedly erudite anthropologist, a university professor at the highest career level, you sure must be stupid to think you can bullshit us into doing your dirty work while you sit back in Boston with an unsullied reputation. One thing's for sure, Tom old boy: if we hit pay dirt and you're not with us, it's like we never knew ya!"

"I know that, Caleb," Tom responded, "and that's why we're still on the phone. And I'll tell you honestly, the staff is damned intriguing, but it's the Indian's monotheism that's pulling me down there."

"What's that got to do with it?"

"It's Anthropology 101," Tom went on. "If the Indian told the truth about his ancestral chieftain, who might be his own immortal self, we've got another chosen person or people, who, like the Jews, haven't exactly become like the stars in heaven, but haven't disappeared either. And if I could confirm that there was no cross-pollination, that the missionaries in their overzealousness didn't influence the Indian's revelation – the Christian Bible was after the fact and not before – then I've got the makings of a major discovery even without Cain, the fountain, or the staff.

"So I'm thinking right now that it may be a win-win situation for me. I can't look bad if it's the monotheism I'm investigating while I happen to be on a joy ride to some islet. And that means I should be down there tomorrow to help you guys outfit the boat and prepare myself to interview this modern-day prophet, or whatever the Indian really is.

"Thanks, Caleb, for crystallizing my thoughts. I'll see you probably midafternoon. If you're not at the hotel, I'll try the marina, slip 24. Put Joseph back on; I'd like to thank him too."

Chapter XXIX

Then the serpent said to the woman, "You will not surely die. For God knows that in the day you eat of it your eyes will be opened, and you will be like God, knowing good and evil."

Genesis 3:4, 5

Then the LORD God said, "Behold, the man has become like one of Us, to know good and evil. And now, lest he put out his hand and take also of the tree of life, and eat, and live forever" – therefore the LORD God sent him out of the garden of Eden to till the ground from which he was taken.

Genesis 3:22, 23

...If you heed the commandments of the LORD your God, which I command you today, and are careful to observe them. So you shall not turn aside from any of the words which I command you this day, to the right or the left, to go after other gods to serve them.

Deuteronomy 28:13, 14

Because all these men who have seen My glory and the signs which I did in Egypt and in the wilderness, and have put Me to the test now these ten times, and have not heeded My voice, they certainly shall not see the land of which I swore to their fathers.... But My servant Caleb, because he has a different spirit in him and has followed Me fully, I will bring into the land where he went, and his descendants shall inherit it.

Numbers 14:22–24

Prelude to Sailing

THE FIRST DAY OUTFITTING THE BOAT passed quickly. Tom arrived that afternoon and joined them at the marina. His interest, however, was not in getting ready for their trip to the islet but in reexamining with John the events of the last few days in their minutest detail.

Caleb took advantage of his time alone with Joseph to test Joseph's commitment to the rest of the trip. While nothing major had dogged Joseph so far, Caleb was concerned that the physical demands of the final leg of the trip might outdistance him. Surely Joseph's nausea during the less rigorous diving episode suggested a weakening constitution that mightn't hold up to unknowns of far greater consequence. But Joseph was convincingly comfortable with the risk, and the doctor in Caleb declined to use his medical authority to undermine Joseph's resolve.

In fact, there were some fascinating insights that Joseph brought to their discussion, one of which made Caleb address some of his own fears in pursuing Cain. For the next undertaking, Joseph told Caleb, he would see himself as if he were about to embark on his first roller-coaster ride, the one Goldie had snookered him onto at New York's Coney Island amusement park ages ago. That experience had become for him the standard for accepting risk and the possible loss of control.

He was terrified of the roller coaster for what he believed was its inherent danger – just as he now felt about the trip to the islet. So he begged off the ride, but Goldie was consumed with excitement – it was her first roller-coaster ride – and she asked him to buy two tickets, one for her and one for him, so that he could sit next to her until the ride started. That way he'd prevent the seat from being occupied by some unsavory character. How could he refuse?

The cars filled quickly, but when he sought to escape, Goldie distracted him until they were on their way and escape was impossible. Their car, the first one, was already making the steep climb, rising with the strain of the gear chain pulling them along the incline. He remembered feeling less tense during the initial ascent, as if no danger lurked, just as he would feel as they pulled out of the marina on their trip to the islet. His fear had heightened, however, with the roller coaster's elevation, especially as the amusement park noise and lights faded below, just as his fear on the boat, he knew, would escalate in relation to their distance from land. Ameliorating that, though, was the comforting constancy of the roller coaster's track, as would be the calm expanse of the sea on the trip. Even at the top of the incline, he'd laughed at being so initially petrified of such a silly ride, for there was a second or two of perfect peace – a suspension of all fears real and imagined – just as the diving experience with Taino contained a moment of perfect peace until the sharks came.

When the roller coaster's descent commenced, he'd gasped, grasped the car's safety bar in front of him with all his might, shut his eyes, and held his breath as if it would be his last. He'd wanted to scream as Goldie was doing, and curse her too, but his stomach was still at the top of the incline and he couldn't yell anything. Then the car hit the bottom of its decline, and as it turned upward again, he felt his body flatten against the car floor, his head jerk forward, and then back. At that moment, he was sure he wouldn't survive the ride, and his mind, when it could think, merely called himself stupid. Such were his recent thoughts when the sharks came.

But then, once more, the car was rising, and at breakneck speed this time. He was alive though, and suddenly exhilarated enough to scream with Goldie at the ecstasy of it – just as he felt when Taino resurfaced with the staff – never to be relived again because he'd already experienced it; yet never to be forgotten either for the lesson he'd learned from it: always judge risk by the true danger, not by any irrational fear you might harbor, for there is no risk in fear alone. And, Joseph told Caleb, since he judged there to be minimal danger in the trip to the islet under Taino's command, notwithstanding his immense fear of losing control over whatever might happen, he would accept the risk and go. He would be on the boat when Taino pushed off, he said, and allow the passage of time to take care of the rest. For he'd adopted Stitches's father-in-law's – Isaac's – outlook on things: a goal to be achieved on a set schedule would be accomplished merely by the passage of time.

And so it was that on the morning of the third day after they'd returned from retrieving the staff, on the day Taino had appointed for their departure to the islet, Taino met them on the walkway to his slip in what was clearly an unhappy state. Oddly, after their earlier conversations, no one had even ventured the possibility that Taino might not show.

"I am afraid there might be a slight change in our plans," Taino said after being introduced to Tom. "I had thought that I would merely guide you to the islet, but that may not be all I must do. There seems to be something more, though I myself do not yet know what it is, and I want you to be aware because I also do not know where it will take us."

"Do you mean we will have another detour like the diving before we can go to the islet?" Joseph inquired.

"I do not think so," Taino replied, "but I am also not sure. It is something I will learn as we proceed on the journey, but I cannot promise that it will not take us from it. It is a dismaying circumstance for me too, but it is the will of my God, and I must obey."

"Is it something that came out of your stay on the mountain, your holy mountain?" Tom asked, eager to begin exploring the Indian's belief system.

"Yes," Taino responded, "it is the result of a vision I had in the cave of my ancestor, much like he had before me. I am to revisit the islet, that I know, and I have the staff. But what I must do with the staff in relation to the islet, now that I have it, I do not know."

"May I ask something quite personal?" Tom said.

"Certainly."

"I have not had the full benefit of your prior conversations with my colleagues here," he began, "so correct me if I am wrong. It is my understanding you said that your God was your ancestor's only God as well, that He promised to protect your ancestor, and that through your ancestor the people of the world would be blessed. Is that correct? And were the Ciboney to become a great nation as well, either in number or in deed, or was the promise made to your ancestor, only as an individual? Do you understand what I'm asking?"

Taino nodded. He appeared neither disheartened nor challenged and merely motioned everyone onto the boat.

"Over the past few days you have learned more about me than any other person my whole life," he said as they opened folding chairs on the deck. "I cannot tell you all the secrets of my people, for that would tax your ability to believe. In some things I have not been entirely candid, and for that I apologize, but with more of the truth, which I now believe I owe you, you may better comprehend why we are here.

"After many years on this island, my ancestors were uprooted and forced to flee to an Out Island when the Danes occupied what is now St. Thomas. As a people we had remained aloof from the world, except for our uninvited contacts with the little man, the Spanish explorer mentioned in your Francis diary, the Danes, and missionaries who brought us your Bible and Christianity. All of this was long before the Americans came.

"We were a proud people, and we had the staff, passed on from generation to generation, chieftain to chieftain, until the *Jason* arrived. We had lived under the grace of Ochinkos and always believed that He was responsible for our health, peace, and prosperity. Never did a chieftain doubt, until the one who welcomed Captain Francis.

"The island to which we had relocated after the Danes had taken our ancestral home had become too small for us by the time the *Jason* came to our shores, and the chieftain had already begun praying for a sign of what to do. So he welcomed Francis's intrusion as preordained – a means, at a minimum, for the chieftain to gather information on the outside world, and, at best, a great ship to take his people to a larger, more beautiful place of plenty. Of course, as strangers ourselves when we first set foot on that island, it was a commandment of our God that we welcome strangers, such as the missionaries, and now Captain Francis. But we were wrong in each case; the chieftain was wrong.

"My people found out that the *Jason* was a slave ship soon after its arrival, when Captain Francis began replenishing his ship's water supplies and stocks of food after completing his repair of storm damage to the ship. It was then that the chieftain told Captain Francis of the islet with the little man and the fountain, employing it as a diversion as my ancestor did with the Spanish explorer. In the case of Captain Francis, it was to avert his kidnapping Ciboneys as slaves to replace those he had lost on the voyage already. But Francis was not interested in the fountain, and the chieftain became fearful that even if Francis did not make slaves of the Ciboney then, he would carry back word of this innocent, peaceful people to other slavers, who would seek to traffic in the Ciboney nation.

"Yes, as logical as it had been to seek information on the outside world, the chieftain was now convinced that it would have been wiser to remain aloof and hidden until Ochinkos Himself led the people from the island. It was too late, however, to reverse the knowledge of the Ciboney people that Francis had. How naive my ancestor was to have welcomed a man he thought might be a messenger from His God, only to learn too late that Francis represented the most ignoble vices of mankind. How easy it is to believe in a false messiah when you fear that your God has abandoned you, when centuries have passed without prophetic events or further revelations to reaffirm your faith and His promise. But that is His way.

"So to answer your questions, Dr. Petersson," Taino went on, "yes, I am a monotheist and the protection of Ochinkos extended solely to that Ciboney. And yes, through him all the peoples of the world will be blessed. But as to your last question: there was a time I thought the Ciboney would become a great people, in number and deed.

However, time often erodes the original intent of oral revelation and its oral laws. Too often what is not shortly committed to writing is manipulated for the benefit of those who are deemed to know it and who are looked to for guidance on how to observe it. Consequently, it behooves a people to have only laws that were written down near the time of revelation, like the Israelites, so that all may have access to it and know that the recorded revelation is complete. The Israelites even had a divine command to publicly read their written revelation every seventh year. This we should have done as well but did not, and then we foolishly adopted many of the laws of the Christian Bible as our own. By doing so, we lost the identity of our God that was embodied in our original revelation, and many of my people came to assume that, like the Israelites, they too were a nation of priests, and they strayed from Ochinkos to pursue gods of their own creation. That was our undoing."

"I am confused, Taino," Tom said. "How much influence did the Bible have on the tenets of your faith? I mean, when was the first revelation to your ancestor in relation to the missionaries' arrival and your adoption of the Bible as your written law?"

"You should not find our independent monotheism surprising, as you seem to," Taino responded, "but to answer your question, our earliest revelation predated by centuries our receipt of the word of your God from the missionaries; yet our oral law at the time we learned about your Bible seemed to comport with most of its teachings. That, however, is the error in having oral law over centuries passed on from chieftain to chieftain, which then becomes written law. By the time it is recorded, it may bear no resemblance to the original. And outside influences, like the missionaries, may further distort the oral law from the original no matter how hard the chieftain might fight to maintain its integrity. As my visions these past two days revealed, the worship of false, personal gods was my people's undoing.

"Unlike the Ciboney, the Israelites had been given written laws for bringing offerings to their God if they unintentionally sinned, and the absence of a sacrificial system like that for the Ciboney proved a major liability. You see, the beauty of the Israelite system was that only the inadvertent sinner could seek forgiveness, and by doing so, it brought him closer to his God. That resurrected him as one of the faithful. The intentional sinner, the murderer or the thief, for example, was removed from the people to set an example as well as extract the bad influence. But when you lack a system like that, then the intentional sinner, remaining among the people, in essence negates your God. And by serving a false god permitting those sins, he begins a process of diminishing what the people believe. That is what happened to my people after the incident of Captain Francis."

"Joseph, that's what I meant about your intentionally eating that BLT at the hospital and creating your own personal god. But go on about Captain Francis," Caleb said when he realized he'd interrupted Taino, "tell us what decimated your people."

"The chieftain foresaw the great suffering that would arise through Francis," Taino continued, "and he devised a subterfuge to preserve his people. He took the staff – which had been safeguarded in a shrine for the people to view, inadvertently becoming to some an idol in its own right – and while Francis was still an honored guest of my people, hid it among the captain's possessions en route to his ship. When the ship was ready to sail, the chieftain informed his people of the theft, and hundreds of the faithful stormed the ship as it began to sail away. In the skirmish that followed, a gunpowder explosion occurred, sinking the *Jason* and drowning most of those on board with it. It also buried the staff and its benefits from those of us who survived.

"Unlike the prior centuries in which we multiplied and enjoyed the blessings of Ochinkos, misfortunes befell us: disease, slavers, and misery. Never once did we acknowledge that Ochinkos had turned His face from us because we had sinned in worshipping foreign gods, and it was only last night that I realized how jealous my God is. Ochinkos gave Taino a promise of protection and future blessings in return for Taino's total submission to His will through the observance of His laws. But when we turned from Him by adopting teachings of the missionaries, and acting as we did with Captain Francis, He turned from us as well, allowing the grip of evil to encompass us.

"Our thousands soon became hundreds, tens, and ones. We made substantial efforts to recover the staff and rid ourselves of Christian influences, but we could never dive long and deep enough to locate the *Jason*, and the written word of the Bible proved too difficult to erase. We, the Ciboney people, became one.

"It took the independent good fortune of a salvage company fifteen years ago to pinpoint where the *Jason* was, and after stripping it of the few treasures a slave ship might carry, they abandoned it to any such as I who might have an interest in it. The other day you witnessed the result of the chieftain's foolish subterfuge. Ochinkos is merciful to those who truly atone. For me, however, there is a much higher standard, and now that I have the staff, I believe that His face will again shine on me. But the manner of it, the full test of my faith, is still to come. Perhaps when I have done all that He will ask of me, and I have demonstrated my undying love for Him with all my heart and being, He will renew His promise as of old."

"What exactly did you learn on the mountain?" Tom eagerly asked.

"I learned, Dr. Petersson, that past chieftains, who were responsible for carrying the word of Ochinkos to future generations, allowed their own beliefs, not just those of the people, to be corrupted over time by their own desires and by the Christian missionaries so that even they fashioned personal gods for themselves, and they paid dearly for it.

"From our earliest revelation, and again yesterday on the mountain, it has become clear to me what Ochinkos seeks of me. As in your Bible's story of the serpent in Eden, only God knows good and evil absolutely; man perceives them only in relative terms. It was Eve's desire to know them absolutely, to be 'as God,' that permitted the serpent to lure her and resulted in their banishment from the Garden and its Tree of Life. That is why your Bible's written laws were given to you – just as my people's oral laws were revealed to us – so that we might yet know absolutely what is good and evil. For, in the same manner as the dos and don'ts of my oral laws, your Bible's positive commandments, like 'Love thy neighbor,' are the absolute good in this world, and its negative commandments, like 'Do not murder,' are the absolute evil in it. If we strictly observe all that God requires of us, we can achieve absolute goodness and become godlike, in His image. That is why your Bible directs you not to supplement or diminish, or veer to the right or left of, any of God's laws. And that is why I must now absolutely submit my free will to God's will, so that I am no longer tempted by the serpent within me. I am willing now more than ever to do so, because I know what it is like to live within and without God's presence."

"Isn't it possible that your God simply chose another person or people to favor?" Tom said. "I don't mean to be disrespectful, but Christianity argues that very point about the Jews – that the Jews lost their chance to be God's Chosen by straying so often, and that Christianity is now the way to salvation."

"I had feared that myself until yesterday," Taino replied, "but I was reminded in a vision on the mountain that even the Christian Bible acknowledges God's eternal commitment to the Israelites."

Caleb's own vision suddenly crystallized. No matter what happened on the trip to the islet, no matter how virulent rabbinic resistance might be to his mission, he would press the Jews to assume their written contractual responsibilities to the God of the Hebrews, the Ivrim of the Torah, as well as to each other and all the peoples of the world. There was no other choice. He himself would become a Hebrew of old – not a modern, derogatorily-named Jew who worshipped his own personal god – and he would take his paternal great-grandfather's name, Yerachmiel ben-Yishye, skipping his family's generations of desertion and deceit. For unlike the once and future, false, rabbinically born Messiah of the royal line of David ben-Yishye, he would be the son of Yishye who would seek God's mercy, Yerachmiel, in enabling a return to the Levitical teaching of the Torah with its clearly proclaimed and welcomed blessings.

He would memorize the poem '*Haazinu*,' and write a redemptive, prophetic book on what the God of the Hebrews expects of his Ivrim – after communing with his God as Taino did, a lifetime and a half, twenty-seven years, so that he might bring the face of God back to the peoples of the world.

What Caleb did not envision at that moment, however, was that Numbers 14:24 was even more critical to his future. For in the desert millennia ago, there were two men who believed absolutely in the divine embrace of their people, of their destiny in a land flowing with milk and honey. They were the only two over the age of twenty who came out of Egypt in the Exodus and survived the full forty years of desert wandering. Yet until today, Yehoshua bin-Nun had been the only one to lead the Israelites to their Promised Land. Now the other, Calev ben-Yephunneh many times removed, a Judean baptized Caleb Call but renamed Yerachmiel ben-Yishye, and his daughter, Leah bat Calev and Michal – would lead the Israelites back to the Promised Land and the blessings of the God of the Hebrews. And they shall cause to be made for Me a *mishkan*, a tabernacle as I commanded the Israelites in the desert millennia ago, so that I may dwell among them. For just as Yaacov had to return Esav's birthright before he could return to his father's house in peace as Yisrael, so, too, the Israelites will have to return Levi's birthright as the teacher of Torah to Israel before My face turns back to them.

Chapter XXX

See, I have set before you today life and good, death and evil, in that I command you today to love the LORD your God, to walk in His ways, and to keep His commandments, His statutes, and His judgments, that you may live and multiply; and the LORD your God will bless you.... But if your heart turns away so that you do not hear, and are drawn away, and worship other gods and serve them, I announce to you today that you shall surely perish.... I call heaven and earth as witnesses today against you, that I have set before you life and death, blessing and cursing; therefore choose life, that both you and your descendants may live.

Deuteronomy 30:15–19

Cain

AFTER CALEB SET THE SLOOP FREE, Taino maneuvered it out of the marina into open sea. With Joseph at the helm, the sails were raised, and as soon as they filled, Taino took the tiller, leaving Joseph, Tom, and Caleb sitting on the cushioned runner circling the stern, avidly discussing within Taino's earshot what Taino had disclosed. John was a party of one in the cabin below.

But Tom was too eager to discover more about Taino and his tribe's religious beliefs to be content debating them with the others. While Taino had earlier addressed whatever had troubled his benefactors, Tom's business was in the study of man's social and cultural links and lapses, and he hankered for more time with the Ciboney.

Taino listened attentively to Tom, smiled at him, and returned to his own thoughts. Assuming a misunderstanding, Tom renewed his inquiries, and again the Indian ignored him. Somewhat dismayed at the absence of an exchange, Tom sulked where he sat, opposite the staff, which Taino had clipped to the larboard side just above the deck but beyond where the cushioned runner ended in its circling of the stern.

In a sequence equally perplexing to Taino and Caleb, Tom spent the next hour fixed in a gaze that wandered among Taino, the staff, and the sea. He said not another word, and Caleb, fearing that something contagious in John's aloofness might be infecting Tom, sat between Tom and Taino to spark a dialogue. That only exacerbated Tom's disappointment, for in presenting the Indian with the missing link in their prior disclosures – Captain Bakchos's search for the islet and his Arethousa – Caleb was warmly received, so much so in fact that Taino asked him for a repetition of the riddle that had been recited to him the night they first met. That done, Taino yielded the tiller to Caleb and walked to the bow, where he breathed deeply and began battling the riddle and its significance, like the rest of them had already done.

As night fell, Taino employed a sextant, purchased the prior day, and made his sightings and time and altitude readings. The tiller was still in Caleb's hands, and after a small correction of heading, Taino went below to solve his sights and plot the boat's position. While Taino exercised his navigational skills a foot away, Joseph went about his cabin chore of preparing dinner.

Hoping that Taino would soon return to spell him, or bring him a rain slicker to dispel the increasing chill and sprays attacking him, Caleb worked the helm. Yet as he held the boat's course, his thoughts weren't only on his discomfort. He was ruminating as well on Taino's purpose, gradually educing that Taino's sight solving and position plotting were a charade – that he had used his new compass only twice during the day and had arrived intuitively at things like wind velocity, boat speed, heading, rigging tension, and sail settings, things Caleb had learned years before to be precise ingredients in sailing a taut ship.

Long after dinner was over, when all but Taino were either below reading or bedded down for whatever sleep their rotation would permit, a band of huge, marauding clouds appeared, draping the sea in blackness and eerily pitching the boat into a building wind. The calm watery expanse became a tumbling sea in minutes, and Caleb and Tom, who had been reading while Joseph and John slept, came up to secure whatever they could.

Taino remained steadfast at the helm, gulping the heavier air and allowing himself a full night's shift at the tiller, notwithstanding Caleb's standing offer to relieve him at any time. Thinking of that offer, Taino smiled from within his rain slicker and hat, as he wiped salty sprays from his face. He'd come to believe that even Caleb, the most experienced hand he had, was a mere novice, familiar with only the most elementary fundamentals of sailing. The sea was fickle, even Caleb knew that, and there was too much danger in the haste with which a tender breeze could work its way into gale strength, or the way a "norther" could hit without warning. Taino just couldn't afford the prospect of Caleb throwing them irretrievably off course, especially since he knew the way to the islet in only one direction, the one they were on.

Taino's crew rotated sleep surprisingly well that night, and dawn came with Taino still at the helm and the sea calm again. Tom prepared a huge breakfast after coaxing John to assist, and all they made went down easily under a gorgeous red sky. Joseph took his food at the tiller under the close watch of Taino, who ate with him and seemed refreshed despite his lack of sleep.

Tom was himself again, ready once more to seize an opportunity to converse with Taino. But he was also growing anxious wondering why no one had defined their objectives at the islet, if they got there, or asked about the return trip. In the event they actually found the islet, was something to be brought back to civilization – waters from the fountain, or Cain himself? Was there really a sea serpent awaiting them? And were the powers of the staff to come into play against it? Perhaps, he mused, the whole adventure was what Joseph had earlier facetiously said it was: the ultimate practical joke of Stitches, John's bankroller, the only one smart enough not to be with them on the trip.

At midmorning, with Caleb at the helm and Taino napping below, the wind hardened again, turning quickly into gale strength and forming a wall of over forty-knot air. Taino came up immediately, and Caleb willingly gave the tiller to him. Joseph and John went below, and Tom and Caleb again secured whatever they could. Driving sprays of frothy sea whipped their rain slickers as the sea continued to build. The temperature dropped almost fifteen degrees in fifteen minutes.

Suddenly a rain squall hit, combining with the sea sprays to make topside unbearable. Tom and Caleb were constantly sliding on the water-heavy deck, and Taino shouted for them to go below, safe from being washed overboard. And as they closed the cabin door to seal the wetness out, they could see Taino enjoying his fight with the elements, stiffening the boat into the crests and troughs of gigantic waves with what appeared to be perilous abandon.

Three of the four below huddled together, totally unnerved by the danger. Only John was calm enough to claim an empty bed for the duration. His sleep was disquieted, however. A half hour after Tom and Caleb had disturbed him coming into the cabin, they noisily opened the door again to see if Taino was still with them. They saw the jib blown out, and a tattered mainsail spilling wind. But Taino was at the helm, chanting what seemed a Ciboney hymn to Ochinkos, and clearly oblivious to the trepidations in the cabin. Minutes later, John sat up in his bed and irately declared that their fears were inane, arguing once more that it was all preordained, that time was running ineluctably parallel to that of centuries before.

The storm lasted until dusk, and everyone below joined Taino on deck as soon as the calm came in. They hadn't eaten since breakfast, and Taino gave the tiller to Joseph while he proceeded to drop the tattered sails into a tangle of sheets and ropes on deck. Tom volunteered to prepare dinner.

The sky remained overcast into night, and a palpable, misty blackness, even worse than the night before, hung over them as they ate on deck amid two kerosene lanterns. It was unusually warm now too, as if the low cloud cover were truly blanketing them.

"Are we almost there?" Joseph asked when Taino had him abandon the tiller.

"In the morning, I believe," Taino answered. "We are now running with the current, and its set and drift will have us at the islet shortly after sunrise, if I remember correctly."

With that comment Tom got up and meandered toward the staff. He stared at it for some minutes in the dim lighting, and seemed, to Taino, to be inching toward it, to touch it, something none of the others had ventured to do, although Taino had cleaned the barnacles away during his stay on the mountain. "Do you mind?" Tom asked Taino at last.

"You had best respect the possessions of others if we are to succeed on this journey," Taino said, blocking Tom's way. "We have only this night before I fulfill my promise to you. Let us not do something foolish to defeat your purpose here, whatever it is."

Tom was embarrassed and followed Taino back to the chairs that had been set out for dinner. They sat in a circle, and John, who had remained sitting while Caleb folded the table in their midst and brought it below, was now opposite the Indian.

Addressing Tom, Taino said, "Dr. Call said certain things yesterday that have helped me understand why I am here, although I do not yet have full clarity concerning my own mission. But unlike the others, who spent an evening with me when we met, I have not heard from you, Dr. Petersson, an explanation of why you are really here. May I please hear it now?"

Tom hastily apologized for his misdeed with the staff, just as Caleb rejoined the group. Tom went on to disclose his anthropologic interest in Caribbean Indians, including the Ciboney, his newly seeded fascination with Ciboney monotheism, his interest in the little man and the fountain, and his desire to observe the power of the staff as the others had when it was first retrieved among the sharks. He gave an extended dissertation on his academic credentials, emphasizing the prestigious publication of his recent Caribbean research, but omitted his depiction of the Ciboney as inferior.

"That seems to explain your interest in being here," Taino said. "The article you mentioned is the same as that recently described to me by Mr. Hauser, which referenced the Francis diary?"

"Yes, it is," Tom replied.

"And that article made a comparative analysis of Indian cultures in the Caribbean?" Taino asked.

"Yes."

"Have you now realized – perhaps it is what most encouraged you to join your friends so late in their efforts – that there is more to the Ciboney people than your article had recognized?"

"Yes," Tom admitted after some hesitation, "that is so."

"Then why did you not mention that fact in your answer just now?"

"I thought it might cause some unnecessary tension between us," Tom apologized. "It is my wish to observe what happens here, not to influence it."

"Total honesty among us is a prerequisite to what happens here," Taino responded. "And with your openness now, there remains only one other who is yet a mystery. That person, Mr. Hauser, is more than any other the one who has brought us all together."

Everyone turned toward John, who in the dim lighting was nodding off, but snapped awake at the mention of his name.

"John, I know we talked of it before, in those many little questions I inquired of you the night we met," Taino said, "but please bear with me and aid me in learning who I must now be to my God. Tell us again, please, your personal reasons for being here."

John stumbled for an abbreviated answer, limited to his life at the medical center, only to be drawn into his years in Germany as a Catholic priest and his bond to Cain as an outcast, frozen from God's grace. He admitted along the way that by finding Cain he might gain closure for his actions in Germany during the war, and be blessed with God's grace again.

Taino interrogated him further, and in response John began hinting at things about himself that were unknown to all of them, things even John didn't fully acknowledge about himself. So Taino persisted in digging, and John fought what Taino sought. Yet all the while, Taino succeeded in fleshing out more and more of John's earlier life, and Caleb increasingly sensed that John was a more willing party to Taino's pursuit than he let on.

By midnight, Joseph was exhausted, and he retired for the night. The rest of them, however, kept after John, eager to probe the roots of the dark secrets John's words had exposed. And so the night passed into morning without sleep for any of those remaining; yet still without the truths they now uniformly believed John was withholding. All the Indian could achieve into morning was the redirection of John's discourse into a piecemeal confession that was being revealed on two levels: those things about himself John was quite willing to disclose, and those things about himself John offered with substantial resistance. But the basest level, which Taino and the others wanted and John didn't even know existed – the source of his nightmares, of his unremembered memories and unrecallable dreams, of nights like those he experienced on the *Argo* – was until then successfully kept from them all.

With the sunrise, Taino addressed John's tantalizing confessions more directly. He stood and stretched, then sat again and said softly, "John." John's eyes opened wide. "You are looking to reveal something deep within you, far beyond what you have already disclosed. All you have told us throughout the night is what you want people to believe about you, and secrets you have previously admitted only to yourself. It is clear, though, that you are not here because of those things, but because there is something deeper within you, something that goes to your very essence, that brings you here, perhaps even against your will, that you will not even admit to yourself. That is what we must uncover to discover your reason, and probably mine, for being here.

Life has become too burdensome for you as the person you are, and you cannot cope with this burden buried within you as it percolates there attempting to reach the surface. It is what you have been saying all through the night – that finding Cain will in some manner result in your finally finding yourself.

"We are here to help you find your way, even though you have already abandoned us to confront the demon within you by yourself. Yes, I saw it in your face when we first met, as I saw it in the faces of the little man and Captain Francis without understanding it then or now. Perhaps it is a sign for all generations. Certainly that sign convinced me to welcome and cooperate with you when I would have preferred to retrieve the staff alone. And if it is such – a sign for all time – I must comprehend its significance in relation to what has been divined for me. Perhaps it is in the riddle you have brought me."

In response to Taino's softly spoken words, John's eyes were once again closing. He fought to stay awake, his head nodding between spurts of wakefulness and fits of sleep, ever seeking to rest peacefully on his chest. The mentally turbulent night seemed to have thoroughly sapped his strength and his desire to confront his demon head on.

Tom had heard Taino and John throughout the night, and he took up the Indian's challenge. He leaned toward Taino so as not to awaken John, his mind actively seeking debate, and he stared at the Indian, who was looking out to sea.

"You have made certain assertions about John which I digested earlier, and now wish to contest," Tom said to Taino, drawing the Indian's attention back. "I will give you the benefit of my knowledge of him if you will clarify your last comment."

"You mean about Mr. Hauser's connection to the little man and Captain Francis?" Taino inquired, turning toward John.

"Yes, about that," Tom replied, "but specifically about your seeing evil in their faces. You and not your ancestors. What you're implying about your age is absurd. It is beyond any scientific basis. Perhaps it is your own sense of guilt for being the sole survivor of your people that obscures the real issues and pressures you to make such ridiculous claims."

"Dr. Petersson," Taino responded, "I did not say the sign was of evil – you just did – although it is surely that. There is in Mr. Hauser the sign of what you call Satan, and the real guilt is not in me alone, although it is there too, but in all of us. Whatever has brought us together will never be realized until each of us sets the others free. Yes, that I have already deduced in relation to our journey: each of us holds the key to the destiny of the others. All of you have a role in mine."

"All of this is right out of the Middle Ages, Taino," Caleb offered. "You're going way overboard in pursuing the reasons we're here, and certainly in your laying claim to being centuries old!"

"It is in the riddle for each of us to see," the Indian replied, "and I must understand its meaning before we get to the islet."

"I don't understand!" Tom shouted angrily, and John stirred for a second. "You're making it more complex as you go!"

"What I know," Taino said, "is what this night has elicited from your friend, John, who may no longer be that. He is a man possessed of some great guilt, perhaps greater than mine, that only you, Joseph, and Dr. Call, knowing him better than I, can surface. It is quite certainly embodied in his pursuit of Cain, and you know more than I about why he seeks that ancient. In releasing him from his guilt, each of us will reap his own salvation."

Tom sat there for a long time thinking about what Taino had said. Caleb did the same. They watched John's head continue to bob, snap awake, and drop to his chest in a rhythmic sequence as they pondered what to do next. Taino repeatedly looked toward the sea and at John's face, as if that cycle of study might solve the riddle.

"I heard what John confessed last night about his life in Germany," Tom began at last, "and there were a number of inaccuracies that I chose not to contest because of what I owed him in my own peace of mind after my brother's death. Now that he's asleep, I'm willing to say that those errors may have confused you, and there really is no deep-seated guilt that must be released."

Taino nodded and smiled, but this was merely in reaction to his sighting the islet in the distance.

"Let me explain then," Tom went on. "He said last night that he was a happy child, liberally loved by his mother. That wasn't quite true, at least from what he told us a few weeks ago. At that time, he commiserated with a friend of ours who had been the unwanted last of ten children by saying that he became a priest to secure the love and attention he'd never received at home. He even admitted that his mother never showed him any affection.

"Now it's possible he said what he said solely to ease the pain of that friend of ours, but I believe he was being more truthful then than now. What do you think, Caleb?"

"I think he was truthful with Stitches and not now," Caleb replied. "I also think his misstatements last night were intentional obstacles to Taino's getting to know the real John – just as he's stayed aloof from us in recent days to camouflage his changing behavior. And from my own personal experience with him on the *Argo*, when I roomed with him during a storm on our way to St. Thomas from San Juan, I know there's evil lurking within his soul. I won't say any more."

"Let's keep going anyway, for Taino's sake," Tom said. "Another error John made last night was his statement about always having admired the Jews, especially the mothers, who fought to maintain their family's identity in the face of their imminent annihilation.

"But he admitted to us, at the same time as the other error I just mentioned, that he left the priesthood because God had failed him in his efforts to protect Jewish children during World War II. He told us that he'd hidden a number of Jewish boys in his church, and one for sure, maybe all of them, were taken by the Gestapo through what I sensed was John's own culpability."

"Dr. Call," Taino said, "it is important that you be as free with information about John as Dr. Petersson has been. Otherwise, we will never achieve our purpose here. Remember, each of us is the key to another's salvation."

Caleb deliberated a response. Finally he said, "That night on the *Argo* he was having a nightmare about a boy that he gave up to the Gestapo. As I understood what he said in the German he used – but I can't vouch for it – the boy wouldn't cooperate with John's desires. I've made every effort to ignore what I thought he meant, to deny to myself that I heard what I heard or that I heard anything at all, but if my life depended on it, I'd bet he did mean it the way I initially took it."

"What do you mean by 'John's desires'?" Tom asked. "Just so we don't get any more confused than we already are."

"I'd bet he's got the hots for young boys."

"So you can see, Taino," Tom went on, rushing from the subject, "admiration of the Jews may not have been high on John's list, and these errors may have confused you. He was too tired during the telling to know what he was saying. If there's a hidden agenda, it's news to me. Maybe it's your own hidden agenda that's feeding on itself here!"

The elevation of Tom's voice jarred John into semi-wakefulness. He shaded his eyes and muttered, "I must have dozed, are we there?"

"No," Taino responded, "not quite. And that applies to our discussion from last night, too, which Dr. Petersson and Dr. Call have now actively joined."

Taino gauged the islet to be a half mile off with the current's set and drift slowly carrying them by it. He turned to John and stared at him before lowering his gaze and saying softly, "This may hurt, John, but it will uncover what you have been looking for, the reason you are here, what is behind your search for Cain.

"Tell me, John. What was Cain in the Bible?"

John was now fully awake and looking quizzically at Taino. "Just answer, John," Taino added. "You will understand more as we proceed."

"Cain was the first son of Adam and Eve, who killed his brother Abel in a rage over God's rejection of his offering. Why do you ask?" Suddenly John was talking in English with a heavy German accent, and it stunned Tom, but not Caleb or Taino.

"It will be clear soon," Taino said. "Have patience.

"Now last night you talked about yourself at great length. I was about to ask you some questions when you fell asleep. You were up so long that I dared not wake you, but now it is appropriate.

"You said last night that you left the priesthood because God failed you during the war. It sounds very much like Cain, like you identify with him in his rebellion against God. Is that correct?

"You said you hated your mother because she gave her love to others and none to you. Was that the case with Cain? Might you empathize with Cain and his unrequited love for his mother?"

John's mouth opened to speak, but the accelerating pounding of his heart kept his breath from delivering words. Sweat beaded on his forehead.

"John, listen to this, my last question," he said, touching John's chin and turning John's head toward him. "Last night you said that you admired the Jewish family, especially Jewish mothers; yet you seduced them into placing their young boys in your custody with the promise of protection. You said children gave you the opportunity to return the love your mother gave you; yet we know you fed a Jewish boy to the death camps because he refused your demands. Could Cain have killed his brother because he, too, would not submit?"

John tried to stand, to flee Taino's onslaught, but his legs wouldn't support him, and he fell back into his chair. Unremembered memories and unrecallable dreams were now fully with him, there to be finally reckoned with, exploding their poisonous venom on his soul. He felt them strap him to his chair and shower him with crushing degradations. He wanted to scream to express his pain, but there was no air in his lungs to do it.

"Taino," Caleb screamed, "look what you're doing to him! You'll kill him!" Joseph raced up from the cabin.

Taino merely turned to Caleb and said drily, "No, I cannot. Only Dr. Petersson, Mr. Kallman, and you can do that. We are so close to the truth, the real guilt, let us continue. Please."

"John, answer me. Could Cain have killed his brother for the same reason you had that Jewish boy killed? Because he, too, would not submit?"

John was clutching his chest, pressing it, massaging it, trying to release the horrendous pressure within, but Tom and Caleb merely stared at his difficulties while Joseph pondered Taino's indictment: could John have had that Jewish boy killed because he wouldn't submit to what? And then the verdict struck Joseph, compounded by all the anger he'd repressed since John had violated him right after Goldie's death, and he screamed vengefully at John, "You bastard, you Nazi butcher!" and he flung himself at John. But the ex-priest, ex-human, gathered his strength and dodged the attack. He leaped sideways into the water, thrashing like a shark in a frenzy, and disappeared.

None of them made any effort to rescue John, who didn't resurface. There was something in the trench below, however, that sensed the thrashing and rose toward the stimulus.

Caleb, Tom, and Taino stared at the water for only seconds before realizing that Joseph was prostrate on the deck. They rushed to him and lifted him to the cushioned runner near him. Caleb took his pulse, which was racing but slowing, while his shallow breathing was also returning to normal. Directing Tom to stand over Joseph to shield him from the rising sun, Caleb loosened Joseph's shirt while Taino brought water to his lips. Joseph was now conscious and moving, attempting to sit up against Caleb's instructions. He rose on an elbow and drank some of the water while Taino held the cup and faced the islet.

They were very close to the islet now, drifting past as the current dragged the sloop around it. Tom stepped next to Taino and searched hastily for John in the water before scanning the islet for the little man and the fountain. Spotting none of them, he was about to question Taino on his choice of islets when he saw a broad smile break out on

Taino's face. He looked hard in the direction of Taino's sight and saw a little man, not more than two-thirds John's height, wading out of the water as if coming from the boat.

"Taino, look! He's got John's face! My God, you were right!" Tom shouted, pointing toward the little man who was facing them now and dancing triumphantly on the beach.

Caleb stood to see the object of Tom's remark, and Joseph sat up to do the same. Each was as amazed as Tom at the preternatural resemblance.

Taino grabbed his staff and turned to them from atop the cushioned runner, saying, "Understand the riddle – we hold its meaning close to our hearts and souls, but never truly grasp it until it is too late. Like John before you, you must choose between life and good, and death and evil. You have the free will to be blessed or cursed; therefore, choose God's will, choose life! I have always loved my God with all my heart and with all my soul, but I never understood until today how I might love Him with all my might. The riddle has told me that." Then he dived over the side of the boat next to where Tom was standing, staring at the little man.

The giant cuttlefish from the trench below was touching the keel of the boat at the same time Taino's feet were alighting on the sands of the shoreline. Its twenty-foot arms, with their huge discs and horny talons, slowly crept up the hull of the boat, precisely to where Joseph was stretching his neck from his sitting position to see Taino walk ashore.

Caleb's gaze was fixed on Taino, as was Tom's, when Joseph shouted, "Serpent!" and collapsed. Tom and Caleb froze at the sight of the huge arms coming over the side. They were unable to assist Joseph, who was gasping for air. Finally, Caleb overcame his paralysis and rushed to Joseph, pulling him from the cuttlefish's reach and prompting Tom to scream for Taino to return with the staff.

Taino was on the beach, walking toward the little man and holding his staff high above his head, giving Tom hope that Taino might yet hear his plea, despite the distance, and swim back. But then the two men on the islet, the smaller with John's face, locked themselves in combat, and the staff flipped into the sea.

Refusing to be mortal in an immortal world, Tom grabbed a folding chair and attacked the cuttlefish. Caleb was about to join Tom when he spotted Taino's staff floating toward them to save them.

And the last thing Caleb remembered before awakening to the soothing voice of Dr. Bakchos, was that he'd been hit by the blaring car on his run, catapulting him into water as he grasped a staff to break his fall, just as the arms of a giant cuttlefish reduced the sloop to fragments.

AUTHOR'S NOTE

As you just realized, the entire novel is a comatose prophetic dream of Caleb, which comprises three levels of understanding:

1) The first level is a number of intertwined character development short stories blossoming into an adventure story. There are a number of clear markers/anomalies (among many more subtle ones) within the novel that reveal the possibility of the novel's surprise ending, alerting the reader that something is brewing:

    a) The title page states that *Haazinu (Listen Up)* is a book of prophecy (See Numbers 12:6 and Rambam's *Guide for the Perplexed*), which, in general, occurs through dreams.

    b) Page 4 describes Caleb's running accident during which he grabs "a protruding dead tree limb...like a staff to break his fall." This anomaly should prime the reader for the novel's last paragraph.

    c) The shifting layers of narrative, as well as two dream sequences (pp. 118-123) are likely dreams within a dream.

    d) Page 203 presents another anomaly, wherein "Captain" Bakchos states that previously he was "a neurologist specializing in the comatose."

    e) On page 247, Caleb's vision is set forth, and an omniscient narrator (God) intervenes on page 248, and speaks to "What Caleb did not envision..." Prophetic visions are the highest level of prophecy according to Maimonides.

    f) Page 263 fuses the above markers/anomalies as Caleb concludes his dream while awakening from his comatose state "to the soothing voice of Dr. Bakchos."

2) Once the reader realizes that Level 1 of *Haazinu (Listen Up)* is a comatose prophetic dream, the reader will likely reconstruct the

AUTHOR'S NOTE

story in light of who the characters might be in Caleb's real life and thereby achieve a more sophisticated understanding of who Caleb, the emerging prophet, is.

a) Caleb Call, whose surname was changed by a prior generation from Kallmanowitz (p. 135) to Call, is who he says he is.

b) Joseph and Goldie Kallman, whose surname was changed from Kallmanowitz at Ellis Island, (p. 12), are elements of the Jewish blood relatives Caleb refers to on pages 3 and 135.

c) Stitches, Jo Jo, and Isaac are the respective parents and grandparent of the last child (and their only child, Becka, pp. 35 and 152) Caleb lost to cancer, prompting his extended sabbatical from his pediatric oncology practice and his search for Mitch and meaning in his life.

d) Tom Petersson (Peter's son) and Jake – Tom is Caleb's older brother, Tommy, pages 50, 51, 135 and 136 (both sons of Peter, p. 125, who abandoned Judaism along with his father and grandfather, pp. 135 and 247). Jake, a shepherd, is Caleb's alter ego, the namesake of the shepherd Patriarch Jacob, whom Caleb believes he is most like (p. 175). From Jake, we learn much about Caleb's relationship with his brother, his sense of the "special," and his maturing moral foundation.

e) John Hauser is who he says he is (ex-German priest, etc.), except that his psychiatric social work is conducted at the hospital where Caleb has privileges and treated Stitches's daughter, Becka, in her final days (and where Caleb, as Dr. Call, observed John's therapy sessions, which included Stitches), not at the medical center where Caleb has learned Mitch is actually being treated.

f) Michelle "Mitch" Levy is who Caleb says she is to the extent he knows the truth.

g) Jerry Watkins is who Caleb says he is to the extent he knows the truth.

h) Leah "Lee" Watkins is who Caleb says she is to the extent he knows the truth.

i) Larry Levy is who Caleb says he is to the extent he knows the truth.

j) Father Conlin is a skeptical Catholic priest who, on call at the hospital where Caleb has privileges, questions his own belief in God.

k) Captain Bakchos is Dr. Bakchos, a neurologist specializing in the comatose, with privileges at the same hospital as Caleb, where Caleb is brought after his running accident (p. 4).

l) Taino is an "immortal" prophet in the vein of Moses (who still lives with each reading of the Torah), who Caleb sees himself becoming – Caleb/Taino/Moses, each with five letters.

3) The third level of understanding, once the characters metamorphose into their second-level personae, is the level of metaphor, a walk through Tanach and Jewish history, which brings the reader to an expectation of Caleb's emergence as a prophet in volume 2 of the *Haazinu* trilogy.

a) The Joseph story is a metaphor for *sinat chinam* (gratuitous hatred among Jews) and *sinat achim* (hatred within the Jewish family, as among the biblical Joseph and his brothers).

b) The Stitches and Isaac stories are a metaphor for Kohelet (Ecclesiastes): the importance of time in Jewish life, and the vanity of success.

c) The Tom and Jake story initiates the multiple metaphors for the *arayot* (biblically prohibited sexual relationships), which are threaded throughout the book, as well as (i) the world's animosity toward the Jews (as embodied in Caleb's brother Tommy), and (ii) Caleb's growing love and protection for the Jewish people (as a shepherd like Jacob/Israel, embodied in Jake's concern for Lulu and her lamb).

d) The John story is a metaphor for Eichah (Lamentations), the destruction of the Temples and the Holocaust. John is a metaphor for the biblical Amalek, the bearer of anti-Semitism throughout the ages.

e) The Caleb/Mitch story is an inverse Shir HaShirim (Song of Songs), encapsulating the erotic and "abominable" ending of Caleb's relationship with Mitch, the centerpiece of the book, which, metaphorically, represents the disastrous decline in the relationship between the Jewish people (Caleb) and God (Mitch). Mitch (Hebrew name Michal, p. 248 – meaning, "who is like God"), abused by Caleb and her brother Larry, both representing the Jewish people, who by their or their parents' intentional actions throughout the ages, denied the God of Israel and caused Him to turn His face from the Jewish people.

f) The Jerry Watkins story is a metaphor for the Righteous Gentile throughout the ages. Caleb's relationship with him is tense because Jerry has cared for God (Mitch) while Caleb and his family have run from God, and denied their love for God.

g) The Leah story is a metaphor for the renewed relationship between Israel and God about to be initiated with Caleb's prophecy, the focus of volume 2 of the *Haazinu* trilogy.

h) The Father Conlin story is a metaphor for the horrors brought by the Catholic Church on non-believers, whether the Jewish people directly or Ciboney Indians as a metaphor for the Jewish people.

i) The Captain Bakchos story is a metaphor for the Book of Jonah and Caleb (as Jonah) battling within himself for the last time to run from what God wants him to do (p. 202), because, like Jonah and Moses, he doesn't think he's the right person for the job.

j) The Taino story is a metaphor for the biblical Moses and the foundation for Caleb's later (January 27, 1986 plus 27 years of study [p. 248] equals January 27, 2013) emergence as a prophet in volume 2 of the *Haazinu* trilogy.

As the third level of understanding, in metaphor, is grasped by the reader, *Haazinu (Listen Up)* presages, in the context of Jewish history, the reemergence of prophecy in Israel and a return of God's presence among the Israelites.

With these insights, enjoy a second reading and the many additional insights that await your discovery.